PRAISE FOR
THE WITCH WORLD SERIES

"One of fantasy's most enduring spectacles."
—*Publishers Weekly*

"One of fantasy's most beloved and enduring creations."
—*Rave Reviews*

AND FOR *THE KEY OF THE KEPLIAN*

"Classic . . . Norton and McConchie mesh smoothly. . . . A necessary addition to the Norton shelf."
—*Booklist*

"Richly textured and exquisitely written, this top-notch fantasy is sheer delight."
—*Romantic Times* on
The Key of the Keplian

"Very readable—more power to the authors!"
—*Kliatt*

"Recommended to all who love Andre Norton's Witch World and its diverse creatures."
—Norm Hartman, *The Book Net*
(Web site magazine)

OTHER NOVELS OF
THE WITCH WORLD

THE KEY OF THE KEPLIAN
Andre Norton and Lyn McConchie

THE MAGESTONE
Andre Norton and Mary H. Schaub

THE WARDING OF WITCH WORLD
Andre Norton

Also available from Warner Aspect

ANDRE NORTON
& LYN McCONCHIE

CIARA'S SONG

ASPECT®

WARNER BOOKS

A Time Warner Company

WARNER BOOKS EDITION

Copyright © 1998 by Andre Norton and Lyn McConchie
All rights reserved.

Aspect® name and logo are registered trademarks of Warner Books, Inc.

Cover design by Don Puckey
Cover illustration by Kevin Johnson

Warner Books, Inc.
1271 Avenue of the Americas
New York, NY 10020

Visit our Web site at
http://warnerbooks.com

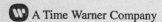 A Time Warner Company

Printed in the United States of America

First Printing: July, 1998

10 9 8 7 6 5 4 3 2 1

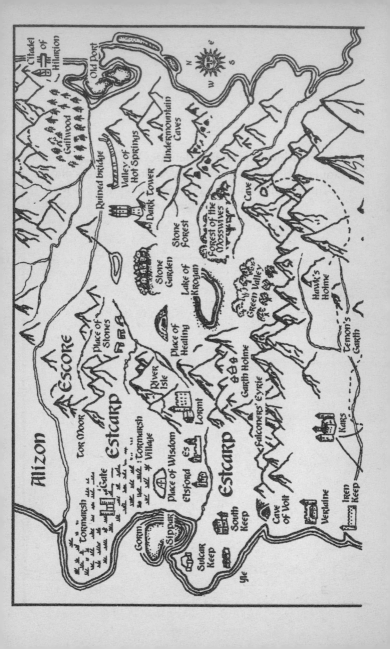

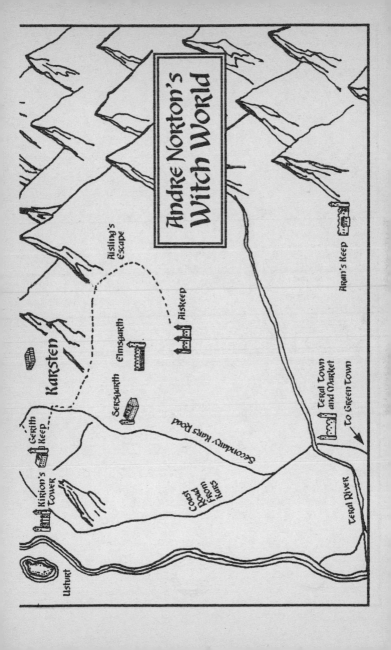

A Word About the Chronicles of the Witch World

Andre Norton

What seeker of knowledge can say with truth that the history of Witch World has been wholly preserved, even in the masses of parchment rolls, the wood-bound books, or those metal plates of yet earlier date engraved in tongues that have not been used for a millennium or more?

Where lie the life stories of those who raised the walls of that ruined city in the far South, site of a battle waged but yesterday? Whence came all the flotsam and jetsam of clans and races, whose only memories and records do not stretch back even to their arrrival through one of the world gates?

Yes, even though those portals giving upon all thc other dimensions have been closed, still there are many tales worth the telling to be found by delving into the Archives at Lormt. For centuries, Lormt acted as a depository for the histories of families and the keeping of clan lines, so that kinfolk widely separated by war or witchery might possibly find those of their blood again. There also, far in the past, the custom began for clans, families, and even solitary rovers to leave accounts of their own journeyings, battles, and victories, thereby illuminating some small facet of the history they knew, having acted within it—and, perhaps, upon it as well. Thus, records left by even single wanderers are to be found there, piled against official reports of vanished kingdoms.

It has now absorbed the attention of some of the burrowing scholars to search out accounts concerning events that they may have been involved in themselves but which they found hard to comprehend as being experienced simultaneously by unknown others. These seekers have included those tied to forceful action in the past and determined to leave for the future some detailing of the roots and branches of the tree of their tale. Such enlargers of the Witch World's store of lore are Ouen and the Lady Mereth.

In a time of relative peace, when the inroads made by the Dark from without are no longer to be feared (though still, and ever, guarded against) these earlier tales are mined by songsmiths, and some mighty sagas have been wrought from even modest accounts. Thus, Lormt is now not only what it has always been—a treasure-house of ancient knowledge—but, in this day, it fosters new wisdom as well, spreading over the land a web of such stories as will make clear to the survivors of a past in which many went armed how well their kindred bore those weapons and to what end.

So, from out of their safekeeping at Lormt, different ages of the Witch World come to life again. In this way, those newborn can learn what passed before: actions of not only potent sorcerers and great lords and ladies but of folk like themselves, meant to live untroubled lives but prevented by fate from so doing.

One such tale, humble in origin only, is that of Ciara, who had to make her life anew under the very shadow of the Dark.

BOOK ONE

Thrice-Horned
to Death
and Destruction

1

Ciara was playing in her secret cave in the cliff when the rider came. She recognized him at once. It was her brother Larian come back from distant Kars. He was studying as apprentice merchant with an old friend of her father's. But why was he home? She scrambled down from her cave to where she could swing across from one tall elm to another. From there she could reach her bedroom window at the back of the garth. She clattered down the stairs calling, "Larian, Larian, Mother! Larian's home!"

Her parents popped out of the cook room, both looking startled. "It can't be." Her mother sounded worried. "He isn't due home again until Year End."

Her father was practical. "Well, my love, we'd better go and see." But before they could move toward the front of the garth, Larian came striding through to meet them. His face was white with exhaustion under the brown, and his eyes haunted. He wasted no words.

"Yvian's gone mad. He's ordered the three-times Horning for all of the Old Blood. I took Falco's relay and came by the mountain paths. The guards will be right behind me. Half of them were fanning out south as I slipped away. They're slaughtering any who even look as if they might be of our kind."

Ciara's mother stared up, and in a voice that the child did not recognize she spoke softly. "They took Falco at the very gates of the city. Merryon died fighting before they burned the house about his family. Even now the death-bringers circle the valley. For only one of us is there an escape."

Talyo stared at his wife. "Do you see true, beloved?"

"I see true. We have less than a candlemark. They are too close for us to flee. But Ciara might hide." She turned to the girl gently. "Don't ask questions. There's no time. You have a place where you go. Can you reach it without being seen?"

Frightened, bewildered, the child gulped. "Yes."

"Can you take possessions with you if they aren't too large or heavy?"

Ciara nodded slowly. She'd taken old rugs to furnish her cave already. Often she'd taken a meal there.

"Good, come with me. Talyo, you and Larian free the stock. Send them running. When you've done, barricade the doors."

She was gone then, dragging Ciara behind her. "I know you get out of your bedroom window. Where do you go from there?"

Ciara pointed. "Across the elms. There's a cave in the cliff up high you can reach from a branch on the end tree." Lanlia stared.

"Goddess, if I'd even dreamed it was so dangerous I'd never had ignored it. Listen, Ciara. Can anyone get to your cave from below?"

"N-n-no. You can't even see there's a cave." She remembered finding it the first time quite by accident as she scrambled about the elms.

"How big is the cave, sweetheart?"

"It's very small. I have to crawl to get inside." Lanlia's look urged her to continue. "I can lie down inside but only just. When I do I can stretch my hands out and touch the wall on each side."

"What do you have up there?"

"Rugs, only old ones, Mother. And candle ends. What are you doing?"

Lanlia was moving with a swift sure speed as she gathered items. She stowed them into a carrysack as Ciara asked her question.

"You must go to your cave. How long does it take you to reach it and return from this window?"

Ciara considered. She sensed the question was important. "Maybe a fifth of a candlemark."

"Good. Now listen to me. There may be no time later to say this. What Larian said was that the duke has ordered all of the Old Race, all of our people to be killed on sight. That's our family. Your father, Larian, and I will stay in the garth. If nothing happens you can return. If we are dead, you are to wait in the cave for five days. Five days, do you understand?" Ciara nodded, gulping back tears of fright.

"After that, try to make your way to Aiskeep. Lord Tarnoor has always been our friend. Ask him what you should do. Do not let any other see you. Now, take this to your cave. Just drop it there and return at once. Go quickly."

The carrysack was thrust into Ciara's hands as Lanlia snatched up another. Still gulping back sobs the child scrambled through the window on to a branch climbing higher and higher before she crossed the line of elms toward her refuge. But once there the peace of it seemed to still some of her terror. She stared down the length of their valley but saw no one. Maybe Larian was wrong. But something deep inside warned her the message had been true. Her other two brothers were dead. Her mother had seen it so. Mother 'saw' seldom, but when she did see what she saw was the truth.

Ciara was the baby of the family. She was barely nine. Falco and Merryon had both been adult men, Merryon married with a family. She had seen them both no more than twice in her life. They were the sons of her father's first wife whereas Larian was her full brother. He had only gone to study in Kars three years ago. Since then he had been home each Year End bringing gifts for all. She had heard of the three-times horning as any child might hear. It was something done to outlaws she recalled vaguely as she scrambled back across the line of trees. The guards blew a horn three times and named the ones who were now outside all laws. After that the wicked men could be killed without blood feud or punishment. Anything they had belonged to their killers. She almost fell through the window. Did that mean *they* were outlaws now?

Lanlia had no time for her questions. "Take this one back, too. Hurry!" Ciara found another full carrysack pushed into her hands and obediently hurried. A third journey, but on the way back this time she could see riders. She dropped into her bedroom gabbling the news. Her father was there. It was he who asked quietly, "How many?"

"I couldn't count, maybe twenty."

"Are they riding fast?"

"No." Ciara was puzzled. "They don't seem in any hurry."

Larian's voice was suddenly savage. "No, they know we're trapped if we're here. Why tire the horses."

Lanlia was practical. "Let them dawdle all they will. It gives us more time. Ciara, you remember what I told you, tell me again."

"I'm to go to the cave and stay there five days or until you call me back. If you can't . . . oh, Mother, I'm scared!"

She was hugged hard. "I know, now go on."

"If anything happens I wait five days, then go to Lord Tarnoor. Only to him."

"Yes. This time don't come back from your cave. Be careful. Don't let the riders see you." One by one her family embraced her. At the last Larian placed two items in her hand. She looked down.

His hand closed hers upon them. "If we live, I'll claim them from you, little sister. If I don't, they're yours." He helped her through the window, watching as she vanished in the foliage.

He could have gone with her. From what his mother said there would be room in the cave for two. But his seventeenth name day had passed. It was for a man to defend his home and family, not to hide while others died.

He'd been fortunate. His father was only partly of the Old Blood, but his first wife had been wholly so. For that Falco and Merryon had both died, their faces too much of the ancient race. But both Larian and Ciara looked more like the incomers. Lanlia had been a half-blood orphan who wed the widowed farmer. Her children resembled her, dark-haired, but with rounder faces and eyes of a clear hazel.

It had saved the boy's life as he thrust through blood-crazed men toward the stables. Once there he had swiftly saddled Falco's relay. He'd guessed his brother would need them no more. That first two days he had ridden all three mounts into near exhaustion to stay ahead of the news. Then he had swung up onto the foothill tracks. In a tiny valley he had unsaddled the leg-weary animals, hobbling them carefully. He had allowed the horses to graze all day while he hunted. Two hares and several rabbits would be good rations for days. He ate ravenously, tearing the roast flesh from small bones.

That night he had slept until midday, risen to eat eagerly again, and then saddled his mounts. Now he kept away from any riders. Several times he dropped down to warn garths where the inhabitants were friends and of the Old Blood. Each time he had been given filled feed sacks for the horses, food for himself. He had been able to press on to the limits of his strength. Two horses had been left behind as he rode.

Larian clamped his teeth shut on a plea to join Ciara. He

knew if he stayed he would die. He stared out of the window slit as the riders approached. He recognized the enemy, and accepted death. With the guards was a neighbor who'd always coveted Elmsgarth land. Under the new Karsten laws he could take it once all males in the family were dead. Ciara had no claim. Only if she had been adult and wed could she have held it.

The neighbor might overlook the child's absence, but not Larian's. He would see the lathered horse that stood head down by the fence and guess. Larian stood straighter. If he was to die, then he would see to it their neighbor did not profit. He strung his bow and waited.

Far above Ciara had reached the cave with her last carry-sack. She huddled into the heavy gray wool of the cloak. It felt like home. Lanlia had woven it for herself only last year. Falco had sent a set of matching hareskins to line it as his Year-End gift. They'd been taken when the hares were in winter garb so that on one side the cloak was dark gray wool, and on the other pure white fur. It was far too large for Ciara, but it would keep her warm in her refuge if she must wait. It even had a hood with drawstrings to tighten it about her face.

She wiggled forward to look down. The riders had reached the garth. From her perch she could hear only a mumble until one raised his voice.

"Come out and you can go free." She knew the man. He was Tylar from Sersgarth in the next valley. He had a pack of brawling sons all looking hard at their father's garth. At least that was what her father had said once. Her mother had retorted that Tylar could look for land for his sons elsewhere. Below Tylar was shouting again.

"Come out and you can go. You leave everything and we'll leave you."

There was no movement from the house and Ciara whimpered. If Tylar was telling the truth it would be wonderful. They could just leave and they'd be safe. Then she wondered.

But where would they go if they had to leave everything behind? How would they live?

She squirmed back a little looking down at the treasures Larian had given her to hold for him.

They were treasures in truth. The slim-bladed dagger laying in her hand had never been sharpened. It had come down from the family of her father's grandmother. Legend had it the dagger had been made by an adept in the Power. Be the story true or not it was true that the dagger remained razor sharp no matter what its usage. For that alone it was prized. Larian had been a favorite of his grandmother's. She had given the weapon to him when he left at fourteen to study in Kars. She had died soon after and Ciara knew how Larian treasured it.

The other object she held was a pendant. It was drop-shaped in silver with small wings sweeping up in a curve on either side. Minute blue stones edged each wing feather. It had been wrought with a delicacy that was sheer beauty.

That had come from her mother's side of the family. It was a bridal gift, held by each son in turn to give to his chosen. Ciara slipped the chain about her neck allowing the pendant to fall beneath her bodice. Then she wiggled back to peer out from the cave mouth again. What were they doing down there?

At first she could see no one. Then a small group of men on foot came into view. Leading them was neighbor Tylar. They carried a log from the wood stack. Ciara was puzzled; what did they plan to do with it? She gasped as below the log was swung forward to strike the door with a hollow boom. She stared blankly. Why, they'd break the door if they kept doing that. Then as the log struck again she understood. They meant to break in. Now that her family was thrice-horned anything could be done to them. There was nothing against the law. Small whimpers squeezed between her clenched teeth. All the stories she had ever heard rose up to remind her of what that 'anything' could be.

Larian sighted his arrow carefully. From among their neighbors, only Tylar was with the guards. If he was dead, there would be none to say Ciara lived. There was no hope for any within Elmsgarth, he knew that now. But his adored small sister might still survive. With Tylar dead his sons would be too busy squabbling over their own Sersgarth and the Elmsgarth land to bother about one small female child with no claim. He hung on the shot until Tylar moved clear. The arrow flew with deadly accuracy. Tylar fell soundlessly, heart pierced. The guards shouted with rage, redoubling their attack on the door.

Talyo nodded to his son in approval. He knew why the boy had shot. Larian had always been the best archer in the family. That had been a tricky shot but Tylar was silenced, and Ciara safer. His wife had vanished upstairs to the watchtower. It had been built by his great-grandfather when he took this valley for his own. The land had been more lawless then and it had been used often. It stood high above the garth. Very high. Anyone who leaped from that would not survive landing on the cobblestones below. Lanlia returned to stand beside her husband.

"The doors are open." He understood, she would not be taken alive.

The massive old door was beginning to split; soon it would fall. He laid his weapons aside and took her gently in his arms.

"Beloved, when I lost Shala I never thought I would know happiness again. With you I have found such joy and love as a man seldom finds." Lanlia said nothing but held him to her with all her strength. There was a final booming ending in a long, splintering crunch as the door gave way. Talyo thrust her behind him.

"Go to the tower now, beloved, and do what you must." In that split second as she turned to run she 'saw.' The gifts of her blood had never been real power in her. But with death reaching out she 'saw' now, as she had 'seen' the deaths of her stepsons and their family. Duke Yvian lay dead, betrayed by his own. Mountains twisted and crumbled, beneath them lay the armies of Karsten. Lanlia leapt for the stairs as her husband and son stood side by side behind her in the narrow hall.

As she flashed around the bend of the stairs she halted to stare back. Larian was down, she felt his death. Talyo was falling. She cried out as he turned to look at her one last time, love in his eyes. Then a sword fell. The guards howled in triumph surging forward to reach for her. But she was already in flight. She hurled herself through the doorways, slamming each door as she ran. It slowed those behind just enough. She reached the final door to the tower and thrust it shut, dropping the long metal bar into place. Then she flung herself up the final flights of stairs. She gained the top and it seemed more terrible to her that it should still be a bright day. All she had loved, all but her daughter were dead. It should be cold, snowing or raining. Not this soft sunshine of late afternoon.

She listened as the guards beat on the door below. It would take little time for them to realize they should bring the log again. Lanlia closed her eyes, her mind sought back to the visions of a dead duke, falling mountains. Below the door boomed. She reached to hold Ciara's face in her mind. Would her daughter be strong enough to survive as she must? The door began to splinter. Lanlia called the faces of her loves. The stepsons she'd cared for, her beloved husband, her son and daughter. She stepped out onto the tower edge. The door broke open and a rush of feet roared upward. She turned to face them then and into her mind came a calm clear voice. She knew it. Her husband's grandmother. A woman of the old pure blood who had loved them all.

The blood shall come full circle. It shall rise to flower again. Come to me, child, and be free.

As the guards threw themselves forward she smiled at them. Then she allowed herself to fall in silence.

High in her cave Ciara could see little. The men had broken down the door and vanished. Then her mother appeared on the watchtower. Ciara would have called to her but she remembered. She must draw no attention, she must keep silence. Her mother was facing away, looking down the stairs. Dimly the child could hear a thudding sound. The men were breaking down another door. She saw them rush onto the roof, saw her mother fall silently. And in that moment she knew she was the last of her family alive. Her hand stole up to grasp the pendant beneath her bodice. The other gripped the dagger hilt. They were hers to keep now, along with the memory. She would not forget how they'd died, that she swore on Larian's treasures.

But she was still only a child. She crawled back into her refuge and wept until her face was swollen and her eyes slits. She cried until she fell asleep wrapped in her mother's cloak. She did not see the guards leave almost empty-handed. What use were sheep or goats to them? And if Elmsgarth had held anything of value, they could not find it. A few had taken minor items. The bolt of cloth her mother had bought to make Ciara and herself new dresses. The set of good pans from the kitchen. A saddle and bridles from the stable. Several bits of clothing and a few sheepskins already tanned. They set a fire but it was already going out as they departed. They grumbled as they rode. The garth had been a waste. No loot, no women, nothing worth the energy.

It was day again when Ciara woke. She could still see her mother's body below on the cobblestones. It set off another fit of weeping. She would have climbed down but for her promise. She stayed, a child's appetite asserting itself by evening. Then she thought to rummage in the carrysacks that lay along the cave wall. Within one was food. She ate mindlessly, cramming the stale bread into her mouth and washing it down with sips from the flask she found. It was watered wine and she slept swiftly again once her hunger was assuaged.

She ate when she woke, crawling to the cave mouth to stare down the valley. Her mother had said she was to remain up here five days. There was enough food, and with the flask and a water bag as well she could stay safely. But the cave would stink soon. She relieved herself right at the back where there was a small dip. The rock was cracked there so liquid seeped away, but not solids. Nor was there any earth to cover them. Perhaps she should climb down when she must do that? But she'd promised, and what if the guards came back and caught her?

She remained, terrified, confused and grieving in her cave a third day. Then, as noon moved into early afternoon, she saw two riders moving towards Elmsgarth. She knew them, Lord Tarnoor and his son. Trovagh was only a year older than Ciara and the families had been friends. Her mother had said Ciara was to go to Lord Tarnoor, but he'd come to her instead. Still she was afraid in case any of the guards were here. She watched carefully. There was no sign of anyone but the two riders. At the garth door Tarnoor was gathering up her mother's body. It would be all right, it must be. She slipped across to the branch of the great elm nearest her refuge. Then to the next and the next until she reached her window. She could hear their voices now.

"Yvian *must* be mad, Gods damn him. There's only Talyo, Lanlia, and the boy here. They'll have got Falco and Merryon in the city. That hell-cursed guard even tried to set fire to the garth before they left."

He was interrupted by a lighter treble. "But, Father, Ciara isn't here. I've looked in all the rooms."

"You're right, lad." Lord Tarnoor's voice was lifted in his familiar bellow. "Ciara? Ciara, lass. Where are you?"

The child remained silent. After a while, she heard Tarnoor speak again, bitterness in his voice.

"It may be that they took her with them. We'll bury the family and then look properly. If she's dead we'll find her to lie with them."

Ciara heard the digging begin, the spade striking rocks now and then as Tarnoor sweated and cursed. Her mother had said she could trust Tarnoor. Aiskeep owed her mother a debt. As a toddler Trovagh had fallen from high in the old Keep. He'd been badly injured and Tarnoor had sent to Lanlia for help. It was known she had somewhat of the healing gift. For many nights she worked over the small child until at last he was out of danger. He would always walk a little lame, and colds tended to settle dangerously on his chest in the chillier winters. But he lived. Tarnoor's only child and the heir to Aiskeep. Ciara could remember her parents talking.

"He loves the boy," her mother had insisted. "Oh, yes, it's true he loathes the man who'd inherit if Trovagh died. But he loves the boy well. I have seen them together." Her tones had become warmly amused. "I do not think the harsh Lord Tarnoor is as hard as he would have many think. I have told him, too, that the child should have a playmate."

Tarnoor seemed to have agreed. After Trovagh was well again his father brought him regularly to Elmsgarth to play childish games with Ciara. Although she was a year younger and slighter of bone, she still was the equal to Trovagh whose injuries had slowed his growth. She had come first to like and then to trust her friend completely, and with him his father. She watched her family laid to rest, heard the old words said. But she was afraid without quite knowing why. She had always been active. Scrapes, bruises, and occasional punishment had been hers. It was not pain of body that held her back now, but pain of heart.

The guards of Karsten were to protect the people. Why, one of Falco's best friends was a lieutenant. The duke was there to give Justice. Where was his Justice in this? Where was the protection? If being one of the Old Blood was wicked, might

not Tarnoor, even her friend Trovagh, turn against her? She
could not bear it if they came at her with swords. Her heart
would break before the bright metal struck home. She hovered indecisively edging first a little toward them, then back.
The movement caught Trovagh's eye as he turned. Already
wise at ten he did not run toward her but spoke quietly to his
father.

"Ciara's here, but I think she's afraid."

"Don't alarm her. Walk to her very slowly, speak quietly,"
Tarnoor advised. He'd seen enough terrorized children in his
time as a soldier. The Goddess grant none had laid hands on
the lass.

Trovagh moved forward, hands held out. "Ciara, Cee? It's
Tro. My father's here. Nothing bad will happen to you. Please
come out. Cee?" She edged toward him, white eye rims
showing like a terrified horse. He kept talking, reminding her
of their games, their secrets, until at last he reached her. Still
murmuring gently, he placed a hand on her arm and felt the
long, slow shudders that rippled through the thin body. "Cee,
no one will hurt you, I swear it. Please come with us." Overcome then with fury, his treble hardened to a lighter imitation
of his father's growl. "I swear, Cee. I'll hang the man who
hurts you. If I can't, I'll order one of our men." He met her
eyes and suddenly the picture of his words set them both to
giggling in slight hysteria.

Trovagh grinned. "I know, I know. My father gives that sort
of order. But he'd say the same." He laid a careful arm about
the shaking shoulders and gently led Ciara to where Tarnoor
stood.

"You would, wouldn't you, Father? Hang the man who
tried to hurt Cee, I mean?"

"Yes. If I could. Or keep him away from you at the least,
child. Now sit down a minute and tell me what you can. Speak
swiftly, for we must be away from here in case any of the
guard return."

She talked, the words spilling out of her like blood. It hurt to remember her mother's orders, and how she had died. Tarnoor swore under his breath. He'd done things as a soldier under orders. But Aiskeep owed Elmsgarth a debt and he'd never been one to forget that. Nor one to harm a child, either, he added mentally. He hid a sudden smile. His son would never forgive him if anything happened to Ciara now. The boy had pledged his word his playmate would be safe. Tarnoor was not the man to see his son oathbroken.

"Can you climb up now and drop the carrysacks to us?"

Ciara nodded slowly. At his gesture she trotted up the stairs, traversed the elms, and from the cave dropped the four containers.

These were slung across the rump of Tarnoor's mount. Then he turned as she rejoined them. This should be official.

"Your mother trusted me to care for you. Will you come with me to Aiskeep? Will you accept me as your guardian?"

Ciara's eyes filled with tears. She didn't know what she was supposed to say. The questions had an air of formality about them. Was there some special way she should answer? She stood drooping before him. Small face white with grief and exhaustion, body still shaking from the shocks of past days. She was unable to think, to speak. She could only huddle into herself, huge-eyed and silent.

Tarnoor forgot formality as he wordlessly held out his arms. She flung herself to him, weeping aloud as he held her. In that moment something passed between them. She relaxed, trusting, knowing she was again protected. Tarnoor held her enfolded, a rush of love for the child he'd been sent. His daughter now. His! And let none say differently.

2

They rode back together, with Ciara's carrysacks hanging over the rump of Lord Tarnoor's horse, while Ciara perched behind Trovagh on his smaller pony. Tarnoor had hoisted her up and wrapped her carefully in the oversized cloak.

"It's too big for her, Father."

"That's no matter while she's on the pony, boy. And I'd rather no one sees who she is while the countryside's still so stirred up."

At the thought of that Ciara shrank deep into the sheltering cloak. She'd seen neighbor Tylar die. Blood feuds had started from far less than a death. From beneath the enveloping hood she peered out, her eyes attuned to her own land, so that it was she who saw the sheep first.

"Oh, stop, Trovagh."

The boy halted his pony. Ciara slipped from her perch to walk quietly toward the small huddle of ewes and lambs. Larian had released them as ordered before the guards arrived. The sheep had drifted well down the valley but kept to cover. It was growing colder toward winter. Soon they would be fed with extra rations of hay. But the odd smells of fire and blood had disturbed them. In their blacks and browns they had vanished into cover blending with the fall landscape. They recognized Ciara at once, though, crowding round to sniff hopefully at her hands.

"I'm sorry, I don't have anything for you. Where's Ysak?"

At the sound of his name the big ram shouldered his way through the small flock. She knelt to hug him gently.

"Look after them for me. We'll return for you." She gazed up at Tarnoor doubtfully. "We will, won't we?"

"Yes, child. As soon as we're home I'll send out men to bring in everything of yours you wish. It's likely we won't find the horses. The guards will have taken any they found."

"Larian let everything go before they got to us."

"Then the men will look for them also. Get up behind Trovagh again. We must get you to Aiskeep."

She mounted in silence looking back at the flock with Ysak as guard. Her mother had cherished each lamb. They were the only colored sheep in the whole area. Father had brought back several frail lambs from the province past Kars to the North. There, closer to the Estcarp border they had such sheep. He'd got the lambs cheaply in a deal and carried them back. With Lanlia's care they had thrived. Now and again she had been able to buy or swap for others. Until at last the Elmsgarth flock numbered some twenty adult ewes and Ysak the ram. All were hand tamed and would come to their names.

They must be brought back to the Keep. She could not bear the thought of them being left alone, prey to men and animals. They were sturdy beasts, but in full winter they required shelter and additional food. In the back of her mind, she wondered why she was thinking so hard about the sheep. Tarnoor could have told her that it was shock, and her mind's defenses. If she contemplated sheep she did not have to remember her family—or their deaths. Now and again he encouraged her with questions so that she hardly noticed the journey back to Aiskeep.

When at last they arrived, she was lifted from the pony. Tarnoor carried her indoors, through the feasting hall, and into a small bedroom beside Trovagh's rooms.

"This will be yours." He turned, speaking quietly to the plump, warmhearted Elanor, who was his distant kin. "Care for her, but touch nothing in her carrysacks, nor do anything she does not wish. See that she eats, if possible. If not, get her to drink something hot. She is uninjured but badly shocked. Ask no questions of her and be sure no one else bothers her, either."

He left them to it. Elanor had been maid and companion to his wife before she died. Now she was housekeeper. Uninspired it was true, but efficient and kind nonetheless. He headed back to the stables in search of Trovagh.

"Do those sheep of Elmsgarth know you, son?"

"Yes. Are we going back for them now?"

"I think so. From what the girl says, it won't be long before those sons of Tylar come looking. The body was gone, which means the guard must have taken it back to Sersgarth. They're troublemakers, that family. But they aren't complete fools. Sooner or later it will dawn on them to put aside any dispute over Sersgarth and gather first what they can elsewhere. Before then I want us to have been and gone."

He called orders as men joined them. Two of the long hay wains drawn by strong teams began to plod off at once.

"Let them start ahead. We'll catch up soon." Tarnoor was speaking to his Master at Arms as the wains departed. "I want nine or ten men, all armed with bow and sword. Steady men, the sort who won't act before my orders even in case of provocation."

Hanion nodded. "Master Trovagh tells me that the guard attacked Elmsgarth. The three-times horning?"

"Yes."

The Master at Arms snorted angrily. "Yvian's gone mad.

What harm did the Old Race ever do us? I rode with some of them in my early days on bandit patrol. Good men, good fighters, and canny, too. A shame to us all this business. Mistress Lanlia aided any with her healcraft who came asking. *She* never distinguished between the Old Blood and the new. As for that Tylar—" He spat at the ground. "Good job he's dead, if you ask me. That family's never been anything but trouble."

"Like to be more before it ends," Tarnoor said gloomily. "They won't overlook the death of their father—even if they were all just waiting themselves for him to die so they'd inherit."

"Humph! Long wait that'd have been, too."

"True, well, never mind." Tarnoor reached for the reins of his own horse as it was led to him. "Let's go!"

A dozen riders clattered out of the gates and off down the road at a steady canter. Tarnoor glanced over them. Hanion had chosen well. Veterans to a man, they wouldn't act too hastily. He might need that quality if Tylar's sons appeared before Aiskeep had been and gone again. Trovagh rode beside him on a fresh horse; the boy might well be of help, Tarnoor thought. Trovagh had run all over the garth with young Ciara. He'd know most of the hiding places there. He scanned the countryside as they rode. No sign of Tylar's lads fortunately. But it had been three days. One of them would think of Elmsgarth sooner or later. That was why Tarnoor had chosen to return at once.

It took hours, until at length Tarnoor ordered torches to be lit. The two wains were filled, heaped high, with more items lashed onto the outside. The sheep had long since been found and started on their trek to Aiskeep. It had been Trovagh who, as Tarnoor had foreseen had been of most use in finding things.

"The horses always hole up in the willows down by the stream if they're left out."

He'd been correct. Four of the strong farm beasts were there along with the saddle horse Larian had been riding. There, too, was the sensible middle-aged mare Lanlia had always ridden. All of the beasts looked well and came willingly to Trovagh's call.

"Good, lad, get them to the stables. Tell Hanion to have the team harnessed. It'll give us another wain."

Trovagh vanished to pass on the order, then vanished again on his own behalf. He returned leading two female goats, both almost whimpering in their desire to be milked. Hanion grinned down at him.

"Well, that's fine." He glanced over at the men. "Erek, you came from a farm, do what you can for this pair, then put them in the wain." It was almost moonhigh before all was loaded. Tarnoor took his son aside.

"Two things. Can you think of anything else Ciara would wish to have before we leave? Do you know of any hiding places within the garth where valuables might be kept?"

Trovagh nodded. "Cee has a hidey-hole in her room. I don't think there's anything valuable there but she'd like to have the things, I think. And there's one in her parents' room, too. Cee showed me once. It's a secret that even she wasn't supposed to know."

"Show me the secret one first, then take a sack and clear out the one in Ciara's room for her."

He was interested to find just how secret the first had been. To open it one had to stand on a stool and swing on a beam. It was clever. At first glance the beam was no more than a roof beam. But with weight dragging at it, one could see that the beam only touched the roof, and it was not attached. Beside him a panel slid open. He studied the hidden contents. Several wooden boxes, one small, the others larger. He opened the first to discover deeds to the land, family papers, and a small bag of gold and silver coins. Talyo's fallback money no doubt, he thought. Best not to waste time checking everything else.

He'd just have the lot removed to the wain. He yelled for a couple of his men.

It was almost dawn before the last items were gathered in. The men were tired but pleased with themselves at cheating Tylar's kin from their loot. All had known the family at Elmsgarth. There were few who had not at sometime or another availed themselves of Lanlia's healcraft. As soon as the road was sufficiently light they moved out. The garth wain rumbled along in their midst. Tarnoor smiled to himself. He had the deeds to the land. With those he could legally register his own name as owner. He would have that done at once, but quietly. If one of Tylar's sons settled, he could be tossed off at anytime. Not that there was any hurry.

He grinned again. The land was too far from the Keep to bother working. But if someone settled here he would wait. Once they'd established themselves he'd offer to sell them the land complete with deeds. That would be more money for the girl. It also gave him control of who settled there as a neighbor. It had been an exhausting, but very fruitful day. He slouched back in his saddle. Trovagh's pony was being led from the wain. The boy himself was fast asleep on a pile of bedding atop the load. Yes, indeed. A good day. He'd acquired the daughter he'd always wanted as well as his son. Found the right to choose a neighbor, and raised himself even higher in his son's eyes.

A rider galloped back from the road ahead. "Lord, there's a rabble approaching. Tylar's sons lead. They've wagons and pack ponies."

Tarnoor acted. Most of his men had served as soldiers in their younger days. He'd kept up the training. He heeled his mount to the head of the line, chose thick brush, and signaled them to leave the road. He added the signals to keep the horses silent, and to make no move until ordered. Everyone was under cover by the time the would-be looters passed. Tarnoor considered them, a motley lot. That miserable garthsman from farther north, a neighbor of Tylar's. The man spent more time drinking than farming, Tylar's four brawling sons, and a sprinkling of others who hoped to profit. Half of them still looked drunk, the rest miserably hungover.

He exchanged looks with Hanion. The would-be looters wouldn't be at all happy to find someone had been before them. It could be a good idea to throw them off the trail if possible. The longer it took for them to learn the truth, the safer Ciara would be. He motioned Hanion close and talked busily, the Armsmaster nodding back at intervals. Once the road was clear Tarnoor emerged. The wain trundled on its way with an escort of half the men. Tarnoor, Hanion, and four of the Keep guard rode at a slow walk back toward Elmsgarth.

They caught up with the group ahead just as they reached the turn into the valley. Tarnoor was at his most bluff and heartily ignorant. "What's this, a drinking party so early? Has someone married?"

Tylar's oldest son answered after a swift glance around. "No, Lord. We heard that Elmsgarth had been attacked. We go to see."

"Ah. That is good, that is right. To help a neighbor who may be in trouble. I, too, have regard for Mistress Lanlia and the family. I shall ride with you."

His small group hid grins with difficulty as they watched the boy struggle with having to tell a lord he wasn't wanted.

"Um, no need, sir, my lord. We wouldn't want to take you out of your way."

"Nonsense. Good friends, good neighbors. Only right. Besides, there may be bodies to be buried. Can't have them around stinking up the garth. Not right, no, no."

"But, my lord . . ."

"Now then, any more and you'll have me thinking we aren't of use."

The boy pasted a patently false smile on his face. "Oh, no, my lord. You do us honor."

"Good, lad. Don't worry, we won't interfere with your work. You get on and help the family. Mend anything broken, yes? Dig any graves if they're needed. I'm just here as lord to see what has happened."

He reined his horse back a little. He and his Master at Arms exchanged glances. Both were having trouble keeping straight faces at the miserable looks ahead of them. The group had come to loot and be rich, not to dig holes, and mend fences. They were unhappily aware that under Tarnoor's eye they might have to do just that.

"Well, Hanion?"

"Very well, my lord. I'd say they suspect nothing."

Tarnoor nodded. The harder part would come when they reached the garth. That they did very shortly. The scruffy group ahead gaped in fury at the neat graves to one side of the house. They scattered, shouts and cries revealing their dashed hopes. Tarnoor dismounted to examine the graves. He'd left no sign as to who had buried his friends. He bowed his head for a moment praying they rested in peace. Tylar's son dashed up to him.

"My lord, someone has been here already. The house is stripped."

He met raised eyebrows. "So? It may be that some of the family survived. They may have departed with their goods to seek a place where thieves do not come in the night."

He watched as the lad opened his mouth to refute most of that, then almost bit his tongue off to keep silence. Tarnoor nodded kindly. "One should not jump to conclusions," he said pompously. "I daresay Talyo will let us know what he wishes. Until then, let no one think to claim his land too hastily."

The young man facing him was all but chewing his tongue to shreds at this. How could he tell the lord that Talyo would let no one know anything ever again. He spoke cautiously.

"Um, my lord, has no word come to you from the Kars guard?"

"I have been traveling. What word?"

"The Old Race was thrice-horned by Duke Yvian, my lord. I fear that Elmsgarth may have been attacked by those . . ." He spluttered to a halt. Well, no, Tarnoor thought. You can't very well explain it was your father who led the murderers here to make a profit. Or that you are here now to take anything you can lever up. Your kind envy anyone with more. You'd use any excuse, this horning was just convenient. Aloud he spoke casually.

"Well, in that case I think you may remove anything you find. Property or beasts. But do not damage the house. It may be of use to whomever settles the land." He saw that thought sink in. Good. The house would be safe. "Nor would I seek to seize the land too hastily. It is possible the duke will have plans for it. He has friends at court who are landless."

That was no more than the truth, too. There were always a crowd of eager, money-hungry hangers-on at the duke's feet. He'd ridden with Yvian when they were both young. None of this smacked of him. If his courtiers were money-hungry, Yvian had been power-hungry. Tarnoor had backed him when the duke first ascended the throne in Kars. Not because he liked Yvian, so much as Karsten needed a stronger hand just then. Yvian had that. He had appetites, too. But they were ones his people understood. What had gone wrong to drive the duke to all this? It was utter folly but too late to mend. Tarnoor would keep his head well down until he knew the worst. Meanwhile he would look to his own defenses.

He stared out across the garth. It was quite possible Yvian would gift the land to one of his hangers-on. Or some toady of his mistress, Aldis. He'd met the lady once and would put little past her. Perhaps this was some ploy of hers? He turned to the lad again.

"There seems nothing I should do here. Should you find anything you believe I should hear about, send word." The boy nodded, a faint smugness coating his look. He'd tell his lord nothing. If they found anything it would be theirs. Not that there was likely to be anything. Some sneaking thief had been before them all, curse him. They'd bide their time. If no one came to claim the land in a year or two, he'd take it. This had been a larger, more fertile farm than Sersgarth. Let his next brother take that. The other two could lay claim to a smaller place now also unoccupied to the north of them. They'd been there in time all right.

He licked his lips at memories of three days past. His father had come here to die. His sons had gone elsewhere and it had been others who died. His share would help to refurbish Elmsgarth again. He could at least graze the stolen beasts here. He sketched a bow to his lord and hurried away. If anyone did find anything he would not be cheated out of his share. Tarnoor gazed after him in disgust before signaling his men to close ranks. They cantered off down the road and were some distance away before Hanion spoke.

"I think they have no suspicions."

"No. The boy's too busy cursing over lost loot to suspect us. He thinks that I came there for the same reason. Well enough. But, Hanion, keep still the tongues in your men's heads. It's likely most of this will blow over. But in case it does not, I don't want that cat's leavings to know the child lives, or that it is Aiskeep that has his plunder."

"No, Lord."

Tarnoor left it at that. Hanion had been with him all of their lives. He was solidly reliable. Full of common sense and born at Aiskeep, the son of the man who had been Master at Arms to Tarnoor's father. Its interests were his own. Aiskeep had always been clever in that. Its guard was chosen from those born and bred there. Now and again they added another family. But a guard was never chosen from that generation. His people were treated fairly, not as other lords closer to Kars corruption often dealt with their servants. Tarnoor was sure his people were loyal, but like most, they gossiped. Hanion would see to it that gossip was confined to Aiskeep.

They clattered back through the gate just as the last wain was being unloaded. Trovagh had been carried off to finish his sleep in a bed, but Elanor waited for her lord in the courtyard.

"Ciara?"

"I persuaded her to drink chicken broth, my lord. She slept then, but I know she had nightmares. She cried out and struggled in her sleep often. I fear she may be ill from the shock."

Tarnoor sighed. "I know. Her mother was the only one hereabouts with healcraft. Do what you can. Let Trovagh visit as he wishes. She trusts him."

Elanor nodded as he strode away. She would care for the child as her own. She, too, had liked Lanlia and trusted her. Unlike others outside the Keep Lanlia had not treated the woman as a mere servant. Elanor had indeed been maid and companion to Keep's Lady when they arrived. But she had also been bloodkin from a branch of the family without wealth. Still, she had been well taught in all the things necessary to care for a large Keep. Seria had been delicate—and lazy. She had been more than happy for Elanor to take over the running of the Keep's day-by-day affairs. When visiting, Lanlia had spoken to Elanor as a friend, and deferred to her knowledge of the Keep when ordering treatment for Trovagh. For her sake, Elanor would now care for Ciara. The girl was of good blood, Old Race or not. She hastily stifled another idea. That was the future. It did not do to tempt the gods.

Over the next few weeks Ciara faded, however, despite all Elanor could do. The girl slept, only to wake screaming. Elanor became aware the child was unable to keep down most of what she ate. Trovagh was gentle with his friend. He could take her mind from memories and willingly played the fool to do so whenever possible. But at last even he was afraid for her.

"Father, I don't think Ciara is well."

"No." Tarnoor didn't think. He knew. It was as if a wasting fever had the lass in its grasp. "Does she talk to you? Say anything about her nightmares?"

"No. I asked, but she doesn't want to say. What can I do to help?"

His father sighed. "Just be her friend, lad. Maybe she'll talk once she's been here a while longer." He returned to a letter from a friend as Trovagh ran off. News from Kars was odd these days. Yvian had made ax-marriage to the daughter of Verlaine. The mother's line had been well enough, but the father's? Faugh! The man was a wrecker and a rogue. And what of Aldis, she'd not appreciate being thrust aside for some maiden. Letters were few and slow arriving of recent weeks. This one was dated before the Horning. He took up another of a later date and read in bewilderment. What all this talk of Kolder was he did not know, but he liked nothing about it.

He finished reading and rose slowly. Out in the stables he found Hanion and took him aside.

"Strange things happen in Kars of late. I think it wise that we mend walls and shut gates. Make no haste too obvious but be sure all is secure." He saw the sharp glance that met his. "Yes. It is possible trouble may travel this far. We host messengers of other lords as they pass. Tread lightly, but I would know how others of our rank have dealt with the Horning."

"That I can tell you already, Lord. Many have ignored it, or openly taken people under their protection. The messenger of Lord Geavon came through last week. He said his lord was very angry, saying that his family had been lords of Gerith for centuries. They took no orders to murder their people from some upstart mercenary. The only man who attacked at the horns bidding, he took and hung."

Tarnoor grinned. He knew Lord Geavon. A crotchety, gloomy man but a good friend and kin to Tarnoor. Geavon's great love was his lineage and his Keep. In Kars Yvian's word ran, but further out, the lords remembered their duke was a man of no family. They might bow politely in Kars. In their Keeps they bowed to none. Yvian had been raised to duke to keep order in the towns and city. If he failed at this, it was likely there would be plots to depose him. No decent lord appreciated the sort of disorder that was now upon Kars. He proved right in that. As days passed small groups of refugees slipped by Aiskeep. Some, bolder, ventured in with letters of introduction from men known to Tarnoor.

He helped all who did so. Some would have taken Ciara with them, had he asked. He did not. Lanlia had trusted him. Besides, the child was too weak to travel. He did not yet acknowledge that he had grown swiftly to love her. The slow seep of those who fled lessened and died. It bothered him. He wasn't above being tempted; there'd been things done he regretted in his life. But this wholesale slaughter of the innocent appalled him. He would kill if he was attacked, or occasionally as a needed example. But Yvian was ruining Karsten with this folly. His grimness lightened considerably with the next letter.

His bellows of amusement brought Trovagh, Ciara, Hanion, and Elanor.

"My lord?" Hanion was interested.

Tarnoor read further and shouted again with mirth. He looked at the circle of puzzled faces. "A letter from a friend near Kars. Yvian is short a bride. The girl vanished into Estcarp to wed some boy there. It appears Yvian was not to her taste. The Kolder, too, are ended. Estcarp made a foray against them and the Kolder are gone from Kars." He snickered loudly. "None of this will sit well with the duke. Makes the man look a fool, not that he isn't. But no man likes the world to know it. He'll have to move in some way to regain authority. Hanion, just in case it's in this direction, move the work along faster. I want the walls mended in another week. You may also look for another half-dozen suitable guards. I'll be sending you with some of the men to Teral market. We want more weapons and I'd like to lay in barrels of beer and salt beef." He clapped his hands still grinning. "That's all the news. Off with you."

Trovagh stayed. "May Ciara and I go along, Father? She's never been to a real market in a town before."

His father considered. It might perk the child up. She didn't look of the Old Race so should be safe enough in Hanion's care, then again was she fit to travel so far? It would be a full day's ride there and another home again. He compromised.

"The market I want won't be for two more weeks. Tell Ciara she may go with you if she is better by then." He smiled as the boy raced away to share the promise. It reminded him, he must look at the boxes found in Elmsgarth. Thus far they had been stowed away unopened. The only action he'd taken had been to record the transfer of Elmsgarth to himself. It had been done quietly so far as he knew, none but he and a clerk in faraway Kars had knowledge of what had been written. Of course he had also taken the bag of coins. That was going toward mending the Keep walls, and gathering extra supplies. It was fair. Walls would help to protect Ciara, while supplies would be shared with her as well.

He watched the girl over the days. She might force herself to eat. It did no good, all that she ate returned, weakening her further. Tarnoor guessed that something within her revolted at living. Unless one of those who cared for her could find the secret and convince her otherwise, Ciara would go to join her slain kin. He would not have that happen. He loved his son as a strong man loves one who will follow him. But Ciara he had come to love as one who protects responds to the need of one weaker. For her his love was a sheltering roof to her frailty. He watched helpless and raging as she failed.

In another ten days she was too weak to leave her bed for more than a handful of hours. Trovagh stayed with her. He brought games, stories, ideas, anything that would divert her. Elanor played and sang to both children. She had a soft voice, but clear and true, and some small skill with the hand harp. Ciara in particular loved the old songs, begging them over and over. Nightmares still plagued the girl. She woke crying out more than once most nights, the lack of sleep also wearing hard on her.

She refused Elanor's offer to share the bed. She did not wish any to know the shape of her dreams. They seemed to her to be a monstrous wrong and wicked. It was Trovagh at last who broke through the wall of her grief and pain to understand what tore at her. Ciara was sleeping but the boy was awake. As he lay quiet he heard the whimpering from her room. On silent feet he stole through the door. Ciara slept, yet in that sleep tears ran down her face. Now and again her mouth shaped a name.

"Mother, Father, Larian?" Her words became loud enough for the listening boy to understand.

"Mother, please, I'm lonely. Mother, where are you?" Her hand slid out, fingers curled as if they sought for another clasping hand. "Father?" Her voice was a moan. "Larian, why am I alone? Why did you all leave me here?" Her voice trailed off into soft weeping once more. Trovagh took the reaching hand in his. With his left hand he shook her gently by the shoulder.

"Cee? Cee, wake up. You aren't alone. You have me and Father, and Elanor now. Cee!" She opened vague eyes to stare at him. The fingers gripping his convulsed. Still half asleep, she spoke her horror for the first time.

"They all left me. There's no one now. I don't have anyone. No family, everything is cold and empty. When you and Lord Tarnoor came I was afraid. Mother always said Yvian dealt justice, and the guards were there to protect us. But they killed everyone by the duke's order. Why? What did we do that was so evil? I was afraid you would kill me, too, so I hid. I'm afraid all the time now and I have no one. Lonely, so lonely . . ." Her voice shuddered to a halt. Trovagh did the only thing he could think of.

His voice became coaxing, "Listen. You can have a family." Behind him Tarnoor stood motionless and silent in the doorway. He, too, had wakened and come to the child's cries, just in time to hear her confession. He could understand it. Older, stronger people than this girl had been broken by the knowledge they stood alone. Children often understood other children better than any adult. He waited to hear what his son would say.

"Honest, Cee. You can have a family."

"How?" Her interest was caught.

"You do like me, don't you?"

Her hazel eyes gazed at him. "You're my best friend."

He stammered a little on the next question, "D-do you love me, Cee?"

"Yes." There was no hesitation.

Trovagh drew in a deep breath. "Then you can have a family." In bemused wonder, Tarnoor listened as his son proposed marriage.

"If we're betrothed, then my father is your father, too. And I'm sort of a brother until we marry. Elanor's cousin to my mother so she'd be your cousin, too. That way you'd have a real family again. All you have to do is say the words, Cee."

For the first time in many years, Tarnoor felt tears prick his eyes as his son led Ciara through as much as he understood of a betrothal ceremony. Somewhere along the line the boy had also heard of knife oath. He added that in, solemnly bringing out his knife to draw a bead of blood from a finger of each of them. The blood was then mingled. Trovagh reached for the cup of water beside her bed.

"Drink a little." She did so obediently. Trovagh drank after her. He took Ciara's hands. "That's it. By the Cup we shared, by the Flame to witness, by the Blood joined. We're betrothed and my family is yours. You don't have to be alone again." He leaned forward to kiss her very gently on the forehead. "That's my right as betrothed."

Then, as Tarnoor shrank further out of sight, the boy stretched. "Gods but I'm sleepy. You'll be all right now, Cee?"

She nodded, her small face happier. Tarnoor watched as his son trotted back to his own room. When he could again peer through the door, Ciara was asleep. The Keep Lord was thoughtful all of the next day. Without her noticing, he kept an eye on the girl. The ceremony, odd mixture though it had been, seemed to have worked. Ciara kept her meals down, slept without dreaming, and woke to eat heartily. She blossomed. Tarnoor spent a week thinking it over, then he made a decision.

It would not be a bad idea to allow the ceremony legal status. He'd never lose Ciara. His son could have a far worse wife and the girl had brought a fair dowry—by now he'd had sufficient time to check all her belongings and the boxes. He quietly called Elanor, confiding what he had seen.

"The child adores him. I think it an excellent idea, Nethyn. Trovagh will never be strong physically. The girl won't hold that against him as another might. Nor will she seek to take power for herself. She *is* of decent family, is she not?"

Tarnoor nodded. "Her mother Lanlia was orphaned. But her grandmother was of a very old family. That pendant the child wears is from that line. There's more. When I opened the boxes, I found a complete setting in solid silver for the table." He whispered the crest and watched her eyes widen. "Yes, that's no line to be scorned. There were plates and bowls with it, all in silver. The carrysack Lanlia gave the girl to hide in the cave had jewelry. Fine work with rare gems from Estcarp. Another of the boxes had gold and silver coins. A goodly sum. Ciara does not come empty-handed to a betrothal even as Karsten would count it." He thrust a paper at her. "Sign this as a witness. It says I approve the match. I'll have the priestess in tomorrow."

Elanor signed, smiling.

The next day the children were called to Tarnoor's study. When they left both were beaming. On one slender finger Ciara bore a ring. They'd spoken words all over again, this time before a Priestess of Cup and Flame. They hadn't cared. Both knew that it was the earlier ceremony that bound them. It would for all of their lives.

3

*F*or a time Aiskeep was quiet after that. Ciara grew strong. The nightmares troubled her no more. That winter it was Trovagh who was ill. His chest troubles flared with the coming of a cold that made him cough painfully. Ciara vanished industriously into the herb room to brew. She returned with a concoction that he swallowed trustingly. Then he smiled.

"That tastes just the same as your mother used to give me."

"It is the same." It helped the boy until he was careless enough to escape from his bed.

A messenger had come, there was commotion, loud, excited talking, all the fuss guaranteed to bring a boy from his bed in the middle of a night that was chill by any standards. Boylike, too, he ignored it, wearing no more than his slippers and nightgown. By the time he had crouched long on the stairs to hear all that was said, he was chilled to the bone. After all that it hadn't been so interesting anyhow, Trovagh muttered to himself. He hunched back into his cold bed and shivered. He felt so cold.

By the early hours of the morning he was hot, tossing off his bedding only to drag it back again as he shivered once more. Something woke Ciara then. She sat up listening. There was nothing to be heard. She would have laid down again but for the tugging at her attention. She dressed quietly. Lanlia had always said to pay attention to feelings such as these. Silently the child drifted from her room. She would look at her family, see that all was well.

She came first to Trovagh's room and stood listening. There came a faint moan, a soft sound of jumbled words. Then she knew. Ciara wasted no time in entering to reach him. The boy thrashed, burning with fever, already delirious. Ciara looked once, then raced from the room to call Elanor. She burst into the Keep mistress's room without ceremony. Elanor woke abruptly to someone who shook her savagely calling her name. Scared half out of her wits she screamed. This brought Tarnoor bellowing questions as he burst through the door in turn. Ciara had no time for any of them.

"Shut up!" she yelled. "Listen! Tro is sick. He's feverish and his chest is rattling when he breathes. Come quickly." She did not pause to see if they obeyed. By the time they found her she was back with her friend sponging his face gently.

Elanor turned to build up the fire. Heat would help to break the fever. It was then that Trovagh coughed. She heard the rattle and winced inwardly. That was pneumonia, she'd heard it before. Many died from it. They labored for two days as Trovagh grew no better.

Ciara sat with him constantly, her herb concoctions seemingly the only thing that helped. Her presence always able to calm him. The whole of Aiskeep prayed. They'd known the lad since his father brought him out in swaddling clothes to be shown to those he would rule. They were aware that Tarnoor's rule was fair and kind by any standards, far more so than the rule in many Keeps. Trovagh would continue that. The heir after him would not. Tarnoor prayed most fervently. He begged for the life of his son—for several reasons. The foremost was love of the boy. The next was love of his people and the great grim gray Keep they shared.

Like the people he knew the habits of the next heir. A corrupt lad. Barely twenty, he was a third cousin in a cadet branch of the line. The boy lived mostly in Kars, and was a hanger-on to Yvian and worshiper of Aldis. If Risho ever came into power he would be ruthless for his own pleasure. Tarnoor prayed harder, on his knees in the small shrine until his back ached. It was all he could do. Upstairs Ciara labored with all the aid Elanor could give. The fire blazed, and blankets were piled on the bed. Trovagh was dosed with every medicine Ciara had learned that might help. None of it broke the fever.

Elanor sat back on her heels. The fire was pouring heat into the room. She glanced at Trovagh, noting the fever flush, the wasted look. They were losing him. The thought was intolerable. She found herself shaking Ciara by the shoulders.

"You're of the Old Blood. Help him! Use it to *do* something. He's *dying*!"

The girl's head whipped to and fro. Do something? She'd tried everything she knew. But she couldn't lose Tro, he was her best friend, her family. Her betrothed. She hadn't been able to save her kin once. This time she would rather go down into the dark with Tro than lose him. She freed herself ruthlessly.

"Go and get more drinking water. When you come back don't speak or touch me. Keep anyone else to that, too." Her eyes came up to stare hard into Elanor's. "I don't know if I can help, but I'll try."

She set herself to remember as she sat on the stool beside the bed. Her mother's mother had died when Lanlia was only sixteen. But Talyo's mother had lived with them until Ciara was seven. Larian had been her favorite but she'd been kind to Ciara, talked to her. Larian! The pendant! Could that help her now? She freed it from her bodice, staring down at the perfect tear shape, the tiny flickers of blue gems that edged the flanking wings. She cupped it in her small hands. It seemed right then to reach out. Tro's hands slid into hers to lie cupped above them. Into that double cup she allowed the pendant to rest.

She was afraid, so afraid. The maids had talked when Ciara was unnoticed. She understood vaguely that it was the gifts of the Old Race that had brought death to them. They said Yvian hated the Witches. That use of the Power was evil and witchcraft. But if she didn't do this Tro would die. She struggled for a time before she could force herself to try. She would *not* let Tro die because she was afraid.

She allowed her mind to relax, to slow into a gentle calm. The pendant helped with that. It radiated peace, warmth. She felt her breathing slow, her heart cease the nervous pounding. She was no longer aware when Elanor returned. Above the cupped hands her face was a serene mask, while within them the pendant gave off a soft silver light shot with blue. Elanor bit back a gasp. Silently she moved to sit in the doorway. She would keep the quiet Ciara had demanded. Tarnoor would have spoken but her gesture was so fierce he, too, joined her without speaking. Motionless, praying, they waited.

At the bedside Ciara slipped deeper into the trance. From the hands cupped in hers she could feel something. All her thoughts appeared slowed, it was—it was—tightness! Ah, yes. Something bound with many ropes that must be unknotted, unwound to free the captive. Patiently she did so. She could not have said how she managed, only that she felt the ropes loosen and fall away one by one. She flung the last of them aside. Rightness returned. But the silver mist in which she walked was peaceful. She could remain here.

From the door Elanor saw the child's face grow strange. It was a mask now, as if the life slowly drained from her. At the same time the rattle of Trovagh's breathing ceased. Now he breathed in and out quietly. His face flushed, but with the normal pink of returning health. Ciara grew paler, more mask-like. Elanor panicked. The girl was exchanging her life with that of the boy in some way. If she went too far down that path they would have Ciara dead instead. Without pausing to re-flect she flung herself to where the girl sat.

Hard hands struck the link. The two sets of cupped hands were thrust away as the pendant fell free touching neither. Ciara fell limply from her stool. Tarnoor leaped forward in time to catch her as from the bed Trovagh spoke.

"What's all the fuss? Cee? What's wrong with Cee?"

There was instant commotion.

It resolved into Elanor tucking the wilted Ciara into the bed by Trovagh's. It was there the girl had chosen to sleep as she cared for her friend. Now it would be most convenient to have them together and damn the conventions. Tarnoor held his son's hand thanking every power whose name he could recall.

Tro was insistent, "Is Cee all right?"

By now Elanor had been given time to check this. "Yes, she just seems to be completely exhausted. I don't know what she did, but it's drained all her strength. A long sleep, a good meal or two, and she should be well again."

Tarnoor heaved a sigh of relief, then another of exultation. He'd done right to make the betrothal legal. With Ciara at his side to keep him well, Trovagh would live to rule for many years. His face twisted into a snarling grin. *Now* let that de-bauched cousin of his try to claim Aiskeep. His son was alive, his people were safe . . . and Gods but he was tired. He sat in the large chair beside Trovagh's bed. When next anyone looked at him, Tarnoor was deeply asleep.

A week later things were back to normal for all but Ciara. She had no idea of how she had saved Tro. That worried her. What if she couldn't do it again? Perhaps if she looked at the pendant again, without needing to help? She closeted herself in her room while Tro rode with his father. Elanor was busy in the stillroom with an infusion of herbs that must not be left.

Ciara pulled the pendant free, then sat looking at it thoughtfully. It was old, that she knew. Grandmother had said it was a bridegift. Somehow Ciara felt that it was *very* old. There was a feel about it, as if it also had a power of its own. Maybe it did.

She cupped it in her hands, reaching again for the stillness and silver mist. It closed around her, warmly welcoming. It reminded her of Grandmother, like a soft lap and comfort. She could have stayed here forever but when she thought that the mist changed. No longer was it so warm nor so welcoming. She understood. She must not stay, though as a visitor she was permitted. She drifted timelessly before resurfacing to her own room.

Ciara was fascinated. After that she used her pendant most nights, just for a short time. Her ability to reach the mist improved until in a few months she could fall into it at will. She had half forgotten how she had used the pendant with Trovagh. It was only remembered when he came running one late afternoon.

"Cee? *Cee!*"

She bolted from the door, there was desperation in his voice.

"What is it, what's wrong?"

Trovagh was white with horror. "Boldheart—Father jumped him over a wall and he fell."

"Is he badly hurt?"

"His leg's broken."

Ciara snorted, "That's bad but it'll heal in a few weeks. There's no need to get that upset."

Trovagh stared at her, then his voice went higher, "*Not* Father, Boldheart!"

Ciara gasped, then acted. She dived for the stillroom seizing her healer's satchel. "What about Uncle Nethyn, he isn't hurt at all?"

"Just a few bruises," Trovagh panted as they ran. "Here, up behind me." He held the overexcited pony still as she mounted, before kicking it to a gallop. They raced across pasture, up the hillside, and around the curve of brush. Before them Tarnoor sat, Boldheart's great head in his lap. Tarnoor's hand stroked the sweat-streaked neck. He glanced across as the children galloped up.

"I can't leave him. If I do he tries to stand."

Ciara saw the pain in his eyes. She dropped lightly to the ground studying the injured leg. For a horse to break a leg meant he must die, but perhaps it wasn't really broken. She ran light fingers down the foreleg. There was a break but it was clean. Maybe, just maybe . . .

"Keep him still, don't talk to me for a while."

She pulled her pendant free, cupping it in one hand while she laid the other across the injured leg. She didn't know if she could do this. She knew she would try. Boldheart had been the best of all the foals of his year. He'd come to a call, proud but friendly. Uncle Nethyn had chosen him when his previous horse got too old for the harder riding. Boldheart was beautiful, dapple-gray over a silver white mane and tail a cascade of pure silver. He was so gentle that once or twice she and Tro had stolen a ride on him, yet he was warhorse trained. She could feel his pain, his fear, but his trust in his rider, and in the humans who had always been kind to him, kept him lying there.

There was no one but Tarnoor and Trovagh to see. She slipped deep into the mist, it was so easy now. She let her thoughts slide, just emotions. She had it! The feeling of damage, of something to be repaired. It was like pulling herself up a rope; she reached the place and sank her mind into the problem. First she had to put all the bits together. Luckily there were only the two main portions and a chip or two. She held them in place with her mind and wondered. What should she do next? A memory surfaced. Metal turned molten in a mold. Did she have the power to do this? But if she failed, Boldheart died. She must not fail.

She reached out, drawing the mist into her. It flowed, filling her with warmth. Then she drove it into the injury, poured it out sinking it deep into the bone. Slowly, so slowly the bones mended, flowed together until all was whole again. She was far into the mist, a glimpse, a hint of a road there. She was thrust violently backwards. In her mind rang a voice.

*Silly girl. Not yet. Go back. Do I have to do *everything* around here?* Ciara surfaced, giggling weakly. She'd recognize her grandmother's tones anywhere.

She found she was clutching the pendant so tightly the wings had left marks on her palm. She lifted her other hand from where it lay curved around Boldheart's injury. With the last of her strength she ran light fingers down the leg. It was healed. There was no sign it had ever been less than whole. Then she fell back too exhausted to move. Tarnoor gaped down. By all the Powers, she had done it. His attention came back to the child, she was so white. His hand sought her throat. The pulse was slow but strong.

He eased himself out from under the heavy head and stood slowly. Then he spoke to his horse. With a thrashing of legs the beast rolled to sit, then to rise to his hooves. Trovagh's face lit joyously.

"I told you so. I told you Cee could fix him." He crouched back to touch Ciara's arm. "Is she all right?"

"She's drained herself of strength, lad. She needs to be gotten to a bed. Hold!" Tarnoor grabbed his arm before Trovagh could vanish. "It isn't as easy as that. I've been listening to the messengers as they come and go. Beyond Aiskeep the mood is growing harsh about the Witches and the Old Race." He looked into Trovagh's eyes. "Do you know what Cee has done here?"

He answered himself. "She healed a broken leg. When you were very ill she healed you, too. Each time she was tired for days. Healing takes a price from the healer. With the Old Blood driven from Karsten there are very few now who have her ability. She's valuable—and what is valuable may be taken. The longer we can keep silence about this the safer for her. Do you see?"

Trovagh saw. "I won't say anything. We could sneak her in the back way. Elanor could say Cee's got a cold and has to stay in bed a few days."

The idea worked. Ciara was well again in a week. It was Lord Tarnoor who was left to think of the problems that could arise if this were known. He talked to Elanor. She had a good practical head on her shoulders. Moreover, she loved both children.

"She's healed both Trovagh and now Boldheart. About the horse we can keep silence. No one but us knew he was ever injured. But Hanion tells me there are some garbled hints around the Keep of her healing of the boy. As I see it the problem is twofold. First the Old Race is still outlawed in Karsten, and Tylar's death is not so long ago his sons have forgotten. If they could do her an ill turn without bringing down my wrath, they would do it. Secondly there is the question of power. Not hers so much, but what others may see in it."

He did not need to elaborate on that to Elanor. Her line might be a cadet branch, but in its time they had fought their way upward just as savagely. Ciara's healing ability could be used as could any ability. One of the powerful coastal clans would happily use the girl as healer in war. They'd use the very fact they had her to encourage their men at arms. Soldiers would fight far more ferociously if they believed they could be healed of crippling wounds after the battle.

"You said she was exhausted afterward?"

"For several days. She said she was unable to call her gift during that time." His look was black. "Do you think any of that sort would care? They'd force her to it, or lie to their men. All that would be necessary would be to show her healing one of their own. The soldiers would believe. After that if she failed her master would have only to threaten to give her to the men she refused to heal."

"To what end?"

"Think, woman. They'd believe her as treacherous as they have always claimed those with the Power to be. That lie could be used to inflame the men against whoever they wished. They could claim the enemy was Witch-ruled, or involved. Oh, any good lie would serve. We need to keep the girl's gift a secret. I'll have an eye kept on Sersgarth, too. Those sons of Tylar's have been troublemakers from birth."

To that Elanor could agree wholeheartedly. "One of the men told me the older son has moved stock onto the old Elmsgarth land."

"Seran, yes. I hesitate to object as yet. Legally the land belongs to Aiskeep but it's too far from the Keep to be used. So long as Seran stays out of the house I'll hold my hand."

He ushered Elanor out saying no more. Seran was as nasty a piece of work as Tylar had been—and more cunning. Tarnoor was sure the man had been talking to Aiskeep people. He couldn't lock the guards in the Keep. Off duty for a few days they often rode to Teral township and the markets there. Too much to drink, the right questions, and Ciara might be safe no longer.

In that he was right. Seran had already garnered some of the Keep gossip about a child healer. He'd leaped to conclusions—unfortunately, some of them were correct. He could not recall having ever seen the child. She'd look like the Old Race, he expected. Sharp-angled face, black hair, and gray eyes.

Elanor, too, had considered that. Ciara did not look like her blood. After all, she was no more than half. It might be possible to make her look even less like to those still hunted. She sent for Ciara; the girl had sense. She might even have further ideas of disguise.

Cee listened. "You can't change my eyes or face shape. Anyhow, they don't look like Old Blood. Maybe my hair. It isn't black, it's dark brown. Could we lighten it just a shade more? It wouldn't show that we'd done it but I'd look more like a Karsten native."

They tried. With an infusion of herb wash Ciara's hair lightened from dark to medium brown. It was surprising, Elanor thought, how much it altered the child's appearance. Nor had Elanor been her cousin's maid for nothing. A skillful change in hair style added a rounder look to Ciara's face. They could do no more but pray now it would suffice.

For a time, it did. Seran was told by more than one drunken man at arms from Aiskeep, that no female of the looks he described dwelt there. It left him furious but temporarily baffled.

Spring slipped into summer, then midsummer before the news came with hammering hooves to the Keep gates. "Open, open for a Clan Messenger!"

Hanion looked about. Only one rider, and that one all but hysterical on a staggering mount. He ran to open the gate.

"What is it, man? Has someone died?"

"Aye. Call your lord."

Hanion put two and two together coming up with six. He fled for Tarnoor's study calling loudly.

"What . . . ?"

"A messenger from Lord Geavon. Lord, I think he may bring news of Yvian's death."

Tarnoor took the stairs three at a time. The messenger was drinking wine eagerly but halted to offer the letter. Then he returned to his cup. Riding like this was thirsty work.

Tarnoor did not wish the contents of his letter to be questioned. He retired to his study before breaking the familiar seal. Geavon might be a crotchety gloomy lord, but he and Tarnoor had been fostered together as boys. They were of the same clan and hence kin, and their friendship had been stronger still. Geavon's Gerith Keep was close enough to Kars for Geavon to hear all the news within days, sometimes within hours. A letter sent with this much urgency must contain news of real import. It was quite likely Hanion's suggestion was right.

Tarnoor sighed. If Yvian had been assassinated by one of the clans, life was about to become dangerous. He read swiftly, then sat thinking. An assassination, it appeared—but not by a Clan Lord seeking power.

Tarnoor remembered. Yvian had chosen to wed Loyse of Verlaine Keep, daughter to Fulk, known as the wrecker-lord. It had been a proxy marriage but legal. Then the bride had vanished.

At first she'd been believed dead at her own hand. There'd been talk of a high window left open, lace left snagged on the rough stone of its sill. Tarnoor smiled. Talk had begun and the people had been amused that the duke's bride would rather be dead than wed. Then other news drifted through on the winds. The girl was alive. She had escaped, fled through the countryside and across the mountains to seek refuge with the Witches in Estcarp.

It was bad enough to lose a bride. But as the news filtered slowly back to the city, the laughter had become too loud to be safely overlooked. For a man to find his ax-wed bride fleeing from him was bad enough. To hear that she had taken in marriage another, worse. But when that other was a misshapen boy, when he and his bride now stood high in the councils and friendship of an enemy . . .

All this made Yvian appear an ineffective fool. He'd gone to Fulk of Verlaine for answer. All that much-tried lord could say was that the witchery of Estcarp had had a hand in events. But where Loyse was now Fulk could not say.

For Yvian it was not safe to allow the matter to drop. Where the people laugh too loudly a duke's throne may begin to shake. Apart from that, Yvian was a proud man. In all of this his pride had been flung into the dust. Somehow he had seized Loyse and succeeded in bringing her back to Kars. It even seemed likely he had bedded her and thus the woman was now Duchess of Kars. But the matter had not stopped there for long. The next any knew Yvian was dead, murdered. By Loyse, some said. By Witches, others claimed.

Fighting amongst several city and clan factions had broken out at the time of Yvian's death. This time all were agreed that the fighting had been Witch-inspired. The duke's mistress, one Aldis, had come with lies to each faction setting them against one another. There was no reason, no benefit to her in this. No doubt it was witchery. Moreover, the Lady Loyse had vanished, so had Aldis, and to complete the set, word had come from Verlaine that a half of its men at arms were dead, the remainder vanished along with Lord Fulk. That must be witchery as well.

Tarnoor snorted. Witchery be damned. It was trouble that's what it was. With Fulk gone the rich pickings at Verlaine were open. If Fulk did not return swiftly a dozen local lords would be at one another's throats to seize the Keep. Still worse, the same applied to Kars. Loyse was allied by her mother's line to three of the more powerful clans. They would be moving shortly to claim the duchy in her name. If she did not return, however, there were plenty of others who'd be interested in a vacant Keep of considerable wealth and the potential for a lot more so long as ships sailed and storms came.

Geavon ended with a couple of paragraphs of warning. Their own clan might well become embroiled in all this. Geavon would find it hard not to become involved if so. Gerith Keep was too close to Kars to be overlooked. He urged his friend to strengthen Aiskeep, to look to his walls and supplies. If none of this was soon resolved war might come.

Tarnoor reread the letter, then yelled for Hanion. "The repairs to the outer wall, are they complete?"

"Yesterday, my lord."

"Then I want you to take the wains for further stone. This is to be used to strengthen any other weaker parts of the walls." He named a figure for this which made Hanion look grave. "After that ready the wains again. We go soon to Teral market to purchase siege supplies." Hanion opened his mouth in horror. Tarnoor overrode him. "If you can think of anything we can take and sell in the markets before we buy, say so once you have checked. Warn the garth owners they should harvest as and when they can. No harvest should be left longer than the time it takes to ripen. Aiskeep will aid with harvesters at need."

He leaned back in his chair and summarized Geavon's letter, concluding, "Clans and city factions are already starting maneuvers. Sooner or later some half-wit will add weapons to the discussion." He looked at Hanion.

"You wanted to ask if we were at war. We may well be very soon. Not with Estcarp, but with our own. The worst kind of war. Go and prepare for it, old friend. The storm is rising, and I'd like to be sure our roof doesn't leak."

He watched Hanion leave before sitting back to swear savagely. Yvian! No country needed outside enemies when they'd enthroned an idiot like that. He wondered where it would end.

4

*T*ime drifted by. Aiskeep walls were thickened in the two weaker places. The children ran about getting under everyone's feet, men at arms vanished to different garths to help bring harvests home, and Teral market came due. As if preparing for trouble to come, the harvests, at least here, had been very good. But by slow, loaded wain, Teral was two days distant. Ciara's eyes on him were so hopeful Tarnoor smiled.

"You two can come. You're to stay together at all times. Don't bother the men or Hanion. Be ready to return when I tell you." He thought of something else. "Ciara, isn't it your name day very shortly?"

"Yes, Uncle Nethyn."

"Well, we'll have to celebrate that." He mentioned it to Elanor before the wains rolled out of the gates, and found himself with a list of small things to buy. Women, they always had some small errand you should do this very minute!

Men, they always left everything to the last minute! Elanor was muttering in turn as she saw them off. How was she supposed to ask him earlier if she wasn't told!

The trip was wonderful for Cee. It was the first time she'd left Aiskeep land since she'd arrived. She and Trovagh rode ponies, ducking and crossing the lumbering wains as the excited pair attempted to see and do everything at once. Tarnoor watched them indulgently. They'd be away five days, maybe six. Two days travel each way and one or two days at the market. Among them, he, Hanion, and Elanor had successfully found enough to part-fill each of the three wains. If it all sold at reasonable prices they would have sufficient coin added to what Tarnoor already had to buy.

He had gone over his lists before they left. He'd buy bar steel for the forging of weapons, horseshoes, and harness rings. More tanned leather, bolts of cloth, and much thread of differing kinds. It was cheaper to purchase the materials rather than goods already made. It should also be possible to find rings ready made to repair chain mail. Enough of them and he could have the Aiskeep smith make up additional armor and save much time. It would also help Tarnoor's purse.

The trip was peaceful. Nothing went wrong. No delays occurred, and the weather remained fine. Tarnoor worried about all that. In his experience when things went right, something wrong was looming on the horizon.

He reflected that he was becoming as gloomy as old Geavon. It was Teral he was approaching, not Kars. The small line of wains and riders topped the long shallow slope and started down toward the town. Teral had been built on the bend of a large stream that cut deep into the softer earth. This meant that even with the water in spate the small town never flooded. The buildings were mostly of wood but the inn and stables were older. These were of the pale local stone, well and solidly laid. Tarnoor had sent ahead to reserve most of the rooms.

He saw to the stabling of their beasts, chased the excited

children upstairs to leave their gear, then freed them to explore.

"Here, that's for you to spend. Remember it has to last the whole time we're here."

Ciara and Trovagh dashed off to count. "We're rich." Ciara was looking at the handful of coins.

Trovagh grinned at her. "Not as much as it looks," he informed her. "Father must have been saving coppers again. But it does mean we can split it more easily. And we don't have to worry about changing it or anything."

Ciara was looking about her. "Oh, jugglers." They watched the entertainment for a while, dropping a copper in the laid-out hats. Then it was the lines and rows of stalls. Trovagh would have bought food but Ciara was more practical.

"The inn's been paid for all our meals. Let's go back and eat there free."

They raced, laughing, back to the inn, there to share well-roasted mutton, new bread with fresh butter, and apples to follow.

"Mmm." Trovagh caught a drip of butter. "Good idea of yours, Cee." He grabbed a couple of the apples, handing one to her. "Let's go see the beast market."

They raced off again. Tarnoor smiled after them. They were having a wonderful time, bless them both. He returned to his discussion with the innkeeper.

"Yes, my lord. Rumors have reached even to Teral and farther south. People are buying all they can afford of supplies. I've had word another trader arrives in the morning bringing beasts for sale and Sulcar-traded goods."

Tarnoor sat up at that. "You mean some trader is in from the coast?"

"Aye, my lord. Trader Tanrae is from hereabouts. He returns home to be with his family for a while." He leaned closer and his voice dropped. "Word is that with the trouble in Kars the man wishes to be well away from any possible fight-

ing. Where there is war, merchants and traders do not profit.
Worse, their goods, gear, and beasts may be impressed by the
army. Tanrae's parents are at a garth several days south. His
wife and children live with them. The man's heading that way
once he has sold most of his merchandise."

"But has he not sold it in Kars before he departed?"

The innkeeper shook his head. "I hear the cargo was landed
from a ship well to the south of Kars. Tanrae planned to go on
to the city."

Tarnoor understood now. "I see, but then he heard the
news, so he chose to travel swiftly in the opposite direction.
A wise man. What goods are you sure he has for sale? It may
be we shall remain a day to see."

The list was interesting enough to ensure that. The children
arrived back to eat in the early evening. Tarnoor seized on
them.

"We remain here tomorrow." He hastily hushed the yells of
delight. "Ciara. I want you and Trovagh to check the herb
stalls for me. Quietly! Buy nothing. Do not appear too interested. If Ciara sees any herb we do not have at Aiskeep and
may need in case of war, remember where you saw it. Come
back and get Hanion. I shall rely on you both in this. Ciara,
you are to take Hanion's arm. He will buy what you casually
pick up to sniff or look at. A squeeze is yes, a light pinch is
no. I want none to guess you have herb knowledge lest they
guess more. I trust you both to be sensible and careful."

It was this transaction that produced danger. Seran might
never have noticed the children if they had been at other
stalls. But Lanlia had been well-known for her healcraft and
herb knowledge. He knew Trovagh, enough to recognize the
boy as Seran passed the stalls. Then he saw the girl. His step
faltered. Ciara did not look like the Old Blood, but she *did*
look very like her mother. And it was that resemblance Seran
recognized. He sucked in a long breath. The brat's brother had
killed Tylar, Seran's father.

It would be fitting if she had an accident here at the market. He was pasturing his stock at her garth now but from what he saw, she and the boy were close. He saw danger to his own plans in that. Under the new laws of Kars and Yvian, she had no claim to Elmsgarth. But Yvian was dead. If the duchess returned she might favor another female. If one of the powerful clans set up another duke they, too, might favor the girl. She seemed to be well in with Tarnoor's son.

The old lord was no fool. Elmsgarth would make a fair dowry. If Aiskeep held it from the girl it might be sold to any who had coin to buy. Good fertile land well away from likely trouble, a large house in weather-tight condition, pens and barns standing ready . . . Tarnoor could gain a fine price for Elmsgarth if he ever chose to sell. Seran glared at the unsuspecting children. Tarnoor didn't live in great state, nor did he travel to Kars to toady to those in power. Still all knew he was related by birth and marriage to two of the clans. But if he did not have the girl in his hands, his claim to the garth would be greatly weakened.

Seran smiled, a look of vicious anticipation. The stream was deep. True in summer it did not flow so strongly but it should be sufficient to drown the Witch's daughter. Over the remainder of the morning he stalked the children, now free from Hanion. In a large, busy market there would be possibilities.

Tarnoor was busy elsewhere. Trader Tanrae had arrived with goods both interesting and useful. The two men were busy talking prices and haggling with enthusiasm. Tarnoor made a last purchase and gave instructions for its handling and delivery. He was about to leave the trader when Trovagh appeared looking distressed.

"What is it, where is Ciara?"

"She's gone. Hanion bought as she showed him. Then he went back to the inn. Cee and I went to look at the beast market again. She was right beside me, when I turned around she'd gone."

Tarnoor wasted no time. Better he made a fool of himself than anything happened to the girl. "Run to the inn," he instructed Trovagh. "Tell Hanion to turn out every man but a couple to guard our wains. I want the market combed, stallholders asked if they saw Ciara. Hop to it, lad."

Trovagh raced away while Tarnoor turned to the trader. "I regret I must leave you so abruptly, but as you have heard, I have something to attend to."

Tanrae nodded slowly. "How old is the little maid?"

"Ten years all but a week. It was for her name day I purchased some of the wares you offered."

"Yes, so I surmised. You will not mind if I and my men also aid the search? I have a daughter of that age myself."

Tarnoor bowed formally. "I would be deeply grateful, trader."

He hurried from the tent with the trader at his heels calling his men.

Tanrae gave quick instructions. Within minutes the hunt was up. In a small tent among the beast tents Seran snarled. Damn that Aiskeep brat. He'd missed the girl so fast, raised the alarm so quickly, that Seran had no time to get her away. He could kill her. But Tarnoor had enough authority to hold everyone here. There was no telling what he would do if he recognized Seran.

There might be no evidence, but what lord required that if he preferred to ignore it? Seran glared at the struggling bundle beside him. Best he left the damned girl here and slipped away. There'd be another day. One he'd win next time. Thanks be to Cup and Flame she hadn't seen his face.

He unlaced the tent flap cautiously. Fortunately the hue and cry had not yet reached this end. He thrust the squirming bundle out and laced the flap again. Then he pried up the rear of the tent and crawled beneath. By the time men were walking down this row he would be well away.

He was. Nor could Ciara say who had laid hands on her. It was Tanrae who almost tripped over the trussed girl. His yell brought everyone from Tarnoor to Trovagh running. Tarnoor slashed the cords and a ruffled, frightened, furious child emerged spitting out horsehair. Investigation of the horse blanket used betrayed nothing. Seran had stolen it elsewhere. The rope was ordinary cord used for many things in a market. Nor could any remember selling it in particular or to whom. Tarnoor kept his guesses to himself.

He did have Hanion quietly check about with several of the men. No one could remember seeing Seran or any of the other three of Tylar's sons. That evening Tarnoor faced the trader over a drink.

"I owe you a debt, trader. I think evil was planned. Your aid made so much more excitement than her taker expected that he chose to leave Ciara and flee."

Tanrae eyed him shrewdly. "You guess who this was, do you not?"

"Perhaps. But I'll accuse no man without proof of some kind. It is true there is a family with good reasons to wish the girl gone. But none were seen here. The child herself can say nothing save that she was gripped about the throat from behind, lifted a little, and carried a short distance. She believes the grip on her throat made her faint for a period. When she recovered she was trussed as you found her."

"What of the tent she lay beside?"

Tarnoor snorted in disgust. "The owner left it laced shut. There's no sign within that it was used. Although the pegs at the rear are loosened as if someone may have entered that way. No one was seen."

"He was lucky."

"Very lucky!" Tarnoor said softly. Tanrae glanced at him. This lord might prefer evidence before he acted, but the trader would not like to be guilty if such evidence were forthcoming. Lord Tarnoor was powerfully muscled. He might be approaching middle-age, but it was clear he'd been a soldier and a fighter. An old sword-cut showed at the top of his left sleeve. The sword at his side was plain with well-worn hilt. Still Tanrae would wager it was a fine blade within the sheath. The lord simply saw no reason to spend on fancy hilts. But the eyes and the lines of Tarnoor's face told a tale to one who could read.

Tanrae had not been a trader for many years without being able to read such. This man would make a loyal and generous friend—and a very bad enemy. He'd rule kindly, until one of his people crossed what Tarnoor thought essential. The trader nodded to himself, drinking off the last of his wine. Then he fumbled in his purse.

"I brought these for the lass. They'll go with the gifts you purchased for her."

Tarnoor looked down at the two small bells. "So they will. That is kind of you, man. Nor do I forget I owe a debt for your quick aid." He rose, ushering the trader out. A good man that. Canny, but honest. He'd look for the man at other markets. As for the children, he'd assigned Hanion to keep watch. Right now they were busy loading the wains for the trip home. He hid a smile. Hanion was under orders to keep them from the end wagon. Ciara's name-day gifts would ride in that, transferred there just before they departed Teral.

The ride home was uneventful. Ciara got over her fright easily. Tarnoor had convinced her that the attack had been no more than a mistake, telling a tale he claimed to have heard in the market of a girl who had run from her home. He made it convincing. Ciara believed, but Hanion knew better.

"You think it to have been that Seran, my lord? I could make inquiries. If he was from home it is likely someone will mention it if asked the right way."

"That proves naught, unfortunately. But listen for word of

him. You've kept one eye on the man, now keep both. I would know where he goes and what he does at all times so far as is possible. He's a soured, dangerous enemy, and I think we'll hear more of him."

"Why not simply have him killed?"

Tarnoor grinned. "You barbarian! It's a thought. But there's more to consider. Sersgarth boasts four sons and two daughters. Already the next generation arrive. If I have Seran murdered, be sure they'd think it to have been at my word. After that there'd be blood feud. It would take a massacre to prevent that."

"What do you think he planned for the child, Lord?"

"Me? I think the stream runs deep there. A few minutes longer without hue and cry and Ciara could have been at the edge. Thanks be to the Powers and the trader that time was not granted."

"Then why not another accident, Lord? I'm sure Seran is sometimes drunk. How easy it is for a man in drink to fall."

"Perhaps. I'll think on it. Now—to work."

A few days later it was Ciara's name day. Elanor was thankful for that. Keeping the girl's gifts hid had required more work than preparing the feast. But it had all been worth it. The beautifully made box was carried in, ribbon bedecked and mysterious. Ciara took it. Her gaze fell on one end where strange holes decorated the side in a pattern. Each was a thumb joint wide and from one issued forth something slim and furry.

"What is it?" Her finger reached out hesitantly to touch. "Uncle Nethyn, what is it?"

"Try opening the box, sweetheart."

Gently Ciara unwound the ribbons. The lid was lifted and two small faces peered back at her. Then a small pink mouth opened. It meowed plaintively. The other promptly followed suit. Whatever they were they seemed to offer no danger.

Ciara reached in to lift one. It clung with small claws, purring vigorously. She lifted the other and stood cuddling them as they snuggled into her.

"What are they?"

"Cats, my dear. Well, kittens yet. I purchased them from Trader Tanrae. The Sulcar often carry them on the larger family ships to keep down rats or mice. We see them seldom here in the South but they are valiant hunters. Worthy beasts to have the freedom of a Keep." To the listening Elanor he added quietly, "They will also be useful for trade in a year or two. I paid high. They are from different litters and should breed well. Once there are sufficient kits I can sell them to other Keeps hereabouts. If war comes they will be worth their weight in gold against vermin in the barns and storehouses." Elanor watched the children each cuddling a happily purring kitten and smiled to herself. All that was true, but she suspected it had been thought up after the purchase. Tarnoor was kinder and more generous than he permitted most to know.

He'd already returned to Ciara, "Here, lass. The trader sent you these as a gift." He held out the two bells. To them he added a matching pair of small leather collars. "Hanion made these for you. See, you may tie the bells to them."

In minutes the kittens were scampering about tinkling merrily as they bounced and played. Trovagh trailed his scarf and the children shrieked as the kits attacked. In days they were often a foursome. The kits grew quickly, friendly to all but preferring to sleep one on each of the children's beds. There was a swift massacre of mice, followed by rats as soon as the babies were a little larger. It made them popular with all in the Keep.

Geavon wrote again several weeks after Ciara's name day. The news was not good. Tarnoor read it, then summoned Elanor and handed her the letter. She, too, read and frowned.

"So the Lady Loyse has reappeared in Estcarp. That makes people certain it was she or the Witches who slew Yvian. That

Aldis is nowhere found makes no fuss. Indeed, it may make things easier solved. But Fulk—now that he's been gone for months the lords about Verlaine squabble vigorously over his hold."

"Indeed. The man was a wrecker and a rogue but he held Verlaine with a strong hand. Loyse makes it plain she will not return nor lay claim to Verlaine or Kars. Thus both rulerships are open. I think it will not be long before argument turns to warfare over Verlaine at least. That should suit Estcarp. Verlaine is close to their border. If the lords nearby squabble over Verlaine, they are not fighting nor raiding elsewhere."

Elanor agreed thoughtfully. "Is it possible that this was why they slew Fulk and Yvian?"

"It is possible. Any soldier could have predicted the outcome."

"So all this may have been a deep-laid plot against Karsten? In revenge for the Horning perhaps?"

Tarnoor shrugged. "Perhaps. It is done now. But it's as well we've prepared. If the struggle grows violent enough at Verlaine it will pull the coast clans in. Then there is Kars. Here in the South we may be called by the clans. If that happens, then there is likely to be open war among the clan lords. Such wars are without quarter. No enemy is fought so savagely as one who is your own." He sighed. "Alas for Karsten."

Elanor left to ready the evening meal while Tarnoor sat thinking. He would write to Geavon suggesting a compromise. For two generations it had worked with a Keep here in the far South. He sent the letter swiftly by messenger. Geavon received it and blinked. Wisdom from a backwater. It just might work. He sat to write letters of his own. There was an advantage to be gained. Two of the disputing lords were of Geavon's clan. If they combined, the others would back off.

They might have done so, had the letter arrived in time. Even in the South they heard how the lords battled over Verlaine. Finally, Tarnoor's suggestion ended it, but not without many dead and hatred stored up. There was a marriage. Verlaine was again ruled. By the second son of one lord, wed to the eldest daughter of his neighbor. In a year he was dead, poisoned. His wife could not hold the Keep and fled to her clan. The war began again and spread this time.

But Tarnoor had used the year wisely. He'd bargained, traded, bought, and sold. Aiskeep was stronger than it had been in many generations.

The kits, too, had contributed. Their first litter had sold for very high prices as Tarnoor had expected. The second litter, already bulging the small female's sides, was sold in advance. Tanrae had visited Aiskeep, once bringing a long train of loaded wains. The same Sulcar ship had met him quietly on the coast. With the trader came a second female kitten for Ciara.

Elanor might wonder that the Sulcar who allied with Estcarp would come to trade. Tarnoor did not. Civil war in Karsten could only profit other lands. If they sold Karsten goods and gear to war, then the longer and more deadly that war, while the Sulcar profited and other lands lay safer.

From overseas news came that the hounds of Alizon hunted. Karsten could not look to them for aid. They had strange allies, men said: perhaps those Kolder who had done so ill by Kars after all their promises. Meanwhile in Karsten war came closer. Twice Keeps near Kars were clan-besieged. The fighting spread to Kars for several days. It died again but sullenly. Then one arose supported by two of the clans. Kieren was young, but a fighter known from the wars with Estcarp. Since many believed that their troubles were all Witch-caused, that stood him in good stead.

He made truce with a third clan by marriage. Another year of peace, and half again. Ciara was growing. She'd been twelve last name day and Trovagh thirteen. She was not beautiful but there was strength and sweetness in her face. She and the boy were as close as ever, always up to some ploy. The letters from Geavon came regularly to Aiskeep. Tarnoor expected another shortly. Instead, Geavon's nephew came quietly in the night.

He stood in Tarnoor's study talking softly. "My father is being drawn into clan councils. Kieren does not treat his wife well. Her clan plans to wait until she bears her child, then declare her Kars Regent in the child's name. My uncle thinks this will bring war again. He asks that you allow his family to come here while there is yet time."

The man he addressed nodded. "Bring them cautiously. Travel as traders or a garth family on the move. They'd be good hostages against Geavon's compliance with orders."

"Yes, my lord." The young man slipped away before dawn, riding back to the Keep.

Events overtook him. It was weeks before Tarnoor heard, then he sat silent. Geavon's letter was open before him. The boy had been slain on the return. By whom Geavon did not know, only that the body lay before their gates one morning. The lad's father was not a man to think deeply for meanings. He assumed that it had been done by the clan opposing his and acted. A third clan had been drawn in. The remaining three might have stayed out of the fight. It was none of theirs. But the duchess's father deemed it a good time now to strike for the duchy. The baby had been a son.

Kieren died in an ambush. The other clans swept in to do battle. Geavon was full of regret. It would not be possible just at this moment to send his family to Aiskeep. Tarnoor swore, tossing the letter into the fire. Outside on the stairs he heard the clatter of heavy boots. That was Hanion in a hurry; what troubled them *now*?

He opened the door. Hanion burst in already speaking. "Lord, there's men at arms at the gates. They tried to enter but we had the gates shut in time. They say they are from Lord

Geavon but we recognize none of them and they are heavily armed. They demand entrance."

Tarnoor followed Hanion to the gates. There he looked down at those below. Men at arms? No, more like a small army. He counted more than a hundred men along with a dozen wains. They had set a half circle about the gates just over an arrow's flight back. This was no message from Geavon. He leaned far out to search for any known face. An arrow sliced the collar of his cloak as he shied sideways.

He swore again. He seemed to have done a lot of that since Yvian's death, he thought. Then he descended to the gates.

"Unfriend, come forward and tell me what you wish."

From the other side a voice called, "Open the gates and yield to Clan Grothar."

"If I choose not to?"

"Then we remain here. Nothing goes in or out save it be one to offer surrender."

"Stay then and be damned to you," Tarnoor bawled back. He marched up the wall steps again to look between the crenellations. Aiskeep was under siege. The war had arrived in the South at last.

5

Ciara and Trovagh were bored. Outside the enemy had been camped at Aiskeep gates for a month. Nothing more happened. The soldiers sat there, firing an arrow now and then at anyone they saw on the Keep walls. Sometimes one of the Keep men at arms shot back. It had been quite exciting that first week where there was a lot of that going on. But the men outside had moved back a few more yards. They stopped bothering to shoot. Now they just sat. They didn't even bother to reply to the colorful insults Aiskeep men hurled at them. After a long consideration of his maps, Tarnoor had identified the probable reason for the siege.

"Look, here's where their land runs. This land belongs to Septan, who's just wed into the clan. His land reaches almost to Aiskeep. Clan Grothar has a very old dispute with our clan." He snorted. "The idiots have decided to take advantage of the general unrest to see if they can add to their boundaries."

"Why is that so stupid, Uncle Nethyn?" Ciara was puzzled.

"Because, my dear, as any effective soldier knows, before you begin a fight, you should know what shape your enemy is in."

Both children stared, then understood. "Oh," said Trovagh. "All the stores we've been getting in."

"The walls are all fixed, too," Ciara added.

"Exactly. We've spent the last couple of years expecting this. The walls are just about the strongest they've ever been. We have enough supplies in the lower storerooms to last a year or more even without our own harvest, and we have a water supply. The armory is filled with arrow bundles, bar steel, and anything else we may need. So this pack of fools pick now to start something." He snorted again. "I never did think Ager had any sense. He heads the clan because he has seven idiot sons who all back him. That's why. Not that even they'll continue if he does much of this."

The sons—or Ager—must have come to a similar conclusion. The siege remained in camp ineffectively another couple of months. Then one morning they were gone again leaving only an awful mess and an incredible stench behind them. Tarnoor promptly sent out scouts, Hanion leading them. They returned to say that Clan Grothar had far worse troubles of their own.

Hanion was grinning. "They have their own siege now, my lord. It seems the boy who wed into them isn't so happy with his bargain. His own clan seems to have taken up his quarrel. Do we head for Teral while our gates are clear?"

"We do indeed."

Tarnoor split his forces. Some thirty armed men escorted the lumbering wains toward the small market town, while another thirty men remained to guard Aiskeep. Most of those remaining were the older or young and inexperienced. Some were simply garthsmen who wished to help their lord. Between the two groups messengers rode. That way, Tarnoor mused, if anything happened at either end he should know within hours. Nothing did. The wains returned heavily loaded, the last of the Keep's fall harvest was gathered into the storerooms, and winter was on its way.

Ciara and Trovagh had sneaked away. When the girl first arrived she had begged to learn the sword with her friend. Hanion agreed if his master had no objections. Tarnoor had merely laughed.

"Let the little maid learn," he'd said kindly. "It will help to take her mind from her grief." He'd then dug into the storeroom to find a light sword that might be used. In the four years since, the children had gained knowledge of both sword and bow. Ciara had proved to have a very real talent for the latter. She could not pull one of the heavier ones, but with a light bow she could place her arrows with a neat precision.

Trovagh was a swordsman. He would never be of more than middle height, but that height was already springy with lithe muscle. His reflexes were excellent, his sight keen, and he'd learned of Hanion all the tricks that shrewd old campaigner could teach. He still developed dangerous colds during the winters, but Ciara was there to help with those. At fourteen he bade fair to equal his father in common sense and leadership.

Beside him Ciara stood, their old comradeship as strong as ever. She could beat him in a sprint although his endurance was the greater. If he was the better swordsman she could outshoot him. They knew each other's minds, each often finishing a sentence for the other.

Tarnoor and Elanor, studying them, were happy with what they had wrought. The children knew Aiskeep from the highest tower to the lowest storeroom. They knew every inch of the lands and the mountains that backed them. Both rode like centaurs. Not that there weren't flaws. Only the previous week, Elanor had found a large and indignant toad in her bed. She'd climbed into the bedding, thrust her feet down to the wrapped stone, and instead of the expected warmth, encountered something cold, damp, and alive. She'd screeched, shot out of bed, lost her balance, and landed sitting on her rump in the middle of the bedroom in a way both bruising to dignity and posterior.

She knew why the toad was there, of course. She'd made Ciara stay inside that morning instead of allowing the child to ride. Elanor had received a very thoughtful look. But one day the girl would be Keep Lady. She must learn everything possible now. Elanor rubbed her rump and smiled unpleasantly. Two could play at that game. She said nothing in the morning—but Ciara sitting down to her porridge found it to be heavily salted.

"I trust you'll eat all your breakfast," Elanor told her with a heavy significance. "If you do I'll find myself silent." Ciara ate glumly. Trovagh pulled the bowl between them and ate his half. Elanor understood. He'd helped with the toad and would share the punishment. She cleared away the emptied bowl and true to her word, said nothing of toads to Tarnoor.

Neither child had ever been beaten. After losing her family the way she had, an angry word left Ciara heartbroken, convinced of rejection. Once, in earlier days, Tarnoor had rounded angrily on her for a piece of dangerous mischief. He had found himself holding a child who wept more and more frantically. Her sobs shifted to gasps for breath, then she fainted. She became conscious only to return to the gasping and then loss of consciousness once more. She'd been put to bed and been miserably silent for a day until Tarnoor had convinced her she was not utterly unloved.

But during their next exploit, Tarnoor would savagely desire to beat both of them bloody. All had been quiet for weeks. Even a recent letter from Geavon had reported fighting to have temporarily died down in Kars. Winter was closing in, and the children decided a last ride into the mountains would be fun before the snows deepened.

"Take your bow, we may see something."

Ciara nodded. "You better take your sword, too. Uncle Nethyn says not to take chances even on our own land."

Trovagh laughed, "All right," he teased. "But what do you think is out there, outlaws or wolves?"

It was true neither were that likely. So early in winter the wolf packs had not yet begun to form. It would not be until several months later that they could become dangerously hungry. As for outlaws, most of those were to be found far more to the north where clan fights had often dispossessed garth families of their homes and land. Aiskeep was not only the Keep, but also the land beyond. The great stone Keep itself held dominance over the entrance to a long steep-sided fertile valley that cut well into the mountains behind, winding almost twenty miles as it gradually rose toward the steeper heights. Because of this position the Keep controlled the valley. The original Tarnoor had seen the advantages at a glance as Karsten expanded south several hundred years earlier. He'd spent everything he had in raising the Keep and walling it in thick solid walls.

This had paid off. He held the land alone for many years, the only lord able to keep his estate free of wolves and human attack. Over the years, those who enjoyed a frontier rallied to him, but they also preferred strong walls between them and danger. Since then garths had risen outside Aiskeep. They were often independent but the trade was useful. Nowadays most of the land about was settled, but with Yvian's death, the usual peace had been permanently changed. The constant clan squabbling of the past four years had left many men with no trade but banditry. But right now neither child had any thought of that.

With a yelp Trovagh sent his horse racing up the valley, Ciara following hard at his heels. On the side of each saddle bounced a filled bag. They planned a trip that would take them to the valley end. It wouldn't do to go hungry. They rode beyond the valley, then the horses leaned into the mountain trail. Farther up and well to the northeast there was a small sheltered cup of land. There was a cave there, and a rock basin usually filled with good water. They would eat, rest their mounts, and then hunt.

It was fortunate that they were walking their horses in silence. They approached the cave only to hear voices. Trovagh signaled Ciara to back her mount. Cautiously he joined her further back and dismounted.

"Who do you think that is, Tro?"

"I don't know. But I know a few other things. They're trespassing, and they aren't our people. And before you ask, I was closer. That accent isn't from here. It's more to the west over by the coast."

"Oh. So what do we do, ride back and tell Uncle?"

"Tell him what. That we heard a foreign accent in the mountains?"

Ciara grinned at him. "No, we tell him how many there were, what they looked like, and what they were doing here."

Trovagh grinned back in relief. Good old Cee. He'd known she'd want to find out about this bunch as much as he did.

"Right. We leave the horses off the trail over there. If we cross the trail and go up the side there," his finger indicated, "we should be right over the cave. With luck we can hear everything they say. We can even look through the bushes at them if we're careful." He had a brief moment of doubt about this. But Cee was nodding.

"It's sunhigh. If they're still here it probably means they're staying the night. We can find out about them, then ride back to tell Uncle. He can come back with Hanion in the morning."

Trovagh quashed his doubts. This was for Aiskeep, to help protect their people from outlaws. Not that in his heart he believed the voices belonged to wolfsheads. Probably some messengers trying to be unobtrusive at a lord's orders. For all that he and Ciara were careful. With their mounts safely tucked away in the lawleaf thicket, the two children drifted quietly up the hillside.

Below them the cave echoed voices. A fire burned in the

mouth. Trovagh looked down at that with interest. Hanion had told him often how to build a smokeless fire for enemy country. Down below was a perfect example of this. It certainly indicated a wish on the part of those below to remain unnoticed. A sideways glance at Cee showed him that this had not escaped her. They lay forward comfortably and prepared to listen.

A rough voice floated up to them as the speaker emerged from the cave. " 'n I say that we go west again. There ain't nothing in these mountains."

"There's as much loot as you'll ever see, you fool."

"I seen nothing yet."

"So shut yer mouth an' listen. Down there's a Keep, see. Only the Keep's right at the other end of the valley. Take a day for word of us to get there, an' even then the lord won't care if too many of his cattle don't get killed."

A younger voice cut in. "Cattle? You said there's gonna be loot 'n' women!"

There was the sound of an oath, a blow, and a smothered yelp. "Shut yer mouth when those older's talking. People down there is just cattle to 'is lordship. That's what I mean. We hit a couple of the families down this end. It takes another day for the Keep to hear, and by the time they come—*if* they bother—we're long gone with whatever we wants. See?"

"So when 'er we go down?"

"Dusk. They'll all be sitting down to 'er nice meal. All unsuspecting like. With it dusk, no one else'll see nothing. We kill them all and take what we want. Then maybe another house or two before it's daylight. If there's any good-looking females we tie them up until we're done looting. When we clear out, they come with us. If they can't keep up, we dump 'em." He laughed viciously, "Even females don't chatter with their throats cut."

The younger voice chimed in describing what he planned to do with any women taken. Trovagh blushed violently, then felt sick. He hadn't thought of war being like that. If these men found him and Cee . . . the blood drained abruptly from his face. He was hearing what would happen to her in every word from that filth down in the cave. They'd have no mercy because she was gentle and loving. No mercy that she was only thirteen, and Trovagh had brought her here. He reached out to take her hand in reassurance. He looked at her then and blinked in surprise. Cee looked furious. He didn't think he'd ever seen her look so angry. He wriggled back pulling her with him. At a safe distance she rounded on him and he understood.

"That's *our* people they're talking about. The nearest houses are Jontar's and Mashin's and Anrud's. The bandits are going to kill them all. We have to stop them."

Put that way Trovagh agreed. "We won't have time to get back to the Keep and send help before dark."

"No," Cee said shrewdly. "But we could get Jontar's daughter to take a message on one of the horses."

Trovagh nodded slowly. It was likely to infuriate his father, but he'd see they'd had no choice. It was the duty of a lord to protect his people. But Ciara could ride for help. Not that he had much faith in her seeing that. He was right.

"I'm a healer," he was told flatly. "I may be needed."

The boy shrugged. He'd done his best short of tying her to a horse and running it off down the valley. Knowing her, she'd persuade it to run the other way anyhow.

"We need to know how many of them there are. We don't want to risk us both getting caught, either. You go back to the horses, mount up, and be ready. If I get caught, it'll be up to you."

That made sense to Ciara. She slipped silently down the hillside to where the horses waited patiently. Above the cave Trovagh listened, trying to count voices. There were three he was certain were different. But they couldn't be planning to attack a whole family with only three men. Many garth families had half a dozen men or more. Jontar's certainly did. There was Jontar's father, Jontar, two sons, and three married daughters. There were also an uncle, and a cousin. Some of the women would fight as savagely for their homes and families as any man.

Taking them by surprise over a meal would even the odds somewhat. But it was still likely there were more than the three men he could hear. He listened, then squirmed farther down the slope. If he could look partway into the cave he might see something to help. He did. Near the fire there was a heap of saddles and horse gear. He could count at least a dozen saddles. The conviction came over him that it was time he and Cee departed. Some of those men the gear belonged to must be around. He'd much rather they didn't find either of them, Cee in particular. He reached the horses without incident.

"Well, did you find out anything?"

"Yes, there's at least a dozen saddles stacked to one side of the fire. I guess they have the horses along a bit further. Maybe the rest of the men are there with them."

"Or maybe they're hunting."

That sounded likely. "Yes, well, we have to get out of here and warn everyone." He started his mount moving down the trail. They traveled at a fast walk. Trovagh didn't want to warn the outlaws. In these hills the sound of galloping hooves carried. It was midafternoon when they reached the nearest houses. Trovagh took charge at once.

"Jontar, we need Ami to take an urgent message to my father." It was fortunate that the girl was a good rider, Trovagh thought. She'd worked in the Keep stables the last two years. She was familiar with their horses and could ride fast. He gave her the message, making her repeat it twice. By now the whole family was there listening, eyes wide. Ami booted her mount off down the valley racing the light. She would arrive by dark.

Now if they could just keep the outlaws at bay until his father arrived. It dawned on him then that there were methods other than a passive defense. He gabbled quickly to Cee— thanks to all the Powers that she was with him. She knew his mind without long time-wasting explanations. After that there was a subdued bustle. One of the boys vanished on Cee's horse to keep watch on the trail. There was a place where he could see far up the hill. But if he kept the lawleaf thickets between him and the approaching riders, he could make it back to the houses without being seen in turn.

Others of Jontar's family had fanned out across the valley rousing the nearest garth families. They gathered in a steady trickle as the news spread. Trovagh gazed at them proudly. His first command. Those outlaws had underestimated the spirit of his people. He said so in plain words, the boyish pride showing through. Then he gave orders. They were obeyed. Some of the older men had fought bandits before; the lad's ideas made sense. They said so in quiet mutters as confidence spread. Cee had vanished to arrange her own side of the work. Women surrounded her listening closely.

The sky darkened toward dusk as all was readied. Jontar's lad came riding at a slow canter. Far up the trail he had seen the group of riders moving downslope.

"Lord Trovagh, they come."

"Good, join your family within." He scanned the area. He could see no one, to all appearances he was alone. He stepped up onto the water-butt beside the house corner, from there onto the roof where he lay flat. Like many of the garth roofs it was covered in a layer of thick turf. Quite cozy, Trovagh thought, as he made himself comfortable. Then he waited.

The bandits came riding carelessly. They made no great noise but expecting nothing they made no real attempt to be unseen. At this hour all beasts were stabled or penned, the garth owners would be at their food. They dismounted, leaving their horses tied to a fence. Above them in the darkness

Trovagh smiled. He saw nothing but he knew what would be happening at the fence very shortly. The intruders padded over to the house. One pressed his face to the logs. Through a crack—carefully provided though he did not know it—he could see the family in the light of a lamp within. They ate hungrily, talking of garth work as they shoveled in the good food.

The bandit drooled. Two of the women were wearing cheap jewelry that glittered in the light. They were young and pretty. What with the smell of the well-cooked food, the glitter of gold, and the women, he was entranced. He finally forced himself away. A series of hoarse whispers apprised his fellows of the plunder. They could see only three men. Taking this family would be like robbing baby birds in a low nest. They failed to see that the family all ate along the far side of their table. Or that behind them a door stood open.

Nor did they know that with ample start, Jontar's daughter was even now pulling up at the Keep. She screamed an alarm as she hauled the horse to a plunging halt.

Hanion came running anxiously. "What is it, are the children hurt?"

"Bandits in the upper valley. Lord Trovagh and his lady brought the alarm. I've a message for Lord Tarnoor."

His master arrived before Hanion could send for him.

"Trovagh? Ciara?"

"Safe, Lord. Your son said I was to tell you that bandits have invaded from the mountains. There appear to be around twelve of them. They plan to attack our garth, butcher my family." She had no need to explain why. Tarnoor knew bandits. "Your son plans an ambush using the people. He asks that you send reinforcements as soon as they can be got to him."

"Is that all, lass?"

She came close so those arriving could not hear. "He and the lady said this, too, my lord. It's their job to help us, you taught them that. And—they both love you."

Tarnoor went white. He spun grabbing Hanion by the shoulder. "Call out the guard. I want half of them to ride, just in case this is some trick to lure us away from the gates. Pick the men who can best manage hard riding in moonlight. I want them ready to ride in ten minutes." He left an orderly confusion to race for the stairs. Back in his room he shuffled into chain mail, sheathed his sword, and dived for the stairs once more. A just-woken Elanor pattered behind wailing loudly for an explanation. He commended her to Jontar's daughter, vaunted to his saddle, and while Elanor still wailed, he was gone, his men trailing him.

Elanor stood glaring after him. He wouldn't be taking half the guard if one of the children had merely fallen. She turned to the girl drooping near her.

"You're Ami, aren't you?"

"Yes, my lady."

Elanor gathered her dignity, a touch difficult when one wore only a long ruffled nightgown with feet bare beneath. "Come with me, girl. I want to hear all about this."

After she had heard she dispatched the girl to a meal and a bed. Then she sat for a long time in her chair. She prayed for a girl and boy out there in the dark. Doing what they did for love of their people. Then she prayed for Tarnoor, that he wouldn't break his neck on this wild night gallop—and that he wouldn't have apoplexy thinking about what was happening before he could arrive. Lastly she prayed for the people themselves. Then she sat silent, waiting for day to come.

Down the long straight road Tarnoor pounded. He kept the beast to a steady canter, though it went much against the grain. Still, it would do no good to push on so fast he left half his men injured from falls behind him. The moonlight lit the road to some extent. The horses knew the trail well, but potholes lurked in shadows, ruts in light and shade. If Trovagh had any sense he'd have sent someone down the road to wait for them, someone else to stand back and watch. That way if the plans went awry there'd be one waiting to say how and what. A chance for Tarnoor to act as rescuer. He only hoped the boy had been able to keep Ciara out of it. He doubted that, he thought with grim humor. But the girl had sense. If fortune favored Aiskeep, it would be the bandits only who suffered.

Behind him in the dark there was a sudden cry and a thrashing. Someone down. He ignored the sounds. If the man was dead there was nothing he could do. If he lived they'd see to him on their return. If he was so badly hurt as to require immediate aid, he'd die anyhow. He hated having to think that way but he'd been a soldier. If he must, he was capable of putting emotions aside. He snarled to himself. He'd give that pair emotion when he arrived. If they got themselves killed, he'd murder both of them. He found he was grinning savagely at the paradox. He glanced up at the sky.

Ami had said the outlaws planned to attack at dusk. It had been just after that when she arrived. With this cursed dark it would take longer to return, maybe twice as long. Three hours? He winced as he thought what could be happening to the upper valley in that time. This might even be an advance thrust against his defenses. All had been quiet recently. He'd expected that to change after winter. Had some cunning enemy decided to damage Aiskeep and allow winter to make that worse? He shivered. The Gods damn that fool Yvian and thrice-cursed Estcarp. All he'd ever wanted to do was care for his people and his Keep as his father had before him. Raise a son, see grandchildren, and be laid in the end in an honored grave.

None of which was looking all that likely right now. When he caught up with that pair, he wouldn't know whether to kiss them or murder them. "Their job is to help their people. I taught them that indeed," Tarnoor muttered ferociously to himself. By Cup and Flame but he'd teach them something else once he had them safe. Underneath he was conscious of a glow of pride. The blood of Aiskeep wasn't thinning into weakling cowards at least. But if those bandits laid a finger, just one finger on either child . . .

He glanced up again at the sky. Halfway. Gods, keep them safe, he prayed. Just keep them safe.

6

Trovagh craned carefully over the roof edge. He could hear the hoarse whispers quite easily, as below the bandits readied for their attack. The boy smiled as he slipped backward to where the mortared stone chimney lifted above him. He dropped the waiting piece of stone into the opening, hearing it rattle downward. There, that was the warning to Jontar that the bandits were about to attack.

He could only hope that his plans could work. He and Cee had done their best, drawing on everything they'd ever heard or learned. But Trovagh could remember Hanion telling him that plans never did work out the way they were supposed to. Something *always* went wrong. You just had to pray it was nothing serious.

Outside, the outlaw leader had tried the door. Nothing held it against them. He turned to smirk with a gap-toothed leer to his followers. Then he thrust his weight against the wooden planking.

With a crash the door slammed open and the bandits poured in. The leader was amused to see the women rise screaming, fleeing through the door behind them. Women always did that. He'd sent a couple of his men around to the back of the building. They would take any women attempting to leave through rear exits of any kind.

He had no way of knowing that his men now reposed in peaceful unconsciousness where they had first stood in expectation. Trovagh had thought of that. Ciara led those who waited for them. Both men had been taken in silence by women who knew every inch of their ground—and wielded massive iron skillets. Ciara had seen to the binding and gagging herself. She leaned against the wall, a wide grin hidden by the darkness. If this was war it didn't seem to be anything she couldn't handle. She just hoped Tro would be careful. Uncle Nethyn would skin both of them if either came to harm.

Inside the house all of the garthspeople had been ready. The sound of the stone rattling down the chimney had warned them. Even as the door crashed open, the women had jumped for the entrance behind them. There they had slid through the opened window. The men—Jontar, one of his sons, and a son-in-law—had also jumped for the rear door. The table had been overturned with a quick heave before them as they spun to face the intruders. To reach them or the women they believed within their grasp, the bandits had to attack.

They had to do this across a high, thick-planked table and through an entrance wide enough for no more than two men at most. Up until now the bandits' attacks had been made against isolated garths, or those garths where the Keep Lord did not care for his people. The garths had been easily taken, the people weaponless and already cowed. Aiskeep was not like that. Its buildings were built solidly; its people loved and trusted their lord, who also encouraged them to be proficient with arms.

Ciara led her women around the building. They fanned out in groups of three into the dark. Ciara reached for her striker. The woodpile should be just here somewhere, she thought.

She found it by barking her shins. She hopped a moment muttering, then ran light fingers over the wood. There! Under her hand was a feel of kindling. She moved to stand before it, shielding the striker's spark. Dry grass had been wrapped around thin, dry sticks. The striker snapped a fat spark into the center of the kindling. In seconds there was a growing flame taking an eager hold.

With the stack of wood beginning to flame, the outside of the building came into dimly lit focus for those in the dark. Inside the bandits still attempted to get across the table. One had fallen already. Part three of the plan moved smoothly into action. Behind them the door still stood open. Trovagh dropped lightly from the roof and whistled, the call of a familiar bird, albeit one unlikely to be about here and now—although bandits from the coast would be unlikely to know that, he hoped. He edged toward the entrance to be joined by three boys with slings.

"Ready?"

"Yes, Lord." There was both excitement and savage anticipation in the answering hisses.

"Go!"

Slings whirled in unison as the lads stepped up to the door. The slings flicked forward. Inside the room three of the rearmost men in the outlaw group crashed to the floor. The boys stepped aside. Stones dropped into good leather again. Another volley. Two men fell, the third screamed as the pebble smashed into his ear.

"Back!" Trovagh snapped, grabbing the nearest lad by a shoulder. Within the house the bandit leader spun to gape behind him. No sign of the two he'd sent around the building. One man dead, five down behind his back. He was horror-stricken. This was no soft group of garthsmen. He must have surprised the soldiers.

True to the bandit code he promptly abandoned his men, diving for the outer door. The three remaining saw this and as promptly joined him in flight, trampling their unconscious fellows in an effort to reach the door first. Outside, two of the farmers pulled tight a thin cord across the doorway. It took the fleeing leader around knee level, pitching him to the ground. His followers trampled him with vigor in turn. Trovagh slid toward them from the side, sword flickering in the light. From the other side came grim-faced garthsmen bearing weapons of various types. They had the look of those who not only knew how to use them, but were very desirous of doing so.

The remaining bandits paused for a few seconds, but for outlaws there is no mercy if taken. They attacked desperately, seeking to break away in the dark. One did. He reached the horses, leaping into the saddle only to find as his weight hit it that both he and the saddle revolved rapidly. He landed on his face with a muffled howl. Ciara's women wielded skillets with enthusiasm. The bandit stretched out to sleep with a weary sigh. At the house the two remaining outlaws fought back to back. Both had swords, but the garthsmen ignored the danger, closing in hungrily.

But thus far only the outlaws had been hurt. Trovagh preferred to keep it that way. His father would be more ready to forgive everyone. He whistled the slingers in again. They whirled their weapons and the last two outlaws folded to the ground. The boy beamed. Praise be to Cup and Flame. It seemed there *were* times when all plans worked out. He jumped violently as a slender figure slid out of the dark to take him by the arm.

"Gods, Cee. Don't *do* that!"

She grinned happily up at him. "We've got three. They're all alive too. The women trussed them like chickens for the pot. Hadn't you better look at yours?"

Trovagh smiled back, hugging her. "One of ours is dead, I know. But you're right. We'll check the others and tie those alive." He rallied Jontar's family who swiftly brought out the bandits from where they had fallen.

"This one's dead, my lord."

" 'N this one here, Lord Trovagh." Ciara dropped to her knees checking carefully.

"Two here alive, Tro. This one is, but his skull is cracked. He'll probably die. This one's dead as well."

The two taken last were both dead. The slingers had struck with all the power they had. The leader, however, was alive, muttering his way back to consciousness as he was swiftly and skillfully bound by hard-eyed farmers. Ciara had vanished again. Now she came trotting back to where Trovagh directed the clearing up inside the house.

"Five dead, one who'll probably die shortly, and six alive. The live ones are all tied. One of them said something awful to Jontar's wife. She hit him with her skillet again so I had them all gagged as well." Trovagh looked at her proudly. She was a grubby, untidy girl, panting with exertion and excitement—and the best lieutenant a leader could have had.

"Let's get them into a barn with guards. Then we need to bring the horses in."

"Already done. The horses are over at Marin's being rubbed down. I told everyone that we were awarding a horse and its gear to each garth that had fought. Was that right?"

"Yes." He made a mental count. "Yes. Sure. That's five horses to them, seven to the Keep. What are they like?"

Ciara looked thoughtful. "Most of them are ordinary farm horses, but there's a couple there that aren't. They're a sort of yellow, with black manes and tails. They've been well-treated, too. Whoever amongst that lot were riding them has looked after both very well. They aren't young, but they'd be worth keeping. The garths won't want them. They wouldn't be right for working land." She shivered suddenly. "Isn't it awfully cold now?"

Trovagh shivered, too. It did seem to have gone really chilly in the last few minutes. Maybe snow was on its way. He shuddered again before realizing.

"No, it isn't the cold, it's the letdown after a battle. Hanion told me about it. Get into the house and start the women making soup for everyone." He studied the moon briefly. "Father will be here soon with the guards. If we can give them all something hot to drink while we show him our bandits, he may be a bit less furious."

That, Ciara thought, scuttling hastily inside to start soup pots simmering, is something to hope for. She felt fey and oddly light as she moved. Under her bodice her pendant seemed to have warmed. Her hand stole up to curve about it. She still visited the silver mist most nights before she slept. But obedient to the dangers of being known, she had not used it to heal again. Was there something she should do now?

She was distracted from that by other demands. On the fire hob two large pots of soup steamed. Ciara rounded up as many mugs and bowls as the women could find her. To that she added all the moderately fresh bread that could be found at short notice.

A third pot of soup was placed at the ready then a fourth. Tonight was a night to forget care, to share in the celebrations. It wasn't every day that a garth earned a new horse at no cost. They had paid no coin, and shed no blood. The young lord and his lady had fought beside them. Someone produced a flute, playing an old dance tune. Another man ran for a small hand drum. The wood stack was burning merrily, not that Jontar worried. He knew his lord. Tarnoor would replace the fuel since it had burned in his service. Jontar smiled at his wife, leading her into the dance. It could have been very different.

Ciara saw to it that the bubbling soup pots were shifted to one side to allow those still cold to warm. She also had a few words with several of the women.

Under a moonlit sky Tarnoor pressed on. Amongst the oncoming guard Hanion suddenly saw something. He reined up alongside his master.

"My lord, look!"

Tarnoor stared. "Dear Gods, the bandits must have fired a garth house."

He drew rein. "We must not rush in . . ."

Hanion cut across his words. "No, Lord, I can hear Marin's flute. He would not play that for any bandits. I think it's a celebration. Nor would he celebrate if the young lord or lady were hurt."

Tarnoor kicked his horse into a canter again. He strained his eyes for a sight of the boy and girl as he came into the firelight. His eyes fell first onto the bandits, twelve of them lying in a neat row propped against the house wall. By the other wall the children sat on a long settle brought out for the purpose.

Ciara had been listening; she heard the hoofbeats and signaled. Tarnoor loomed out of the night, the expression on his face grim. Before he could speak she ran forward to take his hand as he dismounted. Tarnoor found himself sitting on the low seat, a large steaming bowl of savory-smelling soup in his hands. The girl knelt at his feet.

"We're so sorry, Uncle Nethyn. We know how worried you and Aunt Elanor would have been. But we had to do it." Her voice lowered, "We're theirs as much as they are ours. How could we run away from danger leaving them to fight alone? They fought so well, too."

Tarnoor grunted. "How many dead and injured?"

"Oh, none of our side were hurt at all. Well, Marin's son has a bruised—um—behind. He tripped over a bandit in the dark. You should have heard what he said." She made a shocked face.

Tarnoor felt a chuckle rising. A dozen hardened bandits beaten by two children and a pack of farmers. He tried in vain to keep his face hard, before the laughter exploded. He threw back his head and bellowed. Trovagh sighed in relief. He'd thought Cee could soften the old man's anger. He marched forward then with the head of each garth following.

"Father, I wish these men commended. We said that each might have a horse from the bandits' mounts in recognition of garth courage and aid this night. Do you agree to this, my lord." He went down formally on one knee before his father, a junior officer to his superior.

Taken by surprise, Tarnoor made no move. His eyes scanned those who waited. He saw the pride in themselves. They had faced armed men, led by their young lord. They had won and without injuries. It was events such as these which would forge the bonds between led and leader. It did no harm at all for a lord to be held as lucky, either. He remembered the anguish of his ride here. The terror that he might find either child dead or horribly injured. But he could not take his own fear out on those before him. He smiled.

"I agree. But first you who led shall each choose a horse. Bring out the beasts now so that we may see them."

Ciara had vanished to obey almost as he spoke. She returned leading the two she had noticed. These were held to one side. In the dark Tarnoor could see little. The other ten mounts were paraded. All were reasonable beasts, geldings mostly with one mare. The mare, more valuable, was awarded to Jontar's garth. It had been his family who risked most. The other four garth heads each took their choice. The chosen beasts were led away, the remaining five taken to join the guard mounts. Tarnoor turned to glance out into the dark.

"Of what like are the two you have chosen?"

Ciara led them forward. Tarnoor gasped. "Do you know what you have here, lass?"

"No, I've never seen horses like them, Uncle Nethyn. They look different from any but they are gentle. Look." One of the beasts was lipping her hair, while the other nuzzled the girl's shoulder. "This one's a stallion, the other one's a mare." She looked slightly puzzled. "I always thought horses didn't care about mates, but these two do."

Tarnoor spoke softly, in awe. "Yes, they would. Nor am I

surprised you have never seen the like of them. They are rare. Incredibly rare in Karsten. These are Torgians, child. They must not be young. Perhaps they were loot from the time of Yvian. They are a pair, trained to work together very likely. They bond to their riders as ordinary beasts do not, but only if the rider is worthy. Also they live long lives though they breed less often. They are a treasure beyond price to Aiskeep."

Ciara patted the nearest rough shoulder. "Then Tro and I can keep them?"

"You may indeed. They are yours, one for each of you. Who shall have which of them?"

Ciara trotted over to Trovagh leading the Torgians. There was a quick muttered colloquy. She returned. "Tro wants the mare; that's fine because I want the stallion." Tarnoor opened his mouth to object, then noticed the beast nuzzling her with what he could only describe as an air of already besotted affection. He agreed resignedly. Torgians made their own choice of rider. A wise man who knew horses did not interfere.

"If you are both happy with that. Now stable the beasts and come, tell me how all this happened. Ami could give me only your message." At once Trovagh and Ciara competed to explain. Separately and in chorus they told of how they had spied, plotted, and finally fought. Tarnoor hid his expression in blandness. From what the lad said, both had known some of the danger they were in, but not all. Ciara dashed away to bring more soup and Tarnoor turned to his son.

"What did you hear them say while you listened alone?"

The boy blushed, looking miserable. "They talked about women."

Tarnoor was relentless, "What exactly?"

Trovagh spilled out the filth he had overheard, his face reddening until it could be seen even in the firelight.

His father nodded. "Yes, that is how men like that think and act. If they had taken you, either of you . . ."

"I know!" the young voice burst in. "Father, it was all I could think of until we got back to the garths. It was my fault. I risked Cee. I didn't tell her what they said. I think she sort of guessed but I couldn't tell her the words. They made me feel sick."

"As any decent man would feel," Tarnoor said quietly. "These are not good men. They are bandits. Best in daylight we ride back to this cave and look about. It may be that they'd had prisoners or other loot left to wait for their return." He took the boy by the shoulders looking into the young, anxious eyes. "I understand all you did and why. I cannot punish you or Ciara for courage, or for standing by those you will one day rule. Your plans . . ."

"Cee thought up a lot of it!" Trovagh interrupted.

"Yours and Ciara's plans worked well. They were sensible, pitting your strengths against the enemy's weaknesses. But you were lucky. It isn't often plans go as intended."

Ciara had joined them, leaning against Tarnoor's knee. She broke in then. "That's what Hanion always says. Not to expect your plans to go the way you lay them out. He says you should have contingencies arranged, too. We did, Uncle Nethyn. As much as we could, and we had reserves waiting. Tro was wonderful!" She turned a glowing look on her friend as he blushed.

Tarnoor was hard put to it not to chuckle. They were so innocent, so young. Yet—he recalled the sudden ugliness of his son's eyes as he recounted the conversation he had overheard. The lad had understood too much to ever be completely innocent again. He'd known he faced the same dangers with men like these, but his outrage and fears had all been for the girl.

His father grinned, not that Ciara couldn't do her share. He'd bellowed all over again at her account. That first pair of bandits sneaking around the house in the dark hunting women. They'd certainly found them but not quite in the manner intended. Then while all was confusion in the house, Ciara had taken her group to undo the saddle girths on the waiting mounts. A very old trick that, but still good it appeared. Around him the celebration was louder. Many couples were dancing, more food had been brought out, and others ate and drank, toasting their lord's son and his lady. Tarnoor accepted a mug of beer and drank heartily. Then he entered the circle dance. He wasn't too old to celebrate his children's victory either, by the Flame.

Luckily there had been no more than beer brewed by the garthswomen, Tarnoor thought the next morning. The merrymaking had continued until the early hours. He'd found Ciara and Trovagh asleep huddled together in one of the barns well before Tarnoor himself had staggered to rest.

He'd smiled down at them. As yet they treated each other as brother and sister. Time enough for formal marriage when that changed. They were old enough, but he had never had a taste for breeding his stock too young. It paid to wait. Fullgrown beasts produced healthier offspring with fewer losses of dam or baby. From what he'd seen over the years, he thought bitterly, that should be applied more to human marriages as well.

He remembered his own weddings. The first when he was sixteen, the girl had been barely thirteen. She'd died in childbed, the baby with her. It had been more than ten years before he'd wed a second time.

Wiser then, he'd wanted to wait to have children; his new bride was so young. It had been the fault of her mother. Seria must have told her that she was no more than a companion to him as yet. The woman had brewed some poisonous potion, sneaked it into his wine, then coached her daughter. He'd been muzzy, hot with desire when Seria came. He'd done what the drugs drove him to and his young wife demanded before collapsing into sleep.

In the morning he'd feared for her. Left her alone again until she came to him to say she was with child from that night. Then he'd gone to Lanlia begging help. She'd come to look over the girl and told him the truth.

"She's too young to bear safely. Her hips are too narrow. She will die." She'd hesitated. "I could give her a potion to free her of the child. In such cases my craft allows."

Tarnoor would have agreed. It was his wife who refused. She'd been another of those who feared witchery, even the gentle healcraft. She was certain it was a son and she would bear him safely for Aiskeep. It had been a son for Aiskeep, she had been wrong in all else.

Once her labor began Tarnoor had been ruthless. He'd sent at once for her mother. Demanded she attend her daughter so she might see what she had done. For three agonizing days he waited. He'd wept when the babe was brought to him. Wept again when he bade his dead wife farewell. He had not wept when he drove her mother from his gates.

If it had not been for her folly he might still have had the girl he'd adored. He might have had many strong children growing up to name him Father. She'd cheated him of that. He'd wed no more. Nor had he. Trovagh would be his only child. Tarnoor had been panic-stricken when the toddler fell and was so badly injured. Lanlia had come with all speed, her strength poured out to save the child. For that he'd sworn blood debt. It was why she'd sent her child to him at the last. In that he had still paid nothing. He'd loved the girl from the first, loved her as the daughter he'd hoped to have with his second wedding. It was an old saying: A son for the Keep, a daughter for the heart. He had both. What the Gods took with one hand they gave with the other.

Ciara slept. In her dream the familiar silver mist rose about her. On her breast the pendant took on life under the covering cloth. It glowed softly, the gem chips at the wing edges points of blue flame. Ciara saw her mother standing on the edge of the watchtower. Across the distance their eyes met. Love linked between. Someone was saying something as the girl strained to hear.

It was familiar, not her mother speaking but—she gasped in sudden recognition. It had been years but surely—surely it was her grandmother's voice that spoke? She willed it louder. It was speaking to her mother. She watched the change of expression on that loved face. Saw the fear and grief fade to be replaced with an accepting serenity. Ciara felt the same emotion flow across the link. She watched quietly as she saw the tower door spring open, the Kars guards rush through. She looked as Lanlia fell and through the link she knew her mother's spirit had fled before she struck the ground.

In her mind the words Lanlia had heard echoed softly. A promise from one who scorned to lie. "The Old Blood shall come full circle. It shall rise to flower again."

Ciara smiled in her sleep. Estcarp. That was where most of her blood had fled. But the voice spoke again then, very quietly. "Not to Estcarp but to the east shall the blood seek. There it shall flower in freedom. When the time comes, give what you treasure that one you love may fly free. Remember!"

Ciara woke slowly. She'd dreamed something but she couldn't quite recall. She'd heard someone speak, seen something. It didn't matter. Under her bodice the glow faded from her pendant. The time for her to remember was not yet. Beside her Trovagh stirred, stretching and yawning sleepily. He staggered to his feet.

"Didn't Father say we should go to the cave today? Let's see if there's anything to eat, I'm starving."

So was Ciara; she ran with him to seek both food and drink. Then she saddled their horses while Tarnoor gave orders.

"Keep the captives unharmed until we return. They may have water. If they speak uncleanly, gag them again after they have drunk. I will return soon. Go about your work but leave men to guard them."

He nudged his mount into a steady canter up the hillside trail. The boy and girl ranged up the line of riders to fall in behind Tarnoor and Hanion. By sunhigh they were at the cave, spreading out in silence to hunt. There was nothing within but the ashes of a fire, debris from several meals. They continued on to where horses had been pastured. There they found dung and hoofprints, cropped grass. Hanion stood up from inspecting these.

"I see the tracks of no more beasts than those we have already. There are footprints leading away, one set only. A woman, I think. Let you and I, my lord, follow with care." Tarnoor agreed, pausing only to signal Trovagh that he should join them.

There was not far to trail the reeling steps. For much of the way the one ahead had gone dragging on hands and knees. Tarnoor guessed what they would find. They rounded bushes, then with a gasp Hanion stooped.

His fingers touched, seeking life. Then he looked up. "No use, my lord. She's been dead for hours. I don't know her, she must have been some traveler they stole along the way." His hands gently straightened the twisted body, closed the staring, agonized eyes. Behind them there was a sound close to a snarl as Ciara thrust past.

Tarnoor caught her back. "Nothing you can do for her, lass. She's gone beyond some hours, Hanion says."

The girl ignored him, dropping to sit touching the pale face. Then she spoke. "She must have an honored grave by Cup and Flame." She reached for twigs piling them into a small stack at the feet. Trovagh walked away to return with a cup made from a large leaf. In it was watered wine from someone's flask.

"Will this do, Cee?"

"Yes." She stood looking down at the woman as Tarnoor spoke the words of leave-taking. There was Cup and Flame but the dead spirit cried for more. Ciara could feel the rage and hate that still held the spirit bound. It needed the fire for cleansing that it might be freed. Slowly her hand moved to her pendant. Tarnoor saw the movement and spoke softly to Hanion.

"Go to the men, say we return shortly, we do but bury one misused by those sons of filth. Remain with them until we are done."

Ciara had waited. Hanion marched away, then her hand lifted the pendant. She opened her mind to the silver mists. She did not know what to do, only that the spirit should have peace. That she willed with all her heart. To those beside her it appeared she did nothing, but a soft golden glow rose about the woman's body. It thickened, closed tighter. Then as it cleared, it could be seen there were only ashes. A small breeze lifted them, and they were gone.

Tarnoor looked at the girl. Now they both knew what could have happened. He signaled the children to him. "The bandits are your prisoners. It is for you now to decide what you will do with them. Speak together as we return. Tell me your choice once we are at the garth." It was not a pleasant lesson, but both had to learn that wars had aftermaths. The decisions there, too, fell on the Keep Rulers. From the corner of his eye he watched as the pair talked, falling back in their concentration. Then they were riding into the valley. Ciara rode up to his left, Trovagh to his right. Both young faces were stern with decision.

At Jontar's garth Tarnoor stood and looked down at the bandits. He glanced about; there was a line of trees by the stream that would do at need. He motioned to his men.

"As my son and his lady judge, so will you do." It was Ciara who stepped forward, Trovagh at her shoulder. She spoke in a clear voice for all to hear.

"In winter the wolves come, we meet them with fire and sword, nor do we mourn their deaths. Yet they come to feed their cubs, to eat instead of starving. If we give them death and it is just then these men, too, should die. They came to plunder, to rape and burn, for nothing but pleasure in their own evil. So have we judged them." She fell silent.

Trovagh took a pace forward, he breathed in once hard, then spoke. "Hang them!" When they rode out an hour later, it had been done.

7

That winter was hard. Bitter chill, an early snow that stayed late, and wind that whipped up the air to blizzard frenzy. Within the garths of Aiskeep there was no great hardship. The houses were strong, well chinked between the logs that formed their structure. The Keep itself was warm from the large hearths, although drafts abounded in the main hall in which all shared meals. Ciara had noticed that long since and planned for almost two years to surprise her uncle.

The sheep of Aiskeep were white, small hardy creatures that lived in two flocks in the foothills above the valley end. With the death of Ciara's family, the flock of black and brown beasts her mother had reared were added. They grazed separate from the others with their own shepherd. The girl visited them every week; Ysak, the flock ram, was an old friend. The sheep were shorn in rotation by flock. It was a tiring business but wool was one of a Keep's staples. Even the poorer garths had a few sheep. How else were they to have clothes to wear.

The colored sheep remained Ciara's. Quietly over the past two years she had taken possession of several of the fleeces after the shearing was completed. Some she traded with the garths. Others she retained. With all three colors she had worked busily on evenings when Tarnoor was away. Elanor and Trovagh had known her plan, of course; often they had found time to help. The kittens, too, had assisted—at least that was probably how they thought of it. Now this winter, it looked as if the end was in sight.

It would be Tarnoor's name day in another few weeks. Since that was only a few days from the midwinter feast, it was usual to combine the two. Trovagh had found a small sheet of parchment, well used but capable of being cleansed. He scraped it patiently until all the old message had been removed. Then with painstaking care he lettered a name-day blessing on the whitened surface. From the Keep's priestess he persuaded tiny pots of blue, green, and gold, these being the colors of good wishing. The blessing was a work of art when it was done.

Trovagh went in search of Ciara when he finished. "What do you think?"

She studied the parchment. "I think it's one of the most beautiful things I've ever seen, Tro. I wish I could letter like that."

"You can write."

Ciara sighed. "I know. But that's just writing. What you do is art." She pointed. "Look at the kitten peering out around the capital letter. Look at the lawleaves along the border, and the quarewings eating them." She laughed. "That bird is winking. I always thought quarewings were cute. It's just so beautiful, Tro. Uncle Nethyn will love it."

"What's Elanor giving him?"

The girl grinned. "A new robe and slippers. She used some of my brown and black wool, then she dyed more of the white. It's in the house colors."

Trovagh whistled softly. "You mean she managed to get that mulberry shade right at last?"

"Yes. Don't let her know I told you. But it's perfect. She's done it with two different lots of wool now. It wasn't the color so much. It's setting it; mulberry usually doesn't hold once it's washed. Now that she's found a way to make it fast, I expect we'll have something else to trade next market. The gold was easy, that's just onionskins. She got the mulberry just right, so I expect we'll all be wearing it after a few more name days."

The preparations continued whenever Tarnoor was absent. There was much muffled giggling and hasty whipping of things from sight whenever he returned. Tarnoor played his part by carefully seeing nothing. The servants contributed their help with enthusiasm. The Keep Lord was loved and besides, it wouldn't do to miss out on any fun going in a long, hard winter. When the day came, Tarnoor obligingly found work he must do away from the main Keep rooms.

In the large banqueting hall there were loud voices. "To one side—no, the other one, you fool. Higher. More. Yes, that's it. Secure that there. Shift the other over a handsbreadth. Ah, yes. That's perfect."

Elanor stood back to beam in approval. "They look wonderful, Cee. Now go quickly and change, you, too, Tro. I'll just make sure all is well in the kitchens, then Tarnoor will be back. Go, go!" She chased them from the hall so that they ran giggling before her. Feet pounded up the stone stairs. Young voices called back and forth as they changed to festival clothes. Ciara swept from her room to join her friend. He took her arm and they drifted regally back down the great stair, the elegant effect slightly spoiled by quiet giggles. Tro was telling her how an overfresh mount had dumped Hanion in a snowdrift that morning.

Tarnoor arrived to find his family clustered at the hall entrance.

"What's this? Are we to eat standing out here?"

Ciara danced up. "No, Uncle Nethyn. But we have a surprise for you. Now you have to promise to shut your eyes and not open them until we say." Tarnoor shut his eyes obediently. With a child on either side to guide him, he was piloted to his seat.

"You can open your eyes now." Tarnoor did so.

Before him there was the usual pile of name-day gifts. But there'd been no need to hide those from him. He glanced around, his eyes suddenly caught by new color where none had been in the old hall. He stared before walking over to touch, to examine. By the Flames but this must have been work for the child. It was something new, too. The hall had wall hangings, old tapestries woven and sewed by his mother, his grandmother, and earlier ladies. Such tapestries were not only to brighten a hall, they also kept drafts from those who ate there. Many years gone there had been two more tapestries. But the years and the moth had conquered.

The drafts had been fierce of late where those two had once hung. Now two new hangings were in place. Tarnoor fingered them. Felt! No one had ever done wall hangings of felt before. The hangings had a strong, primitive look to them. The colors were clear and brighter, hard edged on each piece. He stepped back to look again. Aiskeep in spring, gray stone under soft blue skies, with green grass and the stream. Thickets of lawleaves, and a flock of sheep grazing nearby.

The other hanging was Aiskeep in the fall. The same gray stone Keep, but with the glowing hues of almost winter. He moved forward once more. It was interesting. Up close the picture vanished into no more than odd-shaped pieces of felt. Step back and you could see Aiskeep again. Ciara waited anxiously. Trader Tanrae had told her of this method of making hangings two years ago on one of his visits. It was quicker than tapestry, warmer, too. It might also last better, but only time would demonstrate that.

She waited, then Tarnoor turned to drop an affectionate arm about her shoulders.

"My dear girl, you'll ruin the Keep." He waited while the hopeful look shifted to worry. "I'll have to begin giving feasts to all my neighbors to show these off to them." Ciara heaved a relieved sigh.

"Do you really like them, Uncle?"

He was serious for a moment. "I think they're wonderful. I know the time and work they'd have cost you. Where did you get the idea?"

"Trader Tanrae. He told me once of a tribe across the seas who make their tents from felt in many colors. It was so drafty in the hall after the old tapestries were gone. I wondered if I could make hangings the same way."

Tarnoor admired the hangings again. "It seems you can. Now, I'd better see what else I have lest the rest of the family grow jealous." He twinkled at her as they returned to the massive table. The remainder of the evening was wild amusement. Hanion came in to sing several of the old hill songs accompanied by garthsmen on flute and drums. Elanor also sang, accompanying herself on her small hand harp. They played foolish games and the evening ended with Ciara and Trovagh doing an impression of Tarnoor and Elanor in which they found each had chosen to invite mortal enemies to the same feast.

The comments on the enemy Keeps, their lords, ladies, servants, and customs, had both adults laughing loudly. Hanion who had remained by the door to watch and listen was almost in tears of mirth. He could recognize, if the other adults could not, some of his own words on those visitors he had not liked. It was well into the night before any retired. This name-day feast had been the best any could remember.

The remainder of the winter passed slowly. Spring was late, sliding into a shorter than usual summer. Pasture for stock was short. At Sersgarth they were overstocked. Beasts stolen years earlier from garths of the Old Race had prospered. Seran had refused to sell as many of the offspring as he should. Now Sersgarth land and stock would suffer unless he found other grazing. His mind turned to Elmsgarth. No one had ever settled. He had pastured his beasts there more than once, each time prudently for only weeks at a time.

This time it would be for a summer and fall. The house would be convenient; he could sleep there warm and dry, and his wife and son could remain at Sersgarth. This he did but with care. It was known his beasts were on the land but not that he himself used the house. Fall arrived in a blaze of color. It would be another hard winter from the signs. Seran sent back his beasts to Scrsgarth, but he remained. He'd always believed there were valuables unfound in the house. He would take a day or two longer to search again.

This time, quite by accident, he discovered the secret cupboard in the main bedroom. He peered in cursing vilely. Nothing! After all that, nothing! Voices alerted him so that he dived for cover partway up the watchtower stairs. There he sat silent, listening to the young happy talk, the laughter and jokes. Now and again he managed a glimpse of the pair.

Trovagh and the Witch's daughter. He'd missed his strike at her once. But now he knew she was still at Aiskeep. If that interfering lord had other things to think of, Seran would be able to use Elmsgarth as he wished.

He waited impatiently until, hours later, the pair had ridden away. Then he fled for his own mount. He knew at least two Keep Lords who'd pay well for this information. Not because they cared about hunting Witches. No, they had feuds with Aiskeep. That should gain Seran land and a fat profit to boot. He caressed his coin that winter. With spring thaw Aiskeep would find it had enemies at the gate, nor would it know from whence they came.

He was both right and wrong. One of the Keeps had troubles of its own that spring. The other waited until early summer. Then they gathered their forces.

They marched first to Sersgarth, there they forced Seran to join them. They camped solidly at Aiskeep gates and commenced the attack. But for all they could do, the Keep stood. Summer wore on as the attacks became more frantic. Twice attempts were made to undermine the walls. But Aiskeep was built on a ledge of underlying rock. The enemy could tunnel only so far before they found their passage halted. They held the siege but privately the Master at Arms knew it was futile. Still his lord commanded.

It cost them dearly. In men and supplies, and most of all in the fear or respect others might have for them. They had made no impression on Aiskeep, but many of their own guard were dead. They were weakened by this and all for some tale from a garthsman with his own ax to grind. The Master at Arms guessed he'd be made scapegoat on his return—unless he could soften his lord's wrath. There was one way to do that. He had Seran bound before the army marched on Sersgarth.

There they demanded a price. To buy the lives of Seran and his family, to save the garth from being razed, let all there bring out what they had. There was a swift discussion between the brothers. They drove out all the stock that was Seran's. All the plunder from the Old Race that Seran had hoarded. The betrayer betrayed. His secret hiding places were emptied, all was offered. It was not enough. The brothers took his wife aside. They would pay coin each of them, but it was against Seran's share in Sersgarth.

He would live, but he must leave to find another home, other work. She would have refused. She had no great love for her husband, but she guessed that if she refused they would claim her to have agreed anyhow. She spoke the words, hating them with her eyes. Small hoards of gold and silver, small items of jewelry appeared. One by one Seran's brothers contributed until the Master at Arms nodded. Seran was released while his laughing guards gathered the price they had taken.

Pushing the stock before them, the small army rode for their Keep. They could have still razed the garth, taken all that it possessed. The Master at Arms had chosen to leave the dirt-grubbers be. His lord might not approve, as such a thing was a game too many Keeps could play once it began. His lord received him grimly, a man who had failed. But the plunder displayed turned his mood to one of approval. It was only men he had lost. More could be found anywhere. The supplies used were more than covered by this display of ransom. He laughed, tossed coins to each soldier, more to his Armsmaster. There would always be another time.

Seran was not so fortunate. He had been long overbearing, even vicious as the oldest brother. Now he had brought down disaster. The younger three and their wives argued all night. By morning they were united. Seran was taken outside to be shown a small shaggy pony. On it was a pack, not overplump.

"This is yours. Take your wife and son and go." He would have protested, but for the look in their eyes, the hands that hovered by pitchforks, wooden staves. With a surly snarl he took up the lead rein, called the two who must go with him. He marched from the gates without looking back. In a way he understood his brothers. It was what he himself would have done. It was Aiskeep he hated. Lord Tarnoor who was the enemy. He'd remember that. Somewhere, somehow he would gain a revenge on them. They'd recall this day and weep tears of blood.

It was long before Tarnoor discovered these events. He shrugged when he learned. Seran had betrayed many in his time, that matters were reversed was only just. He would have helped the woman and boy had he known where they went. He did not. None seemed to know or have seen the small group as it fled. But it was almost a year. Well into the fol-

lowing summer before word came to Aiskeep. All three had
vanished.

On the road Seran had suffered a second loss. His wife had
refused to travel far beyond Teral. Her family's garth was
there, and there she would stay. She was taken in again willingly, not so Seran. He stayed the winter but in spring it was
strongly suggested he move on. His wife remained. His son
went with him. Over the years, Sersgarth was forgotten. But
Aiskeep and its lord were not. Seran grew old muttering tales
of revenge into his son's ears. The boy listened. Seran died,
still swearing revenge. His son joined a lord's guard to learn
soldiering. Revenge was all very well, but it put no beans on
the table.

At Aiskeep the years were quiet after Seran's departure.
They slipped by like beads on thread as unrest ruled Karsten.
Yet it passed them by. The knowledge that twice other Keeps
had tried Aiskeep walls nor found them wanting encouraged
Aiskeep to be left in peace. Tarnoor started no feuds, and he
lived quietly; he believed it was better not to stamp on the tail
of a sleeping snowcat. Geavon continued to write from his
Keep near the city. The news was rarely good as Keeps and
clans warred, now with this one now with that.

Trovagh and Ciara were happy. The girl was seventeen,
slim and round of face. Her eyes glowed a warm laughing
hazel, her skin a sun-ripened peach. She was agile and supple,
interested in everything and everyone. Trovagh was her friend
and partner in it all. Sometimes his father wondered how long
it would take the lad to wake up and look at his young friend.
The lass was not beautiful, but there was an integrity there. A
strength and pride. From towers to furthest valley she knew
and loved Aiskeep.

One day the boy would open his eyes. Ciara was born to be
Keep Lady. Elanor smiled to herself. Events would take care
of themselves. She made sure that Tarnoor said nothing. In the

Year of the Pronghorn they celebrated Ciara's eighteenth name day. The Torgians had produced two foals in that time. The oldest had been carefully broken and trained for the girl at Tarnoor's orders. Trovagh led the girl to the stables to show off the fine colt. Ciara clapped her hands.

"He's lovely. Tro, let's go for a ride?"

Her friend grinned cheerfully. "I guessed you wouldn't wait to try out everything." He patted the magnificent saddle that had been his own gift. Beside it hung the bridle Elanor had given and a beautiful saddle blanket of rabbit furs that was Hanion's gift. Trovagh looked across at the stalled present.

"But it's a pity you can't use the colt. Father was so annoyed the poor beast picked up a stone bruise right on your name day. Never mind, you can take Quickfeet; she's good in rough land." He grinned at her. "You'd better change. The stable boy will have my horse ready by the time you get back here." He added as she turned to go, "And tell Father that we'll ride down to the cave and be gone all day. I'll get food from the kitchen, then wait here." He watched as she picked up her skirts to run lightly back up the inner stairs. It was only on feast days and when visitors were present that Cee ever wore real skirts. At other times she wore the shorter knee-length type divided for riding. She always said that she was too busy to drag about in skirts to the floor with all the weight of wool.

If pressed she recounted that tale of old Geavon's about some Keep Lady who'd broken her neck by tripping over a long skirt. Anyway, he liked Cee the way she was. Most of their visitors didn't mind. Geavon had been here twice in the past few years. He was a stickler for proper dress, but he'd smiled at Cee and said nothing. Geavon had been involved in some conspiracy in Kars before the first visit. It had gone wrong and Geavon had chosen to be out of sight and mind a few months. The second visit had been last year. The old man had complained that as Tarnoor never came to Gerith Keep, Gerith Keep must come to him. Trovagh was silently of the opinion that the man was lonely.

At least he had been. Elanor had mentioned that Geavon had hip pains from an old wound. That he was taking extract of poppy to ease the pains when they came. Maybe the old man was wanting to see his only friends while he could. Last time he'd arrived with quite a train of guards and a couple of travel wagons. It occurred to the boy as he remembered, that this was rather more than needed for a visit. Even for Gerith's lord who liked to travel in style. He'd have pursued that idea but for the necessity of persuading Cook they must have food. Once the saddlebags had been filled he'd forgotten all about it.

Ciara joined him just as he returned to the stables. She wore her new riding clothes made by Elanor during the winter. Almost absently Trovagh noticed how well they suited her—and how well they fitted. He found he was admiring the supple sway of her body as she sat through the excited cavorting of her young mount.

"Hey, sleepy. Are you going to sit there all day or do we ride?"

Trovagh snorted. "Ride. Bet I can beat you to the first garth." He kicked his horse into a gallop before he finished his words. Ciara was behind him though as his horse accelerated. They raced whooping and laughing down the valley. But at Marin's garth, he and Jontar met them with grave faces.

"Lord, the Lady Ciara's flock did not return to their barn last night. The boy with them has not come back."

"Maybe one of the sheep became lost. If the lad was looking too late to return, he'll have kept them in the cave for the night."

"That's likely, Lord. But we'd be happy if you could be sure."

Trovagh glanced at Cee, and she nodded. The lad was Marin and Jontar's grandson. It was natural the old men should be worried. But the day was bright, too nice to spend worrying. They followed the trail to the fork near the cave. One track led to the cave, the other deeper into the mountains. As they turned toward the cave, Trovagh halted.

"I can see something down there; look, Cee, just by that rock at the bottom."

She stared over the small cliff. "It's a lamb. That must be why the boy's late. He'll be up at the cave with the rest of the flock. You see if you can get the lamb. Even if it was killed yesterday it should be all right for eating. I'll ride up to the cave to find Kiv and tell him."

Trovagh nodded agreement, then dismounted to peer over the edge. It shouldn't be hard to get down, but it puzzled him why Kiv hadn't found the lamb. Maybe he had only lost it on the way home, then turned back to look. It was always wise to have some sort of rope on one's saddle in rough lands. He unhooked the braided rawhide, fastening it to a stump near the cliff edge. Then he walked down the steep slope to gather the lamb across one shoulder. He was about to climb back when a flutter caught his eye. He glanced across. Something lying behind a larger boulder? But only cloth would flap that way.

He took two casual paces forward, to find he was staring at Kiv's body as it sprawled on the ground. Trovagh dropped the lamb. Flames! The poor lad must have fallen trying to reach the lamb. His eyes focused on the boy. There was something sticking from the lad's chest. Trovagh investigated. The stump of an arrow, the broken portion lay near the body. Bandits? The cave! If there were outlaws around the cave would be the most likely place for them to be. Oh, Gods, Cee had gone to find Kiv there.

Trovagh was on horseback and cantering before he thought. He had sense enough to slow before the final stretch to the hideaway. He dismounted, slipping through the brush on foot; luckily he had taken his bow, he thought. They usually hunted while in the foothills. Cee would have hers, too, but he feared she might not have had the chance to use it. That was her horse standing there. Damn, if only her name-day gift hadn't bruised his hoof that way. The Torgian colt would have attacked on command, or even without if he saw his rider seized.

Quickfeet shied violently away from the cave as within it Ciara screamed. The girl came staggering back clear of the cave-mouth, her upper clothing torn. Her fingers hooked into claws, her eyes flaming fury as she fought in silence now against the man who held her captive. Trovagh glanced about swiftly. There was another horse past the cave. It was a typical bandit mount. Overridden, ill-used, but of originally good quality. Why steal poor animals when you can steal the best. But only one horse, most likely only one man, two at most.

A savage slap sent Ciara spinning to the ground again. She came up fighting, sinking her teeth into her captor's arm as he grabbed her. For a moment her face was visible to Trovagh. He saw the desperation behind the rage, the terror behind the determination to fight. Blood trickled down her cheek from one of the blows. Something rose in Trovagh. A chill, deadly fury. He stepped forward, spying the man's bow. He darted silently toward it even as the outlaw heard the rush of feet. A quick stamp and the bow broke, now Trovagh turned on his prey.

Never fight in a temper, his father had taught him. Trovagh's mood was beyond that description, it was ice, the deadly winter blizzard that comes to kill. It, too, did not slay in a rage, but those who met it died. He feinted. The man he faced was good enough for untrained farmers, but Trovagh had been taught by Hanion since the boy could walk. Swords crossed, flickering and shimmering. Another feint, a bind, and a sword whirling high into the air. The bandit made his final mistake. His eyes followed the blade upward. Trovagh brought his sword lashing around. The outlaw folded in silence to the bloody earth.

Cee? Where was Cee? Trovagh jerked his head around hunting for her. Over Quickfeet's back an arrow pointed. He slouched in relief and pride, gasping for breath. Even after that she'd run not for a place to hide but for a weapon to aid him. Behind her horse Ciara allowed the bowstring to relax.

"Are there any more?" Trovagh was remaining cautious.

"No, he said he was alone, and the others were wiped out days ago by Aranskeep." She emerged from behind Quickfeet as she spoke. Her hand went up to wipe away the trickle of blood. The man's ring had cut high on her cheekbone when he struck her. She walked unsteadily toward Tro.

"Are you all right?"

"Yes." He hesitated; how did you ask a friend if she'd been raped? "Were you . . . he didn't . . . ?"

She managed a small, shaky smile. "I fought him too hard, then you came." He looked at her standing there. Hair torn half loose from its braids, clothing wrenched apart. She was bruised, bloody, but still Cee. His arms went out to close about her. Her face turned up to reassure him as their lips met, almost by accident. Long moments later he put her from him a little.

It was his smile that was shaky now. "I think perhaps we should tell Father our marriage could become official. That's if you feel the same way, Cee?"

She smiled up, long affection and new love in that look. "Yes!" was all she said. It was enough.

8

The wedding was small as Keep weddings went. Trader Tanrae and his family, Geavon and all his, and a sprinkling of the clan who lived within a few days' travel. There were also the people of Aiskeep, the garths, and those others outside the valley who still looked to Aiskeep as overlord. The preparations took until almost midsummer. But then their own priestess united Trovagh and Ciara by Cup and Flame. Aiskeep rejoiced.

Hard on the heels of that event came another that also delighted everyone. It was all Geavon's fault, Tarnoor declared. That was no more than the truth. Geavon had sat with Tarnoor after the wedding. Both felt a little flat after all the excitement. The children were safely bedded down in the tower suite, which was now their own. The guests had mostly departed, and things were returning slowly to normal. Tarnoor sighed.

"I suppose I have only a doddering age to look forward to now."

Geavon snorted in amusement. "You're still young enough to consider a third wife. Now that the boy's off your hands, why don't you look about? Flames, man. You're only in your sixties; you aren't trembling into the grave as yet. Find some widow with a little dowry and no children to complicate Aiskeep's inheritance."

Tarnoor flung back his head and laughed. "And find myself landed with someone who'd want to change the Keep about, and who doesn't know the place! Meddling with the garths, upsetting the servants. If I was going to wed again, I might as well take Elanor; at least she knows Aiskeep and . . ." He fell abruptly silent. Geavon eyed him shrewdly as Tarnoor sat there. It looked as if his friend had finally realized something Geavon had been hinting at for weeks.

No more was said on that subject. They finished the wine, talked of harvest, then wandered off to their beds. Tarnoor lay in his old four-poster bed thinking late into the night. It was legal to wed Elanor. She was only a distant cousin to Tarnoor, a closer one to his late wife, but that didn't matter. She was sensible, comfortable, and kind. She'd run Aiskeep for the last twenty-odd years. There'd be no changes just for the sake of it.

He smiled slightly. As for the dowry, Aiskeep was obliged to provide her with one should she wish to wed. That really *was* keeping money in the family should he marry her. The more he thought about it, the more he liked the idea. There'd be no children, but there'd be a comfortable old age together. She was younger, but then she was wholly of Karsten. Aiskeep didn't talk loudly about it, but there was the blood of the Old Race in the direct line here. Not a great amount. Just enough to lengthen their lives, keeping them hale barring accidents or sicknesses, until they died.

Ciara had done no more than bring back a stronger infusion of the blood. Aiskeep had always been a little different. He slept then. But in the morning he dressed carefully, going quietly in search of Elanor.

"I would speak to you; walk with me in the herb garden."

Best to move slowly, Tarnoor considered, as they walked. He'd lived long enough to know that telling Elanor he had begun considering her because she had no children and wouldn't turn the Keep upside down would not win him favor. Instead, he complimented her on her latest gown, plucked a sprig of rosemary to pin on her bodice, and left her baffled. Tarnoor followed the same plan every morning for a week until Elanor looked for him out of habit. Then he shifted his ground.

At the next evening meal he waited to hand Elanor ceremoniously to her chair. This drew interested looks from his children. They could hardly wait to get away once the meal was done.

"Did you see?" Trovagh was incredulous.

Ciara giggled, "I certainly did. Did *you* see the defiant way he did it? As if he was daring anyone to comment?"

Trovagh nodded, "It would be a fair match," he said. "Elanor's kin, so there'd be no problems there, and she'd cause no trouble at Aiskeep."

"And she's a dear!"

"That, too. Remember the time we put a toad in her bed and she made us eat that oversalted porridge?"

Ciara smiled, "I remember, but she didn't tell Father. I think it would be good. After all, they're old, and it would be nice for each of them to have company."

Meanwhile Elanor, no fool, had also come to a conclusion. She'd never known quite when she began to love Tarnoor. Sometime after her cousin had left him widowed, she thought. When she'd seen how good he was with his tiny son, his people, and his Keep. How kind, honest, and caring he was. She'd never let him see it. She ran the Keep, but in a way she was a servant. If she allowed him to see she cared, he might fear it was only to raise herself. She guessed at the reasons she was considered, but there had been real affection when he looked at her.

She waited patiently as Tarnoor moved toward his question. He spoke gently of love then. Could she care? She assured him happily that she already did. Their wedding was quieter still. Just those within the Keep and Geavon who had not yet departed. But a week later Geavon, too, was gone. Aiskeep settled down. Elanor was happier than she had ever been, and Tarnoor seemed to be discovering a new energy.

It took three years before something occurred to disrupt the Keep.

"You're sure?" Trovagh was delighted.

"Positive!"

"So we can tell Father and Elanor tonight?"

Ciara looked doubtful. "Just so long as they don't go broody. I don't want to be wrapped up and kept inside. I'm young, healthy, and the women of my line normally birth easily. Apart from that I know healcraft. I won't take chances, love, but I don't want to be driven mad by a fuss."

Trovagh broke the news that evening. Privately he also managed a word with his family. The fuss was kept moderate. Ciara rode as usual, walked, and worked in the stillroom with her herbs. She bore a healthy boy. Four years later she added a girl to the family. But by then strange events were beginning.

A man had risen in the far South. He'd begun as a guard and proved to have fighting aptitude. From that he'd gone on to take over a garth. Then with a tail of men he'd taken a small clanless Keep. No one knew where he came from or what his blood. He called himself Pagar of Geen. But Geen was only a small town, and Pagar was a word in the old tongue for 'One who stands alone.' Nonetheless the man was a strategist as well as a fighter and leader of fighters. His next move was to take more land. It had lain long fallow, too far from clan land to be defensible, yet close to the Keep Pagar had taken, which had been small and not so defensible itself. Now the man was building a base, it appeared. Over the next two years Pagar strengthened his Keep, widened his holdings, then struck for real ties with power. It was a letter from Geavon that brought the news. Tarnoor read it with interest. So this Pagar had offered for the daughter of one of the smaller clans. He told his family over breakfast.

Ciara hooted. "Is that the one with a truly evil temper?"

"And a reputation for exhausting the Kars Guard?" Trovagh added.

"So I believe," Tarnoor informed them. It was funny, but not for long. The woman apparently settled to a respectable wifehood, producing a son only days after nine months from the wedding. Her death in childbed was not surprising. Many women died that way. The child, however, lived, giving Pagar a solid clan claim. He used it to add men and clan soldiers to his train, striking within months at a keep belonging to a rival clan. It was taken swiftly. Then another, and a third. With growing wealth and status, his offer for a daughter of a larger clan was acceptable.

By this time there were voices suggesting Pagar be raised to duke. Merchants from Kars, some honest, others paid for the service, lobbied loudly. Here was a man who could finally bring order to the land. A man who knew the people. Three years later Pagar was crowned duke of the duchy of Kars. His alliances spread after that. His second wife died, again in a perfectly acceptable way. There was some gossip, put about by the ill-intentioned of course. Pagar ignored it loftily. He wed a third time. His prize was the only daughter of a powerful man in the most powerful of the coastal clans.

Pagar was thirty-three when he announced a campaign in the North. For too long the land around Verlaine had been lawless, Pagar said firmly. Fulk had never returned. Various lords had held Verlaine, the current one being a weak fool who permitted outlaws to ravage unchecked. Those living in that area agreed heartily. Pagar blooded his troops. Behind him he left Verlaine in the hands of one of those who looked to him. A strong guard reinforced peace over the area. Sycophants in Kars told all about them to look at how their duke handled things.

Geavon told a different story on a visit. "I don't know the man's eventual aim. But everything until now has been a carefully thought-out series of steps upward. I think soon he will attack Estcarp. It's an old enemy to Karsten and the man must lead his men against someone."

Elanor was puzzled. "Why?"

"Because of those he leads. Too many are mercenaries, bandits turned temporarily honest soldiers, outlaws impressed by the loot from the northern campaign. Without a war the army will fall apart. Pagar can't pay them, but to keep them together he must. Or he can offer them the possibilities of vast loot. If he carves a path into Estcarp, he buys time to strengthen his power. Loot to rebuild Kars, plunder to pay his men. You do know he's already started raiding along the border between us?"

Tarnoor was horrified. "Without declaration?"

"Exactly. Estcarp won't take it for long. They'll do something we may all regret." Geavon sighed. "It all harks back to the Horning. Too many in our land benefited from that or have guilty consciences over things that happened. Too many have always feared that one day they'd be called to pay blood debt. Pagar has played on that. He has the city and most of the clans behind him in what he does. The worst of it is, Estcarp cannot win. If they do nothing, Pagar will raid more boldly. If they act, then he will cry out that we are unjustly attacked by an old enemy. This is only the beginning. He will claim that if we do not fight, we will soon be a subject land."

Tarnoor glanced at his friend. "Which do you think will come?"

"Those of Estcarp are not cowards, they'll fight," Geavon said thoughtfully. "Pagar is expecting an easier war than I think he will get. But once he is committed, then so are we all. I never liked nor trusted the man, I think he leads us where we would not wish did we but see the path ahead clearly. I fear for Karsten."

It was well that Tarnoor persuaded the old man to remain. Two weeks later word came from Gerith Keep. Geavon left at once traveling light and as swift as aging bones allowed. His next letter was grim.

Estcarp had made some formal alliance with the Sulcar so that their fleets had been loosed upon Kars. Twenty ships broke the Kars river patrol, slashing into the very heart of the city. The results of that kept the duke busy in his own backyard for a year. The Kars merchants were outraged. The Sulcar had dealt death in moderation, but some wise one among them had counseled another blow. As the fleet withdrew they had burned every warehouse they could set alight. The duke had no sooner quelled that trouble than more came to him from the far South.

Hanion was amused. "They say the man claims to be Pagar's half brother. That the father lived with some woman for several years before he died and got a son on her. This man is a bare twenty, but he's ambitious and a couple of the clans with no love for Pagar will back him. Pagar had better deal quickly with him, else there are others who may decide this one to be the better bargain."

Aiskeep was wise enough to remain apart. But as Hanion had said, there were others willing to fish in troubled waters. Three years passed before Pagar was secure on his throne again. The half brother, however, had been so evilly slain that others rose in his place. As fast as the duke suppressed trouble in one province, it broke out elsewhere. Nor were supplies for war so easy to find of late with the Sulcar firmly on the side of Estcarp. For a time the duke lay low, keeping peace in the land while he built up trained men and quietly bought weapons to store against need.

In those years Aiskeep continued to thrive. The children grew, prospering in health and knowledge. Ciara's daughter was sixteen when she wed. Ciara wept as she kissed her farewell.

"Be happy, do not be strangers to Aiskeep. May Cup and Flame go with you in blessing, little one." For a time they did. Then it was the turn of Ciara's son.

"But who is this lady, we have heard of no Aisha?"

Kirin laughed. "No, but is her name not a good omen? She is the sister of a friend I made in Kars. I met him when I stayed with Geavon at Gerith Keep last year. We visited my friend's house in Kars often. She is young, only fourteen, but we could be wed next year."

Ciara was uncertain. As ever she took her questions to Trovagh. "I know nothing of the girl; could we not invite her here for a time? We can thus decide with more knowledge. The match is well enough from what we know, but we know little."

The girl came. She was small in stature, maybe a little sly, Ciara thought, quiet and gentle seeming but lazy and rather spoiled. She would not expect to run Aiskeep. In that she would produce no contention. She also appeared fond of Kirin, although Ciara wondered how much of her son's determination was merely an infatuation with a very pretty girl. They were wed a year later, though Ciara wished both to wait a little longer.

Meanwhile, Pagar had again commenced raiding the Estcarp border. He was strong on his throne, since many of those who opposed him seemed to die conveniently. There was more gossip about that, which ceased when people noticed that the gossipers also seemed to have a surprisingly high mortality rate. The raids carried on over the next few years, growing in strength and intensity. Pagar did not seem to mind his losses, nor, loaded with plunder from Estcarp's border, did his men.

Then for the first time in many years, grief came to Aiskeep. Ciara's daughter died. There had been no living child of the marriage, and Trovagh and Ciara mourned together as did Tarnoor and Elanor. They had been so fortunate, it had been a long time since death had touched any of them. It was to become a familiar visitor. A month later, Trader Tanrae's son came bringing word that bandits had struck a merchant train. In the fighting his father had been slain.

Talron's face was black with anger as he told them. "I do not believe it to have been the raid it appeared. One of the outlaws was taken alive. He swore their leader was paid for the attack, and that they were to be certain my father died."

"Are you sure of this?" Tarnoor was shocked. "Your father had no enemies I know of. He was a good man and honest."

Talron shrugged. "I'm sure the one who talked believed it. The truth of it is another matter."

Ciara wondered. She wondered still more when her daughter's maid found her way back to Aiskeep. She, too, had a story to tell.

"Lady, I loved your daughter. She was my lady twice over, once as her servant and once as I belong to Aiskeep. I cannot swear to my fears, only that they are there. The marriage was happy enough, though there were no children as yet. Then a cousin of the clan nearby began to visit often. He and my lady's husband seemed to spend more time together talking close, as if they wished none to overhear their words. Then my lady fell ill. They said it was the ague but there were differences. I spoke so but was told I was an ignorant servant knowing nothing. My lady died, and even before her body was in the ground her husband's friend was there, whispering in his ear.

"My lady was buried and I was told I should return to Aiskeep. That there was no need of me. They gave me a little coin, an old pony, and bade me join a merchant train coming south. All this I did, but, Lady, the merchants were kept late in Kars by storms. I did not leave the Keep when they believed."

"What did you see?" Tarnoor asked quietly.

"My lady's husband going very quietly to the shrine. Before the shrine priestess he made declaration that his Keep was now allied with that other clan. His friend stood witness." She turned to Ciara. "I can prove nothing. I have no proof. But I believe my lady was slain in some way. I think her husband to be innocent, but he merely took the opportunity offered him by his friend. But my lady disliked the man, nor is that clan a friend to Aiskeep. So long as she lived she would never have let such an alliance be. I heard them argue often enough."

Tarnoor dismissed the girl gently. Once the door had shut behind her he turned to look at his family.

"What do you think of her tale?"

Trovagh looked distressed. "The girl herself admits there is no proof. She even believes our son-in-law innocent. How can we accuse some cousin of another clan—and of what? That he poisoned our daughter so his clan might ally with one Keep? That's the clan the duke wed into last time. It would be more than dangerous to accuse if what rumor says is true."

It rested there until winter came. Of late many had been mild, but this one was harsh and long once more. When it faded into spring Ciara chose to ride out.

"I will if I wish, Tro. I'm not so old I can't sit a horse. Come with me, and we can take some of the guard and ride toward Elmsgarth. Aiskeep owns it; we should be sure it survived the winter."

Trovagh chuckled. "Well enough, let us ride." They took six of the guard and a pack pony. It was a day's ride to the garth that had once been Ciara's home. They would stay the night there and ride back in the morning.

They walked the horses across boggy ground toward the edge of Elmsgarth land. Leading the small group was

Trovagh. His hand suddenly flung up in a signal to halt. Ciara followed his look. Beside the willows huddled several starved goats. The bark had been eaten high, to branch forks in the case of some of the trees that had proved climbable.

"There's something wrong. Sersgarth has been using this land as pasture for years but not in winter. Why would they leave the beasts here to starve? These are only the ones that have survived." He pointed to a scattering of humps, black and white against the brown earth. He turned to the men. "Spread out, and look for other beasts and any people. Be wary. Listen in case I call."

He sat his mount as Ciara craned about her. "Tro, should we ride on to Sersgarth? If they were in so much trouble that they'd leave valuable stock here to starve, then . . ."

"Then they are probably dead," Trovagh cut in. "It has been possible to ride to Elmsgarth for at least a week. If any were alive, then surely they'd have come by now. Still, you are right, we should ride there to see. Wait a little until we hear if our men have found anything."

One by one the guards trickled back. They had found no one, but the last of them reported signs.

"Signs? What sort of signs? Riders?"

"No, my lord. I think that there were cattle here, too. The fence at the back has been broken down. The beasts will have gone into the hills once they became hungry enough to push through the railings." He paused to consider. "My lord, I believe there to have been perhaps a dozen cattle, maybe more."

Ciara spoke with the sound of steel in her voice. "Sersgarth would never have left so much wealth to die here. Not unless they themselves were already dead. Let us ride quickly. We can be there before dark."

Trovagh agreed. "Spread out in line. Harran, go well ahead. Two of you others fall back. String bows and ride with your eyes wide open."

The small cavalcade swept down the road, half-melted

snow and slush flying from many hooves. They rounded the bend before Sersgarth, then pulled to a hasty halt as Harran rode back.

"Lord, Lady, Sersgarth stands, but the door is shut. No one appears to answer my calls."

They rode on with care. It was as Harran had said. Within the house there were ominous stains here and there. Anything small of value had vanished. More interesting, even the secret hiding places, usually well-guarded family secrets, had been emptied without signs they had been broken open. There were no traces of the beasts here. Even the horse harnesses and wains were gone. But there was no damage. Nothing smashed or burned such as bandits usually did.

They stayed the night, riding back to Aiskeep distressed and bewildered. In the South all had been quiet for some time. It would have taken a strong band of outlaws to win the garth with so little damage. Why then had they not stayed the winter? The buildings were weather-tight with good hearths and much firewood stacked behind the house. With the increasing pressure against Estcarp's border, the loot to be had there drew outlaws and bandits north. Had this been a band of such traveling in that direction? But the other questions remained.

They were not answered that year. Instead, a large family appeared less than a month later to settle in the deserted garth. They claimed the goats found at Ciara's old home as well. Trovagh and Ciara rode over to speak with them.

"From where do you and your family come?"

"From beyond Teral, my lord. A wearying journey."

"We do not dispute your use of the land. But by what right do you claim it?"

The family's leader was brief. "We purchased it, my lord. One who has been very long gone agreed it should be ours."

Trovagh and Ciara blinked at each other. The only ones ever gone from the garth had been Seran and his family.

"Seran?"

"It was a woman. I do not wish to be impolite, my lord, but we have much work to do."

That was so clearly true Trovagh asked nothing more. They walked the horses back, talking as they went.

"It must be Seran's wife; there's no one else it could have been," Trovagh commented.

Ciara looked at him. "That's true. But there's something you haven't considered. We only found Sersgarth abandoned a month ago. Isn't that a rather short time? Think, Tro. It's clear whatever happened occurred at the beginning of winter. But there's been almost no travelers as yet this spring. How did Seran's wife get word that the garth had been abandoned, that all the rest of the family had disappeared when we ourselves didn't know?"

"How, too, did she then find this family to buy from her, and gather their goods and gear to be there so swiftly?" Trovagh added thoughtfully.

"If they came from beyond Teral as they said," Ciara added, "the trip with all those children and animals must have taken more than a week. That shortens their time to have heard and made ready still further. I dislike this whole business."

"And I, beloved. But there is naught we can do. Sersgarth has never looked to the Keep. We have no right to demand a sight of these purchase papers the man claims. We can only refuse them the right to use your own home as Sersgarth did."

That time came quickly. Harran rode in just weeks later to say that Elmsgarth once more hosted beasts. Trovagh said nothing but rode out with ten men. The new family had moved into Ciara's old home as well. The house was clean but to this garth they had no shadow of right. He said so. Politely, kindly, but very firmly. If they wished to buy, it would be considered. If they wished to rent, that, too, would be given thought. But until then, the land and buildings belonged to Aiskeep.

The family head returned to talk at the end of the summer. He would buy. Ciara sold reluctantly. Still the land had always been too far from Aiskeep, nor did any of the family wish to live there. The purchase price would be of use. But both she and Trovagh wondered how a garth family could afford to buy two large garths in outright holding. They did not ask. In some ways, they did not wish to know.

The marriage of Ciara and Trovagh's son was blessed that year. A healthy son to balance the loss of friends and neighbors, which still puzzled Aiskeep. After that there was an interval. Kirin was often away in Kars. To the distrust of all at Aiskeep, he seemed to be moving into the circle of those about the duke. He grew further apart, too, from his wife who turned to spoiling her son as compensation. A second son was born three years later. He, too, was soon spoiled despite all that Ciara and Elanor could do.

It was rumored that Kirin backed the duke in his war. That he encouraged the raids, sometimes riding on these with his men. Ciara did not wish to believe this of her son. Her eyes were opened ten years after the death of her daughter and the disappearance of those at Sersgarth.

"You will ride in outright war? Surely, my son, you have other duties. What of your wife, your sons? One day Aiskeep will be yours."

Kirin sneered at that. "One Keep in the poor South. If I please Pagar, I will rule as a duke in Estcarp. With their allies elsewhere engaged they cannot stand. One strike to their heart and we'll crush them as one crushes a walnut for the meat. My sons will rule a province, not one Keep."

Tarnoor had listened quietly to this; now he spoke. "Estcarp has protections other than its soldiers. Also you have not thought. I am your lord. You are my heir's heir. Under law you may not ride without my permission. It is not given nor shall it be." He closed his mouth in a way that all knew his mind was made up.

Kirin smiled, a slow, vicious smirk. "Say you so, Grandfather? There may be one who says otherwise. As for Estcarp and its witches, they fail. Our scouts tell us the men of Estcarp move back little by little. They may plan to make a stand on their side of the mountains. If so, they are fools. Pagar will roll over them. Their land will be ours. As for your permission, I think you shall give it once you have thought about it."

Before Tarnoor could speak again, Kirin strode from the room leaving the four remaining to stare in horror after him.

9

Pagar was harrying Estcarp forces when Kirin reached him. He returned at speed for several reasons, though he chose not to name them all. One was a third offer from Alizon.

"No," he told Kirin. "I drink no cup of Brotherhood with Facellian. He has unchancy allies. Moreover, I do not trust him. Let him keep busy with the Sulcar; it keeps them from joining with Estcarp any further. Also," he said, looking thoughtful, "Facellian moves against other lands. I think he takes more on his knife-point than he can thrust into his mouth. It may be that if his war does not prosper he will return to us with better offers."

Kirin grinned sourly. "You say he harries the Sulcar, Lord. But the spies bring word of a great fleet assembling in Es Bay. Those of Alizon who would make a treaty with us have the same story. The accursed Witches may escape us all yet."

"Not so. The army gathers. Very soon we shall strike into the heart of Estcarp. A portion of the army, led by you, my friend, shall ride hard to the northwest and the great bay. If any attempt to retreat to some land across the seas, they shall find you waiting."

"Yes, but what of my grandsire? He speaks truly when he says my riding with your army is against the old laws." Kirin sat, his elbow on the table as he stared gloomily into the wine cup. "I am the heir's heir. If he says me nay, I may not ride. My sister is dead. My parents will not breed again. There is none else."

"You have two sons," Pagar pointed out.

"Both children. The law was made to prevent dispute in such matters. My grandsire is old, my father's health has ever been chancy in winter. If I fall in battle, Aiskeep would be under regency for years."

Pagar pursed his lips. "Leave it with me, my friend. I will consult those who are wise in such matters. Let you prepare for the time we move. I swear to you, you shall ride as you wish."

He waited until the fool was gone. Oh, yes. Kirin would ride, but Pagar had other plans for the man he named friend. Other plans, too, for the doddering swine of a grandsire. It had taken half a lifetime but the oaths he'd sworn were almost accomplished. But before he made his final moves here, there were a few small matters to tidy away. He called for wine. He would think each move out that he must make. Too much haste was folly. He'd learned that as a common soldier.

At Aiskeep Ciara was unhappy. Was there something wrong with her that her son turned against them so? Had she not taught him well, loved him greatly? Yet now he cursed them all and would go against even the oldest of Keep laws. Tarnoor comforted her.

"The lad's always been a bit hotheaded. He'll calm down and realize he has responsibilities here. What about poor little Aisha? He's planning to desert her, too, for the Flames know how long."

Ciara snorted crudely. "Poor little Aisha will manage very

well without him. She's ruining her own sons to compensate. They have no curb on them at all. She does nothing either with them or for the Keep. She infuriates me."

From his seat near the fire Trovagh chuckled. "You mean you can't make up your mind, love. One minute you're complaining she takes no interest in Aiskeep. The next you're thanking the Gods she does not, lest she ruin it as she ruins her sons."

Ciara threw up her hands. "I know, I know. Between her and Kirin I'm saying things I don't mean." She turned the talk to other things, but later in her room with Trovagh she was more thoughtful.

"I didn't like the way Kirin spoke. There's something behind that attitude of his. I know he and the duke are close; the boy's spent most of the last couple of years in Kars. He's hardly home at all. Geavon's always said Pagar had his plans all laid out. That he was moving up step by step."

"Geavon's an old man who sees plots in every dark corner."

"Geavon's an old man who's *survived* a lot of plots in dark corners," Ciara retorted. "I don't always agree with him, but I do here. I don't know what it is"—she twisted her fingers together—"but I feel as if something is closing in on us. As if we are being watched, and in danger."

Trovagh caught her restless fingers into his hands. "Hush, love. It's all right. Kirin is only a young fool. He's rushed to Kars to check the law. Once he finds Father spoke true, the boy will be back. Although, he could go." He looked down at their linked hands. "I know why the law was made. It was to prevent children from being used as pawns in the old days. A child ruling anywhere has always been dangerous for those ruled. Father is old, but he's strong and healthy. He should live long. Then there is me. I know I take colds, sometimes badly in winter, but I have you to aid me. Kirin has two sons to follow him here."

Ciara was listening to him as he continued. "The problem

is, sweetheart, that Father *is* old. I am known to be often winter-sick. And Aisha comes from a powerful clan. By law if Father, I, and Kirin died, you should be regent here for our grandsons. But can you see Aisha's clan sitting back to allow it? No, they'd be here on some pretext within weeks. Aisha's lazy. She'd agree to anything they demanded rather than argue."

"And you think I'd sit by and allow Aiskeep to be overrun with her damned clan?"

"No, my dear, I don't. For which reason they'd move against you first of all. Pagar is allied to Aisha's clan, and you know the talk. It's amazing how many accidents one can have if someone else puts their mind to it."

He realized she was no longer paying attention to him. He fell silent, content to sit holding her hands in the quiet firelit room. His love. She'd always been that behind the friendship. It had taken him too long to see. But they'd had almost thirty years together in the big bed next door. He hoped for another thirty or even more. Their family lived long, and Cee was half of the Old Race. They'd be safe at Aiskeep. When other fools spent their coin on fancy clothes, trips to Kars, and looking fine at the court there, Aiskeep had been built.

Their outer walls were massive. The gates were strong and doubly so with a second curtain wall within and beyond the gates. There were now three escape routes where once there had been two. The garths in the Keep-guarded valley were snug, the buildings kept in repair. The people of Aiskeep lived far better than any Keep farmers, Trovagh knew. As for the armory, it would have armed a Keep of twice as many guards. The lower storerooms were kept filled. None at Aiskeep ever forgot the sieges of the restless years after Yvian's murder.

Ciara sat quiet, body motionless, but within the stillness her mind raced. It had been Tro's comment about accidents. It was true. If one ill-intentioned put mind to it, it was amazing how many accidents could happen. The question was, was there a mind here and if so, whose? First there'd been Trader Tanrae, a friend of Aiskeep. He'd died in a bandit ambush: bandits paid to make sure that whatever else happened, Tanrae died. There'd been no reason for it. Tanrae had been an honest trader. He'd had no enemies any could name.

Of course who knew what one who'd been offended might name an injury. It could take very little. Then there'd been Sersgarth. The whole series of mysterious events ending in a new family there—who'd also had the wealth to purchase Elmsgarth. They'd settled into both garths over the years.

They were peaceful enough but somehow, not friendly. Always polite, but without warmth. Ciara felt measured whenever one of them looked at her. As if they waited and watched to be sure what kind of opponent she'd be when the time came.

After that—her eyes blinked back tears—after that there'd been her daughter. The suggestion that the girl had been in the way of a powerful clan. There'd been nothing but the word of a suspicious servant. But an Aiskeep servant, devoted to her mistress and trustworthy. Yet what had the suspicions amounted to, after all? The idea that a large, wealthy, and powerful clan had a young wife poisoned so her husband could swear his Keep to them without objection? One Keep against the scandal that would erupt if poisoning had even been suspected? There were things a clan did not lightly risk. Open that gate and others were free to follow.

It was unlikely, she thought. Yet the servant had listed the details. The ague from which her mistress died *had* had unusual symptoms. It was odd that they had rid themselves of the servant with quite such haste. Odder still that the grieving husband should be swearing his Keep to another clan and so very hastily in such secret. She had a sense of something moving here, but her mind refused to put the puzzle pieces together. There was a vague link. Tanrae had been Aiskeep's friend, Ciara's savior. Sersgarth had been Aiskeep's neighbor. A daughter of Aiskeep was strangely dead.

Well, worrying over it would not help, she decided. She'd done enough of that lately. Better to fix her mind on something she could remedy, like the way Aisha spoiled those brats of hers. She rose, taking Trovagh affectionately by the arm.

"I'm for our bed, my love." He followed, glad she seemed to have found peace.

Kirin paid another visit, this time to speak with his wife. He found her infuriatingly unhelpful.

"I'm not becoming involved. I have to live here while you play at lords all over Kars. Your mother picks on me, your grandfather thinks I'm a fool, and you pay me no attention." She burst into tears. "I'm with child again, too. Go away and do whatever you want. Just don't expect me to help you."

Kirin went. He rode back to the city convinced that a dukedom in Estcarp would be a boon greater than he'd thought. He could find some way of ridding himself of Aisha, and taking a younger, prettier wife. Perhaps a girl of Estcarp who would be properly grateful to be wed instead of taken as mistress. He'd take his sons in hand, too. They seemed more unruly and ill-mannered each time he saw them. A tough Armsmaster and a few beatings should cure that.

Once in Kars he was angered all over again to find Pagar was still on the border. The week it would take to ready the army had already stretched to two. Still Kirin could not legally join without causing an outcry. He must persuade Pagar to intervene before it was too late. He rode on to find him there. On the border his duke was triumphant. It seemed that the forces of Estcarp had learned the lessons Pagar had been teaching. He was closeted with his scout head as Kirin stamped in to join him.

"They pull back, my lord. If this continues, we may be through the mountains shortly. The heart is going out of them.

We win and win and they see no end to this war. My spies say that the fleet in Es Bay will bear away many of their lords and their households. For that reason, too, no doubt the men fall back. Few soldiers fight well when they know their masters plan to abandon them." He sneered at the thought.

Pagar agreed. "Keep pressing them, but do not make them too desperate as yet. The bulk of my army will be ready shortly. Once we have that we can advance at speed." Kirin nodded agreement. Pagar waved the scout chief to depart before continuing his speech to the intent Kirin. He laid his finger on a map. "Here I will split the army. The greater portion of it, led by me, will strike into the heart of Estcarp direct for Es City. The remainder led by you, will turn northwest and travel as fast as they may to the great bay. As soon as we are through the mountains I'll have a screen of scout-fighters flung far forward in front of that portion."

He smiled viciously. "I want none of the Witches to know they will be cut off from their fleet in the bay. Let it come as a surprise to them. Those who suddenly have hope taken away break more easily." He drank deep from his cup, and looked up, face flushed red with wine. "I have laid my plans a long time, but now they ripen. In a month I will sit in Es City as master. Alizon is finding their own enemies a harder nut to crack than they'd hoped. My spies say it looks possible that Alizon will be defeated. I will take perhaps a year to recover our own strength. To train soldiers, to replace those we lose. After that I will consider Alizon."

Kirin gasped. "You would rule three countries, my lord?"

"Why not? A man takes what he can in this life. Now, as for your grandsire, I will move there soon. You lead a third of my army. Do you think I will allow some old dotard to deprive me of a commander?" He patted Kirin's shoulder. "Come, man. More wine and look to this map." He guided the talk thereafter, before saying he would rise early and must go to his bed.

Once retired, Pagar called for one to attend him.

"Wake me early, at first light. I ride for Kars at speed. A light escort to ride with me. Two horses for each of us. Send a courier now with these orders for my lord Draven in the city." He thrust a roll of sealed papers into the waiting hand.

He saw the man off and relaxed. At last all his plans were in motion. So few things left to do before he ruled a subject land. He smiled to himself. He'd risen high and meant to rise higher. Estcarp, Alizon, but beyond them were lands the Sulcar knew. Why stop before he reached even further? Here in Karsten he was limited. Officially he must answer to the merchants of Kars, to the heads of his wife's clan. But in Estcarp, Alizon—he must answer to none but his own desires. Alone with no one to see, his smile was evil.

With daybreak he rode for Kars, where fresh horses waited. Pagar rested, then rode for Aiskeep. Once there he hailed the gates. Tarnoor appeared, to look down in surprise.

"Do you wish to enter, Duke?"

"No, let you come out to talk with me, Lord. I have that which I would say in private."

Tarnoor sighed, turning to Trovagh and Ciara. "This will be some of Kirin's work. The boy has convinced the duke to speak for him. Well, I must go down."

He did so, finding a tent waiting, with a table, chairs, and wine laid ready. He sat heavily. This would not be pleasant, but the law was the law. Even the duke did not break Karsten law with impunity. He listened politely at first, later with paled face and glittering eyes. Then he signed the paper offered.

"You understand you will keep silent on this. Let your family believe Kirin is sulking in Kars awaiting my return. But I have one more request, Lord of Aiskeep." Pagar spoke again, in lower tones.

Tarnoor reared back in his seat. "I will not!"

"Are you afraid?" The duke's voice was silky.

"I have been a soldier before, My Lord Duke."

"Good. Then you will know how to fight. You will do as I say. The consequences otherwise will not be in your favor." He gloated as the old man bowed his head. He had him at last. He would deal with two now, two to come. Divide and conquer had always been a valuable method. He sat there impassively. Just another mission completed.

Behind him he left chaos. Tarnoor marched, back erect through his gates, then stood silent in anguished thought. Trovagh and Ciara came running.

"Father, what did the duke want?"

Ciara saw deeper. "What did that man say to distress you so?"

"It's nothing, child. Just a decision I have made. I'll talk later. For now I must have speech with Hanion."

They watched him walk away as they gazed in bewilderment. "Hanion?" Trovagh muttered. "Why Hanion?"

"Oldest friend, perhaps. One he can trust to obey without question. Which means there *is* something wrong."

They knew what it was soon enough. Through all the uproar, the weeping, the protests, Tarnoor held firm.

"I have made a bargain with the duke. If I ride with him he will see Kirin is safe. If I do not, he will take the boy anyhow. Once that is done, I must disinherit him—and his sons with him."

"But, Father, that part of the law may be withheld at your choice. Kirin's son could still be Keep heir."

"Pagar threatens to have the clans rule otherwise. It would leave Aiskeep without heir, prey to any once we are gone. Pagar would see to that. I will not have it so."

"But men, what soldiers will you take? Aiskeep guards?"

Tarnoor sighed. "I will not weaken Aiskeep. I have sent word to Tanrae's son. Talron will spread it about that I am hiring soldiers. That I will not inquire as to character."

"You'll get only bandits and outlaws," Ciara warned.

"That I know well. It will remove them from Karsten at the least." Tarnoor smiled gently at her. He could not tell her the reason he acted thus. Pagar had threatened and Tarnoor had believed him. The reason Tarnoor had given his family had been only a portion of the threat. The other had been even more deadly. He held to his plan and his silence even when Elanor wept. It must be done.

Men trickled in, the most depraved-looking bunch Trovagh had ever seen. His father shrugged.

"You'd be surprised what unlikely material can make good soldiers." He talked to the men of loot, and of the chances to do well in a subject land, until he was sure they would follow him at least until they reached Pagar. The duke should not be able to say a bargain had been broken. Still, unknown to his family, he hesitated. What if he did this thing and Pagar was the oathbreaker? He had not impressed Tarnoor as a man to care greatly. None knew of the words between them. None would know if Pagar returned triumphant to destroy those Tarnoor wished to save.

It was then that Ciara sought him out. "Father, I don't know why you're doing this. But isn't there something I can do to help?"

He looked at her remembering the small terrified girl she had been. He'd buried her family while she stood by, then he'd taken her as his own. It wasn't her fault Kirin had been rotten at the core. There'd been others in the Aiskeep line like that over the generations. Power-hungry seekers after more than one Keep. But he needed to know. He would ride, but what came after?

"Ciara, my daughter." The words were slowly formal and the woman caught her breath. "Will you foresee for me?"

"You've never asked that."

"I have never wished to know what lies before me. Now I *must* know. I know you cannot do this for yourself, maybe not for Trovagh. But perhaps for me it may be possible?"

Ciara clasped her hands. "I have never even tried." Her voice dropped. "I, too, have never wished to know. Is it so important?"

"Yes." The word was implacable.

"Then I will try. Where is Tro?"

"I sent him to the upper valley to speak with some of the garthspeople. He will not return until late. There is all the time we need, daughter."

She bowed her head in acceptance. "Then let us begin." The door was closed, the fire built higher. Ciara sat, pulling her chair around to face the chair in which Tarnoor waited. "I said I've never done this before. I can only do as I feel is right and pray."

He nodded. Ciara lifted the pendant by its chain, taking it into her hands as she reached out to Tarnoor. "Take it between your palms." He did so and she closed her fingers in turn about his wrists. Then she called the mists. She knew not if she would see: perhaps since his need was so great it would be he to whom the seeing came. Within the mist all was familiar. She wandered timelessly as always until something told her she should leave. She came to herself, sitting straighter, chilled. Before her Tarnoor's face was wet with tears. He must have seen—but what? He allowed her to make up the fire once more but would tell her nothing.

When she had gone he remained gazing into the Flames. If that was the way of it, he could accept. He had seen all he required. Praise be to the Powers that they had allowed him to know. He later went in search of Hanion again. There he added to his words, and to his orders. He despised the men he would lead. They were filth Karsten would be well rid of—his face twisted into a bitter smile—and rid of them Karsten would be.

He rode out one morning. Aisha and his grandsons had not bothered to rise but Elanor, Trovagh, and Ciara were present. There, too, were all the people of the garths. They watched as

Tarnoor rode down the road at the head of his men. It made a brave sight, the Aiskeep war pennant fluttering above the flag bearer. They stood watching long after the column of riders had vanished. Finally the garthspeople drifted away, back to their chores. Elanor retired to weep again. Trovagh took Ciara's hand and held it tightly.

"Why do I feel there was something more behind all this?"

She sighed. "Because there is. What, I don't know, but he had me foresee. I saw nothing, but I am certain *he* did. He would tell me nothing but, Tro, I think he saw his death. Did you know he's left papers with the shrine? They order that you or I rule Aiskeep so long as either of us lives."

Trovagh blinked in surprise. "The law allows. But what made him think it might be necessary to have that written?"

"I do not know but copies of it went to Geavon and to the main shrine in Kars for safekeeping. There is more also. If both of us die while Kirin's children are yet minors, Geavon is guardian. If Aisha refuses to accept that, then Geavon's son inherits Aiskeep." Trovagh gasped in shock listening as Ciara continued. "Tarnoor did all this before the foreseeing. After that he seemed both sadder and easier in his mind. As if he knew the worst but there was compensation."

They waited fearing word. Geavon sent messengers almost daily so that they should hear news of the army. It assembled, marching to the Estcarp border as each portion was ready. With one part Kirin marched as proud commander. In Aiskeep Aisha cursed him. She would bear him a third child before he returned, she was sure. He was selfish, and she hoped he never came back.

Trovagh and Ciara heard that news as their worst fears confirmed. Pagar had lied to their father, or Tarnoor had lied to them. He would have done that only if the alternative was worse.

At the border Pagar listened to his scouts.

"Lord Duke, the forces of Estcarp fall back further before us. If we move tomorrow it may be that we will reach the mountain's heart by nightfall. We can rest the night, then strike forward with the dawn. Estcarp falters; if they see us determined, I believe they will break and flee once we reach their own land beyond the mountains."

"What of Lord Kirin?"

"He and his men are already partway through the mountains. At your orders, Lord Duke, the rest of the army follows."

"I so order."

He listened to the trumpets as they sounded the advance. Close formation, rapid walk. Victory was close. Another day or two and he'd sit in Es City. Pagar called up his escort. He'd ride on down the lines of riders. Show the men he led from the front as a good commander should. His small group cantered past the moving lines. He noticed old Tarnoor with the men who followed him. More heirs were with the army here than the old man knew. Risho was in the tail of the wagons as supply master. Risho was heir after Tarnoor's direct line was ended. Pagar smiled as he glanced back at the oblivious Tarnoor. Poor old fool, he really shouldn't have acted as he did all those years ago. A man should honor his father and his oaths. Pagar had honored both.

He reached the head of the army just as it made camp. By now the tail would be well into the passes, too. They had orders to keep moving, making camp only when it was too dark for the horses to continue. They might be making a wet camp. Pagar studied the sky: the stars had vanished. Heavy cloud gathered. The wind was chill and there was thunder in the air. He snorted. Likely the Witches hoped to give him a head cold. It would take more than that to discourage Pagar of Geen.

Behind him in the half light Tarnoor directed his men. They picketed the beasts, built fires to heat food, and laid out bedrolls. Tarnoor was grimly weary. For a man of his age the march had been grueling but he would march no more. With the fraction of his blood that came down from another people he could see the Witch lights that flickered from tree to tree. They lit the rock edges, shimmered from leaves of the low brush. Tarnoor turned from the camp, walking away down a tiny gully that opened before him. At the end of it was a stretch of mountain ice-flowers. Their sweet perfume reached out to welcome him. In the midst of them, he knelt to pray.

He'd always done his best to be a decent man. He'd cared for Aiskeep and its people. Bred a fine son to follow him. There'd been things he regretted here and there, but few serious sins. Let him be forgiven them. Let poor foolish young Kirin be forgiven, too. Let blessings abide with Trovagh and Ciara, and all he loved. Moving slowly and deliberately he doffed his helm, waiting. Above him the thickening clouds broke apart for a moment. A single shaft of moonlight slashed downward to gleam from silver hair.

Tarnoor smiled. It seemed that after a lifetime the Gods chose to remember his service. The mountains stirred. High on a peak one rock dislodged, hurtling downward to strike Tarnoor squarely across the forehead as he lifted his face to the moonlight. He died instantly. His body fell back, stretching out among the ice-flowers. In a dying reflex his hand went to his sword hilt.

Then he lay still. About him the mountains bucked and heaved.

It was as if they had become as fluid as the seas in storm. They rolled, beating down all in their path, turning to lift then crush all life within their boundaries. Tons upon tons of stone filled valleys, to be thrust up into new mountains in turn. The rocks screamed as they tumbled, grinding against one another. The bellow of earthsound was enough to stun those who heard. It was sound beyond sound, terror beyond terror. Within the millstones of power called by Witches, Pagar's army ceased to exist. In Estcarp, the circle of Women of the

Power strove. They bled all they had from them, mind and body to save their land. Their power tortured and twisted the mountains until the hills shrieked agony.

Women died, power wrung from them to the last drop and beyond. They died, willing sacrifices to a land that was theirs, as all along its border the landscape churned in torment. Pagar had believed Estcarp defeated, beaten. He had wondered casually if they could find anything at the end to halt his advance. He lived just long enough to know.

There were those in the invading army who died in crazed terror, others who died striving to live. But Tarnoor of them all died first, and he alone of all the thousands, died without fear. He had seen this, and accepted his fate. Like an old wolf he was content if his enemies died with him. Let the son of his body, the daughter of his heart rule Aiskeep. Pagar would trouble them no more.

BOOK TWO

If the Dream Is Worth the Price

10

The quiet years ended when Aisling was almost eleven. Those years had not always been easy, but war had remained more in the North than in the poorer, less populated South. Aisha had gone to the main Keep of her clan near Kars city. There she had mixed with those who believed themselves born to rule. Her sons had learned to ape the manners, the beliefs, and far more dangerously—the burning ambition of those in the upper city. Aisha's clan had been powerful under Pagar. Now they talked constantly of those times and plotted that they should return once more. Among the other young men Aisha's sons listened to the talk.

The older, named Kirion for his father, was the more ferocious in that. His visits to Aiskeep had slowly made two things clear to him. The first was that he did not wish to molder his life away settling dirt-grubber disputes while living too many days' ride from Kars and civilization, luxury, pretty women, and all that made life interesting. The second was a bitter anger that the choice was unlikely to be his to make.

Trovagh had watched the boy for those years. He had seen the impatience, the belief that Kirion was more important than any farmer or servant. And he had seen that his people would never be happy with Kirion ruling Aiskeep.

The younger boy, Keelan, was a better choice, yet Trovagh doubted him, too. He was the more intelligent. It might just be that the younger lad had learned to conceal his beliefs better, learned to hide the contempt Kirion felt openly. Neither Trovagh nor Ciara liked the attitude of the brothers to their much younger sister.

"Kirion patronizes her," Ciara said.

"A natural attitude for a much older brother, beloved. But I dislike far more his belief that she is inferior because she is a girl."

Ciara smiled. "Of course he has to believe that. The child rides better, knows Aiskeep and its people better, and is secure here. Kirion resents it all. That mother of his seems to have filled his head with all sorts of ideas about his importance. He comes here and finds a child almost half his age being listened to over him."

"Of course she is listened to," Trovagh snapped impatiently. "She knows Aiskeep. If we went to Kars, we would doubtless listen to Kirion."

"Quite. However, Kirion doesn't see it that way; watch the boy, Tro. I'm not happy about his way of treating Aisling. One day he'll push things too far."

Trovagh agreed with that but what was he to do about it? The problem was partly that of age and little in common. Kirion was now twenty, while Aisling had just celebrated her eleventh name day. Keelan at seventeen was kinder to his young sister. Kirion made it clear he regarded her as an inferior nuisance. In fact, the lad's attitude to women in general bothered Trovagh.

It was true Aiskeep was far from Kars, but Kirion didn't make allowances for Geavon or for Trader Talron. Each in their own way brought or sent news from the city to Aiskeep. Twice of late Geavon had sent an extra separate note enclosed in his main letter. Both had carried warnings that young Kirion might be getting himself into danger. The lad had taken up with a faction that wished to see their figurehead on the throne. Trovagh had groaned. Hadn't Yvian and Pagar done enough damage to Karsten?

Talron had brought news from the lower levels of Kars. "They say Kirion has a nasty temper. He's not averse to beating a woman if she displeases him."

Trovagh had been staggered. "Who?"

Talron coughed.

"Oh, I see. But even a paid companion has the right to decent treatment. What do they say of him?"

The trader sighed, "To be blunt, my lord, they say that he has no care for any. That people are merely tools to his ends. They say he would sell his honor if it bought him his ambitions or a good price." He glanced across to see if he had given offense.

Trovagh shook his head. "It's all right. The truth of the matter is that the boy is like that. It's why I've been busy recently." Talron said nothing, but raised an eyebrow in question. Trovagh spoke abruptly.

"I get colds in winter. These last few years they've been worse. I thought it time to act now, in case aught should happen. I have been to Teral's shrine and sworn several documents. Copies have gone to Geavon to be held both by him and in the shrine records in Kars." He hesitated. "You and your father were always good friends to Aiskeep. It may be as well that you, too, know."

Talron sat silent. He would not ask, that would be intrusive, but he would listen. He hoped the answer would be what he wished to hear.

"Tarnoor made a similar deed," Trovagh continued. "He said that when he died, I was heir, but if I died Ciara was to follow me as heir and to have Heir's Right also."

The trader blinked. That was strong wine to drink. Under Karsten law it was legal, yes, but unusual. The more so when the woman named was not of the clan or kin blood. It was a Right usually given to a sister, to a mother or daughter of the one bestowing it.

"I, too," Trovagh said quietly, "have said this. I am undecided as to who shall inherit Aiskeep. I have formally disinherited Kirion but Keelan may yet be worthy. But if something happens to me, Ciara now has the Right under law to choose her successor. Geavon has several likely grandsons. Unlike Kirion who seems to feel this Keep beneath him, they would be happy to live and rule here. My father decided something similar before he followed Pagar."

Talron grunted agreement. He knew that bunch—full of life and energy. At least two of them would rule well; they understood the garthspeople and the needs of a Keep. Geavon might live near the city but he had old-fashioned ideas on what a young man should know. His grandsons had been well taught.

Trovagh stood up. "I thought it best you knew. A man should know where he stands. You and your father were long friends of Aiskeep." He tossed back the last of his wine, and placed the mug on the table before moving to the door. "I'll ask you to say nothing of this to any. Elanor and Ciara know, and now you, but none else."

The trader bowed. "I'm honored," he said sincerely.

He considered the conversation once he had retired. Trovagh was wise. Kirion was a viper in any bosom. Talron had heard more than he'd passed on. Much of it was gossip and rumor but even that could have a solid base. If it was true, the foolish boy was tampering with dangerous forces. Keelan ran in his brother's shadow. Yet there was something more likable there. In Talron's opinion, Keelan did what he had to, to survive in a household that revolved around the older brother's wishes.

He sighed for Trovagh and Ciara, both of whom he greatly liked. Odd how a solid, decent line seemed to birth a rotten apple sometimes. Kirin had been more stupid than evil. But his son—Talron was afraid there could be real evil there. Of course it hadn't helped that Aisha had spoiled the older boy all his life. Kirion had only to whine and whatever he wanted was his. The younger lad was less indulged. To some extent, the way he'd been handled on his visits to Aiskeep had also helped to counteract his spoiling. Still, it was quite possible Trovagh was right and neither boy was Keep Ruler material.

A pity that would be. Geavon was some sort of cousin, but a grandson would keep the rule within the family more or less. Talron sighed again. It was none of his business. But he'd give a lot to be a fly on the wall if Kirion found out about all this.

Kirion did. Being Kirion he jumped to several additional conclusions. The first being that Keelan would have been disinherited as well, the second that it would be Aisling who received Aiskeep and all that the inheritance carried. He'd never liked her, now he hated. He arrived at the Keep on his next visit seething with rage.

Since he could not legally know any of this, he kept silent. It made his anger rise even higher until just the sight of his small sister made him feel sick. He'd never felt any affection for her. He'd been nine when she was born. Almost at once his mother had packed up to live nearer Kars in the Keep of her father's clan, leaving the unwanted baby to be fostered by Ciara. It had been another three years before Kirion had returned to Aiskeep to visit. Aisha had simply made excuses each year until Trovagh had made it clear he would accept no more. But as a result, Kirion had known nothing of Aisling until he arrived that first time. For several years more, he had barely seen her on these trips. It was only over the past three or four years that she'd been in evidence.

By then Kirion regarded himself as a man. It had infuriated him that a girl of eight could outride him. That she knew more about Aiskeep, its people and its needs than he did. Twice during the last visit she'd made him look foolish. It did not occur to him that it had been his eagerness to impress those about him that had done that. He'd taken responsibility for little in his life before, and it was natural to him to seek a scapegoat.

In Kars he'd made friends with one who had the run of the great records rooms at the shrine. Kirion kept a watchful eye on anything filed that might affect himself. Thus he had known at once when he was disinherited. But his access was illegal. He could not speak of what he knew. It made him savage.

It was in this mood he ordered his horse saddled and rode to the upper valley. There he found Aisling discussing a sick child with Jontar's granddaughter. He hid a sneer. So the brat thought herself to be Keep's Lady already, did she? He waited until the talk was done before he approached.

"Ride back with me, sister?"

Aisling eyed him warily. She was well aware of his dislike for her. But what harm could come of a ride beside Kirion? They were only riding up her own valley toward the Keep where Trovagh and Ciara waited for her. She accepted politely when Kirion continued to wait. The horses walked side by side, their riders silent. Kirion was calculating. As they reached the stand of oaks that marked half of the valley's length, he began to talk. He could be amusing and entertaining when he wished. For some miles he beguiled Aisling with his tales of life in Kars, funny incidents and people he knew.

He glanced around as he spoke, and saw no one. Good. It never occurred to him that just because he could see no one it did not mean that there were no watchers within the garth houses as he passed. The brat was laughing loudly. No training as a lady for all her pretensions. A lady would titter, hand over her mouth, eyes flirting over the edge of that hand. But then a lady would respect Lord Kirion of Clan Iren. He waited, as the laughter died a little, then he suddenly stared at her, face twisted into a sweetly winning smile. Above the smile his eyes were brightly challenging.

"Race you to the Keep, sister. A new bridle if you win."

Before she could reply he was gone, leaning low over the withers of his mount. Aisling signaled her horse to follow. That hadn't been fair, Kirion had started before she'd understood what he was saying. It would be fun to beat him anyway and win a new bridle. She was lighter, astride a mount that knew her every touch. Kirion was heavier, riding a horse that was good but never the equal of the Torgian strain. They thundered down the road, Aisling gradually pulling up alongside her brother.

She looked across at him and grinned happily. It was not intended to infuriate. To the child, it was no more than an expression of her delight in the race. But to Kirion, it was a look of gloating triumph. He lashed his mount, but could not draw ahead; indeed he was starting to fall inch by inch behind the other beast. It was intolerable. All of it. This brat had stolen Aiskeep from him, now she was even stealing Kirion's pride in his own horsemanship. Aisling turned a little to smile.

"I think you may owe me a new bridle, brother," she called.

It was the last straw. Kirion glanced about again, but he could see no one. He goaded his horse into a final burst of speed so that the two beasts were level momentarily. Then he slipped his foot from the stirrup. It was an old trick but the Armsmaster who had taught him had said it could be lethal when it worked. The word Kirion had not remembered had been 'when.'

He reached out his foot to hook it under Aisling's boot. One swift heave and she'd be flung from the racing back of her mount. At this speed and on hard ground, with luck the brat would be no bar to his inheritance. At the least she'd be injured, enough to show her what it meant to laugh as she cheated Kirion from his dues. His foot thrust upward.

In the stable Harran was standing watching the race with amusement. If that city fop thought he'd beat a fine horsewoman riding an Aiskeep horse against one of a very ordinary line, then the man was a bigger fool than Harran had thought. And the Gods knew he thought Kirion a witling anyhow. He was in the shadow of the stable; Kirion's glance had passed over the motionless figure. But Harran was in a direct line between the horses as they raced up the road toward him. He had long vision. Enough to see what was about to happen, though he was too far away to intervene.

He waited in horror for Aisling to fall. It was natural for Kirion to underestimate his sister. Harran should have known better; part of her training with her horse had been under his teaching. She felt the foot hook under hers. Automatically she shied sideways, her mount obeying the sudden body shift. Caught suddenly off balance, Kirion felt himself falling. He clutched for the neck of his mount as it slowed, then, with slow, slithering grace Kirion swung around and under his horse's neck until he landed sitting below it.

It was unfortunate that the horse had moved across the road. Toward the edge where it had halted there was a long soft patch of mud. Kirion landed in this, then went to rise and lost his footing. He measured his length forward, rising with muddy seat and mud-covered front from toes to hairline. Aisling had reined back to see he was uninjured. Childlike she broke into peals of laughter at the spectacle.

If she had ever thought Kirion's friendship of the past hours to be real, she was disabused in seconds. His face twisted into a snarl of rage so savage that she was momentarily frozen. He took a step toward her as she stood too terrified to move. His hands came up for her throat. He'd show her what it was to laugh at him. Fingers fastened in her clothing as he shook her slowly, the intensity increasing. Harran was running toward them shouting. Kirion heard nothing. He'd teach the girl to make a fool of him. He'd show her. He stooped still holding her, for his whip.

In utter panic, Aisling reached within herself. Ciara had taught the child to find the mists, to use them for healing. Now, instinctively the girl reached for the only thing she could use to defend herself.

Kirion lifted the whip. His fingers burned suddenly as if he'd thrust them into a fire. He shouted with pain, releasing the whip and clutching at his reddened hand. Aisling twisted loose, blue fire still outlining her body. Crying in fear she ran for the stables. Harran passed her even as Kirion, face almost inhuman with fury, moved to follow her.

"No, my lord."

He was thrust aside. "Out of my way, you fool. By the Gods, I'm going to kill her."

"No, my lord." Oh, Lord Trovagh understand, Harran thought as he drove a swift skilled blow and watched Kirion crumple. Voices reached him then. Ciara and Trovagh were coming at a run. He drew himself up to explain but there was no need.

"Good man!" Trovagh dealt him a gentle buffet on the shoulder. "We saw most of that from the door." Ciara arrived with an arm about a weeping Aisling.

Ciara stooped to check Kirion, then straightened. "Only stunned," she noted. "Haul him into the stables. Call a couple of the men, Harran. When he comes to, tell him to get on his horse and go before I forget myself. And tell him not to come back unless one of us sends for him."

Trovagh walked over to where Kirion's richly ornamented horse gear was hanging from pegs. He chose a bridle lavish with silver on black leather. This was handed to Aisling. Then Trovagh paused, looking down the line of pegs. He added the saddle and lush-furred blanket that matched it.

"After that you can tell him I picked out his wager to pay Aisling. The saddle is a forfeit. Bad enough he would have injured his sister, but I do not forgive what followed. Tell him to think about events as he rides home. And to help that, give him the oldest bridle and saddle you can find that'll hold together."

He strolled off carrying the saddle, Ciara in his wake with her arm about her granddaughter. Aisling was still sniffing, but she held the bridle tightly.

Harran smirked after them. It was a pleasure to serve a lord and lady who knew the score even against their own kinblood. He concentrated on finding the oldest, dirtiest, most-mended gear in the stable. But in mercy to the horse he used a thick, comfortable saddle blanket. Kirion was groaning his way back to consciousness as a servant arrived with two leather bags.

"The young lord's clothing. How is the little—master?"

"He'll live." Harran tied the horse to the wall ring, then expertly added the filled saddlebags. "I've orders to see him on his way. Stay with me in case he tries to make trouble about it."

The servant spat on his palms. "I hope he does."

But Kirion knew when to lie low. One look at the two men told him they'd be only too delighted to tie him on his mount before chasing it through Aiskeep gates. He kept silence as he checked the bridle and saddle. It wouldn't surprise him if they'd fixed those to dump him again, either. He mounted and rode off, still silent. But Harran catching a glimpse of Kirion's eyes thought he'd seldom seen such a wicked look. If Harran were Lord Trovagh, he'd be keeping a very wary eye out for this one in the future.

Neither Trovagh nor Ciara were unaware of the dangers. Kirion had some powerful friends these days. Aiskeep had a long reputation as a Keep unlucky to attack. But if Kirion gained real power, there were no guarantees he'd care. Ciara remained with Aisling until the girl fell asleep, then she rejoined her husband.

"Bad news, love."

He queried her with a look.

"The child used Power to make Kirion release her. From the sound of things, he may even have realized it."

Trovagh swore. He spoke with a range and fluency that would have surprised any not familiar with his father in like mind.

"That's just what we didn't want any of that lot to know."

"He may still be unaware. Apparently, Aisling called Power to burn his hand. It made him drop the whip and let her go. But from what she says, it would not have been great enough to leave marks. He may discount it. You know Kirion. He'd hate to think there was just one more thing Aisling could do that he could not."

"That's true," Trovagh said slowly, "But he may also see her as a possible tool if he can force himself to accept it. I fear that she may be in danger if this is so."

In an inn on the outskirts of a town a half-day's ride to the North, Kirion brooded over wine. He'd been unjustly treated. First, because he preferred a decent city to a miserable chilly Keep, he was disinherited. Then because he attempted a jest on his sister he was attacked, despoiled of his property, and flung out of his own place. His grandparents had allowed a low-born servant to strike their grandson. Even more, they'd sent the same man to threaten him. He went over events again and again.

Soon he'd convinced himself the whole thing had been only a trick, a joke on his part. The girl had no right to laugh at him. His grandparents had no right to steal his best saddle and bridle to give to that brat. He'd show them, he'd pay them all out somehow. He slept heavily and woke with a sore head and surly of temper. He drank more wine before leaving.

The road was rough over the next day's ride. Kirion was obliged to travel at a walk. It gave him time to brood, to count his wrongs, and swear revenge again. He found he was recalling the race. Damn, if only the girl's horse hadn't shied. He rapidly convinced himself that this had been an accident rather than riding ability. The brat had probably been about to fall off. Why his actions might even have helped her regain her balance as the horse shied back under her.

There was some vague memory teasing at the back of his mind. He couldn't quite recall, but something nagged at him. Something had been wrong in the scenes as he considered them. He should have given the girl the beating of her life. More of those and she might have learned respect for the head of her house. He'd like to have the teaching of her for a year or two. She'd learn politeness and respect for Kirion then, and he'd see to that with pleasure. The feeling of having forgotten something continued to tease him. Oh, well, he'd remember it if it was important. But he was tired and his head ached. He fell into a half dream as he rode.

He found the reins chafing his fingers. They seemed to burn—burn—Sersgarth had burned. He'd known the story most of his life, though not the sequel. Only three now alive knew the why of Sersgarth. Pagar's bid for power. It seemed unlucky to be duke in Kars. They said it harked back to Yvian who'd had the Old Race horned as outlaws. Once he and his friends raised that fool Shandro to the throne, things would change. And rumor had it that all Yvian's luck went with the Old Race when they fled. Certainly Pagar hadn't been fortunate.

Everything, a dukedom, three beautiful wives one after another, the most powerful clans backing him. Then Estcarp, and all at once everything was gone—including Pagar and Kirion's father. That was the Witches. It was said they could do anything. Burn a man to death with their witchery. Blue fire to burn a witch's enemies.

His breath caught. *Yes*! That was the memory he'd hunted. When he'd lifted the whip, the girl's eyes had been so frightened that it had given him a delightful sense of his own power.

Then, all of a sudden, his hand had been on fire. He'd dropped his whip, the girl had fought free of him, and fled. Harran had arrived, preventing Kirion from following, and had struck him. But it was in that fraction of a second before Aisling fled that he'd seen her shine. A sort of faint bluish light from her skin. *Power to burn their enemies.* The brat was a Witch!

He knew there was Old Blood in Aiskeep. His mother had told him, primming up her mouth in disapproval, although it hadn't stopped her family from offering her to Kirin, her son thought in amusement. And somewhere as a young boy he'd heard about his grandmother. She was said to have been a half-blood from the Old Race. Tarnoor had taken her in after the Horning, and wed her to his son for the dowry Ciara had to bring. An inheritance. She could have given another inheritance to the line. Something his young sister had just displayed. Aisling could have inherited abilities.

He smiled slowly. Power! It could be used in so many ways. He rode on, but now he sat straighter, a small unpleasant smile on his lips. There were ambitions he would accomplish. Those he could influence in his favor. Enemies he could be well rid of. Power can come in many forms, he mused. If he played this unexpected card well, he could have it all.

11

Kirion went to the records at the Kars shrine on his return. There he dug through documents until he found everything he could uncover. It made more interesting reading than he'd anticipated in the end. There was the document giving title of Elmsgarth to his great-grandfather. He noted the dates. Tarnoor had been no fool, by the Flame. He'd taken in an orphan and done well from it. He noted the price subsequently paid for the garth and whistled.

He discovered the Heir's Rights paper Tarnoor had sent and was stunned. Witchery! His grandmother must have bewitched the old fool. This allowed her to disinherit any in direct line, naming whoever she chose in their place once Trovagh was dead. He then found that while he had been disinherited, Keelan had not. So! The little brother had ambitions above his station, did he? Kirion would have to teach him a lesson about that. He rechecked all the documents and saw this time a tiny notation on a corner of each. There was no way he could simply destroy everything, they'd thought of that. At least someone somewhere held copies.

It was likely to be Geavon, Kirion thought, as he replaced the papers. The man was a little younger than Tarnoor had been, although his way of talking made him appear ancient. But Geavon took care of himself; he was good for a lot longer yet. And he didn't like Kirion. There was no way Kirion was going to get into the records at Gerith Keep to destroy any copies there. He left the shrine looking unpleasantly thoughtful.

Over the months, he investigated. It would be convenient if he could come up with some kind of spell that would burn all the relevant papers at once wherever they were. He turned to reading. There were books still to be found on the subject of witchery if one searched hard enough. Kirion searched, ending up with a shelf full of volumes. All told him what he didn't want to know. That witchcry was not what he'd always believed. It wasn't spells and chants so much as the focused will of the one working it.

This was not popular information. However, there were some vague, obscure references to other methods.

Kirion settled to more research, pausing only to make Keelan's life a misery. To escape, Keelan fled to Aiskeep, arriving more in charity with those there than he'd ever been. He was received dubiously; no one was forgetting Kirion's action on *his* last visit. But Keelan was so clearly unhappy that they gradually allowed him some acceptance. The boy would have liked to respond but had long since learned to show nothing.

It was Harran who broke through some of the shell in which the boy had encased himself. Harran was Master at Arms since Hanion was finally past the harder, longer work. He was Hanion's nephew, and was intent on following family tradition in service to Aiskeep. Harran hadn't much liked what he'd seen over the years of Aisha or her sons. But finding Keelan ready to listen that first day, Harran was ready to teach. He found Keelan not ill-taught already.

It could be seen the lad had been given reasonable Arms-masters, but of the very conventional kind. Not for them the tricks and ruses that might be the difference between life and death in an alley brawl. Harran took the lad in hand.

Keelan learned as well as listened. He found it far more interesting than he'd have believed. For most of his life, Kirion had insisted that his younger brother was inferior. It was good to do something where Keelan was praised. He worked harder to earn what he knew to be honest comment.

Harran was slowly impressed. He knew the boy was unhappy, knew that this was in part why he was turning to hard work. In Harran's opinion, that was good. Sweat and exhaustion tended to burn out misery. You were too tired to be emotional. He gave generous praise when it was due and until the noonday meal, worked Keelan until the boy was ready to drop. He was pleased to find the novice had a strong wrist, a good eye, and an excellent sense of point.

"That's it, yes. Now lunge—and parry—lunge, yes! Good, lad."

Keelan wiped sweat from his forehead as he relaxed back. Kirion had always said that a noble didn't fight like this, but it was fun. It was also pleasant to know Keelan would be a lot more dangerous to bandits or back alley thugs now should he meet any. He grinned as the thought also occurred to him that Kirion didn't know these methods. It would be a good idea to keep silent on the subject. If he and Kirion ever fought, it would be very pleasant to have a few tricks up his sleeves.

He spent the afternoon riding with Harran, too. For the first time, Keelan found himself mounted on one of the dun strain that Aiskeep had become known for. They had more endurance and more intelligence than ordinary mounts. He'd never known where they began. Now, riding down the valley, he asked to be rewarded with the tale of how his grandparents when mere children had beaten a bandit force with the aid of the garthspeople. He was surprised and impressed by the tale.

"So the horses were Torgians. What were they like; are they really that different?"

Harran was happy to expound. He followed that by taking Keelan out to the herd that ranged to the end of the upper valley and beyond into the foothills. The boy was awestruck. He'd never seen such beasts. It was not the looks so much but the intelligence that shone from their eyes. The feeling that even as he admired them, they were estimating Keelan's worth. He was afraid that however such animals chose a rider, Keelan was unlikely to measure up. His gaze was wistful. To have a horse like that would be wonderful.

He returned to the evening meal tired, wind-burned, and unusually happy. He found the family in front of the hearth in the smaller hall. With them were assorted cats and a bevy of kittens all climbing merrily into any mischief they could find.

Keelan winced. His mother had always said of Aiskeep, that one of the things that had decided her to leave had been all those infuriating cats. She had claimed them to be dirty, flea-ridden, and dangerous. On subsequent visits, Keelan had ignored them. The cats had reciprocated. And since his usual visit was made in late fall to early winter, the kittens had mostly gone to their new homes.

Keelan didn't know it but Aiskeep had been doing a brisk trade in kittens for years. Trader Talron brought in a new cat every so often from the Sulcar with whom he still did a good trade. But these were the only cats to enter Karsten. As a result, the Aiskeep kittens sold to almost every garth and Keep in the South. But few were sold in Kars or to the North.

Keelan had never met kittens until now. Not really young ones that were no more than balls of fluff with wide eyes and small, unsteady legs as they scrambled about the room.

He did notice that there were odd wire guards across the hearths. "What are those for?"

Ciara smiled. "Kitten prevention. They love to sit and watch the sparks go upward. But without the guards sometimes a kitten tries to go up with the spark."

She saw the boy wince as he visualized one of the enchanting fluff balls landing back into the fire. Ciara was caught by that. Keelan had always been in Kirion's shadow, but his brother hated cats. He would not have winced at the thought; more likely he'd try it out for amusement, Ciara thought. This boy could be worth a closer look. People did change.

The next morning she managed to drift silently by as Keelan was receiving his next arms lesson. To her surprise, once more he was taking quite a beating, without complaint and with hard work as he learned. She took Harran aside later that day.

"Have you found out why he's here? It isn't his usual time, and he's not indicating he intends to leave anytime soon. I think he was unhappy about something when he arrived."

The Armsmaster nodded. "He's let the odd word slip. Some girl he was crazy over. Apparently, Kirion took her away from him just to prove he could."

Ciara blinked. "Is that it?"

"No, Lady. The truth is that I think the lad's taken a good hard look at his family for the first time in his life because of that. He's found he doesn't even like his mother, doesn't trust his relatives in the Keep there, and hates his brother along with not trusting him, either. He's in a state of confusion. He's always come second to Kirion and he's been brought up to believe he's less than Kirion because he's smaller, knows less, and can't keep up. Suddenly it's dawning on him that *anyone* three years younger would have those problems. It doesn't make him inferior."

"No, it doesn't. How would you rate him?"

Harran snorted. "He isn't the stylist that his brother is. But that's fine for formal duels. I'd back this one against Kirion in any knockdown, drag-out sword fight where the rules don't apply. Give me a while longer with him and I might even back him in a duel as well." He looked at her. "You know, Lady, the boy's never had anything he could really call his own. Any time he has Kirion makes it his job to get it away again. Now Keelan's afraid to care about anything in case he loses it." Harran snorted. "And that mother of his sees all this but does nothing. There isn't a cat here who isn't a better mother than that woman."

Ciara laughed. "I'd agree." She strolled slowly away, thinking as she went. Later she talked to Trovagh.

"I don't know how long he's going to stay. I'd like him to have a pet of some kind. It seems to be what he needs, but if he leaves he won't be able to take it. Not with the kind of things Kirion does. What do you think, Tro?"

"Hmm. We could perhaps let him have an Aiskeep horse. Say it's on loan. That it can't be wagered, given away, or ridden by any but Keelan. It would bring down untold wrath from Aisha, though, probably mostly on Keelan from what you say. Would he think the horse worth it?"

"I think so, but there's another fear there. From what he's told Harran, Kirion doesn't just stop at taking anything Keelan has. Sometimes he ruins it in spite as well. If we let the boy have an Aiskeep horse and Kirion lames it or has it stolen, what will that do to Keelan?"

Trovagh grunted. "Umph. I see what the problem is. Leave it, love. Let's wait; once we have an idea of how long the lad will stay, we may be able to make better plans."

Keelan did stay. He was finding that being part of a family who were kind to you was an unexpected pleasure. It was summer, the weather mostly good enough to ride, and when it wasn't, there was always the lessons with Harran. Imperceptibly, Keelan was being guided to learn about more than fighting. With Trovagh, he met the garthspeople, hearing their problems and listening to Trovagh's suggestions and solutions. He saw to his surprise that there was a very real and solid affection between lord and the garth families.

He heard the garthspeople argue with Ciara, and saw she listened. It wasn't so at Clan Iren. There if a lord spoke, a servant shut up and obeyed. He heard the story of the bandit raid from old Jontar, this time from the garth side. The pride was unmistakable. Pride not only in beating the outlaw group, but also in the leadership the garths had followed. He hid a grin at the differing attitudes. One minute Jontar was praising his lord and lady for their leadership, the next muttering about foolish children endangering themselves.

Gradually he came to understand the ties between the rulers and the ruled. This was how it should be. Mutual respect and balance. He saw that the garth houses were all warm and weatherproof. There'd be no one dead from cold or hunger here. No lord taking what he wanted and letting the people manage how they could. He considered the story of the bandits afresh. In many Keeps he could name, the bandits might have had the lord's children with the people's goodwill, and in some cases their active assistance.

The people certainly wouldn't have fought like that. Not because they wanted to at least. They would have fought from terror at what their lord would do if they did not fight. Or because they were given direct orders. Or because it was the only way to survive the outlaws. They'd probably have made a mess of it, being without arms or initiative.

Weapons. That was another thing that had stunned Keelan. In Aiskeep, the garthspeople all had weapons. Not just the odd dagger, but bows and swords.

Keelan had almost leapt out of his skin the first time he realized. One of the women had come out bearing a bow and filled quiver as Trovagh rode up with his grandson. Trovagh had simply nodded.

"Deer or rabbits, Marina?"

"Rabbits, my lord." She grinned widely. "Though I'd not

hold my arrow should a deer pop up." She strode away as Keelan gaped. Once she was out of earshot, he glanced at his grandfather.

"Will she hit anything?"

"Oh, yes. Marina's a very good shot." Trovagh was hiding a smile at the look on the boy's face. Let him think over all the implications. Keelan did.

First—that if a garthswoman could carry a bow freely, either Trovagh and Ciara were incredibly casual about their own safety, or their people were incredibly trustworthy. Second—that if a woman carried a bow, presumably so did the men. If she was a good shot, so presumably were the men. Why, at a pinch Trovagh had an army of archers here, he realized. No wonder Aiskeep had never been taken. That led to him questioning Harran.

"They say Aiskeep has never fallen?"

"Humph! Don't let that make you overconfident, lad. There's no Keep that can't be taken if you're prepared to spend enough time, men, and coin. But it's true doing so here would ruin most lords." He took the boy out to study the walls. "See, our lord doesn't spend his money on fancy clothes. It goes into stone; see here—and here. That's where we strengthened it after Yvian's death. And here, that's where we added the curtain wall inside the main one a few years before Pagar came to the throne in Kars."

Keelan was amazed. The walls were massive, the most impressive structure he'd ever seen. Somehow he'd never really looked at them before. He went quiet, staying that way for days as he summed up what he was learning. He'd always felt that his clan was somehow wrong. Everyone in the Keep seemed unhappy, or happy in the wrong ways. The servants cringed when spoken to, the dogs cowered, and the inhabitants seemed to be plotting whenever they had a spare moment from drinking, or wenching.

He'd seen that no one got drunk here. Ciara and Trovagh drank wine with meals. Watered wine and only a reasonable few glasses. They treated each other with respect and a love that was evident in every word. His small sister wasn't the brat Kirion had described. He took that one to Harran, too, who promptly and very forcefully gave the true story. Keelan was unhappily convinced by it. He knew his older brother too well not to believe. It also made sense of some of the more obscure comments Kirion had snarled while giving his version of events. Keelan snorted; no wonder his own arrival had been received with doubt.

The summer wore away slowly into an even better fall. Keelan was beginning to feel an acceptance here. As if it was home, a place to be yourself. A place where people might even like the self he was discovering. He'd heard that Kirion was barred from Aiskeep. That knowledge helped him relax further. Whatever else Kirion spoiled, he could not reach Keelan here. Gradually, Aisling had unbent toward this new brother. Ciara had spoken quietly to the girl, giving her a suggestion.

Aisling had acted on this, asking help of Keelan anytime there was something she could legitimately request.

"Keelan, could you reach that halter for me, you're much taller?" He could and did, with a tiny feeling of pride.

"Can you open this salve, my wrists aren't strong enough?" Keelan twisted the top open, handing it over with a pleased grin. The admiring look he received made his grin widen. Having a little sister was—why, it was pleasant. He almost strutted as he left the stable. He learned slowly that Aisling was intelligent, and interesting to talk to. That she listened to his own ideas with flattering attention. He fell into the habit of talking with her quite often. They began to ride together. Trovagh nodded to his wife at that.

"Nice job, dearling. The boy's found Aisling to be real company once he's got to know her. Plan one, I suppose?"

"Why not?" Ciara laughed softly. Her glance was affectionate. "He isn't really bad, Tro. Not like Kirion. In fact, they have that in common, so Aisling tells me. Kirion's played some pretty dangerous and vicious tricks on Keelan over the years. Aisha has always ignored it, but the boy's been bullied within an inch of his life by his brother, spoiled rotten by his mother, and despised by just about everyone who dislikes Kirion and assumes Keelan is the same. I think a lot of his change here has been the knowledge that Kirion isn't welcome. He feels as if Aiskeep is the one refuge he can't be tracked to and made miserable in again."

Trovagh agreed. "I'll tell you something else, too, beloved. A man needs something to protect. What has the boy ever had? Anything he's cared for his brother has taken away. That makes Keelan feel bad for losing it and helpless because he couldn't prevent the loss. With Aisling he's being a big brother at last." He grinned as he looked over at Ciara. "Harran tells me the boy is really working at weapons training. He's let it slip that if bandits come again he's going to be sure Aisling is safe."

Ciara looked up. "He'd do better to protect her from Kirion."

"I'm not so sure he wouldn't now. Harran says that with a few more months' work the boy will be better with a sword than his brother. Apparently, Kirion is mostly style with no stamina. Good for short, flashy duels. Not good for a real grudge fight. I wouldn't wager Keelan couldn't take him if Harran thinks so." He watched her brows rise. "Yes, I think now you should put plan two into action, my cunning love."

"Plan two?" Ciara looked innocent.

"Plan two! I've known you too long not to know there's a plan two."

His wife grinned but said nothing. It was true, but she didn't want Tro to let something slip. Keelan had sharp eyes. A knowing look at the wrong time might spoil her schemes.

She waited with as much patience as she had ever been capable of finding. One of the cats was due to kitten. Her last two litters had each contained a spare: one the mother decided to discard for reasons unknown to humans.

It happened again, to Ciara's secret satisfaction. The kit was a female, tiny and pathetic. She brought it to Keelan quite casually.

"The mother doesn't want it. If someone doesn't look after it, the poor little thing will die." She unloaded the tiny, shivering scrap into his hands.

She saw the uncertain glance up from the corner of his eye. From all she had pieced together, she could guess at his fear.

"If you can raise her, she's yours. Not to be sold or given to anyone else. She can stay here or go with you, whatever you choose. She *is* unlikely to have kittens herself. We've found those we rear this way are often infertile." She shrugged, "I'll leave you to it. If you can't be bothered, take it down to the stable and kill it. A quick, clean death. All right?" She registered the involuntarily protective movement of his hands with blank face but elated heart. "If you decide to rear it, talk to Aisling. She helped me with one of the others." She strolled out, leaving Keelan to sit holding the faintly 'yeeking' baby.

He reared it. There were times when he considered that quick, clean death. Then he would look down at his troublesome, time-consuming charge and fall in love all over again. She needed him. In weeks she was stumbling on unsteady furry legs all about his room. A few weeks more and she was a skittering racing ball of fluff into everything and under his feet. He adored her. After long consideration, he'd named her Shosho. It was a dialect word for something that was everywhere, ubiquitous. She was certainly that.

At times he wondered despairingly if all kittens were this bad. That was after Shosho had fallen down the jakes. Luckily, it was immediately after the first hard frost. The muck at the bottom of the shaft was solid enough to bear her weight so she didn't drown. But Keelan had to climb down a rope after her. The muck at the bottom hadn't borne *his* weight. He appeared at the top of the shaft with a kitten that refused to know him any further until he bathed. The waiting humans made it clear they agreed. Keelan left grinning to seek a hot bath with plenty of soap.

Shosho forgave him once he was in the hot, soapy water. She demonstrated that by falling in with him, then climbing out using small frantic claws on some tender places.

His howls brought Ciara running, only to be passed by a very wet, virtually airborne kitten, which explained it all to her. She stifled her giggles and left again without Keelan's being aware. That had happened to Ciara a few times before she started shutting her cats out when she bathed. She'd suggest it to Keelan sometime.

The boy was happy all that winter. Shosho grew steadily. She was going to be a magnificent cat with eyes of deep amber, and a thick plush coat of glossy black. She slept on his bed, brought her kills to him, and generally made it clear that Keelan was her human.

Slave might have been a better word. Not that Keelan minded. He was a lap whenever she wanted one, trailed string for her on demand, and loved her with all his heart. In loving her, he found the capacity to love others, too. He was Aisling's lieutenant in many things that winter. Often now he would take a job away from her.

"That's too heavy, let me lift it."

Aisling graciously permitted him to help. Keelan discovered the joys of shared jokes, harmless tricks, and a family circle elastic enough to admit another one in.

Back in Iren Keep, Kirion had vaguely noticed that his younger brother was nowhere to be found. It did not matter. Kirion was too busy with his studies into forms of power. When he wanted Keelan, he'd find him. Right now he wanted only peace to read and privacy to experiment with some of what he learned.

When winter was over Keelan was still at Aiskeep. He was afraid to talk about it. If he said he wanted to stay here for good, perhaps they'd say he couldn't. He said nothing, just in case. If he didn't ask, he couldn't be refused. He'd grown to love the Keep and his family here. Anyhow, he couldn't leave. What would happen to Shosho? If he took her back to Iren, Kirion would find some way of hurting her. Keelan might be able to beat him in a fight now, but that wouldn't heal Shosho if Kirion had injured her.

Apart from her, there was Aisling, Ciara, Trovagh, Harran, and old Hanion who told him stories about Keelan's great-grandfather. Jontar, who was always happy to talk about the bandits, and the host of garthspeople who greeted him now as if they were pleased to see him. They were. The consensus on the land was that the lad was training up quite well, and would make a reasonable lord one day. Had Kirion known any of this, he'd have spat blood. Since he did not, all was peaceful both at Aiskeep and at Iren Keep.

Aisling, too, was happy. She'd always wanted an older brother. A real one, not like Kirion. She celebrated her twelfth name day with Keelan assisting.

His name day would come in early spring. He would be eighteen. He hoped they'd mark it in some way, but he'd say nothing just in case. There was an air of subdued excitement around, he thought some weeks later. But it was probably because spring was on the way. He noticed Aisling vanishing into her room a lot with the door shut. She appeared flushed when he knocked and the door was opened. He hoped harder. Always at Iren Keep his name days had been miserable with Kirion resenting the attention focused elsewhere.

Two days before Keelan's name day, Kirion arrived. He'd run out of books he hadn't read. Then it occurred to him that if the brat did have the power he believed, there might well be books on witchcraft in the old Aiskeep library. He rode there, casually confident that his grandparents hadn't meant his banishment to last. He was disabused on arrival. It was Harran who glanced out, to recognize the approaching rider. By the time Kirion reached the gates, Ciara and Trovagh were there with their Armsmaster.

"Hail the gates, open for Kirion, Kirin's son of Aiskeep." Kirion slouched on his weary horse, waiting for the gates to swing open. Instead, a tart voice addressed him from above.

"You were told not to return unless we asked for you. You have not been asked here, you have our leave to depart."

Kirion gaped upward. "You can't *do* that!"

Trovagh took over. "We can, we have, and we like it that way. Take yourself and that poor animal to Teral, to Kars, or to Hades. You aren't welcome here. Do I have to make it any plainer?"

He did. Kirion sat his mount, his voice rising to an infuriated whine as he pleaded, protested, and then ordered.

"I'm heir now that my father's dead. You can't keep me out." That should get the truth told, he thought. Ciara eyed him. Something in the tone told her the boy knew he'd been formally disinherited. But then she didn't have to confirm that. She leaned out.

"An heir has certain rights, that's true. But automatic entry to his family Keep is not one of them. Not when all are in agreement he isn't welcome. Go away, Kirion. Shut your mouth before you get snow in it."

Aisling heard that last comment. She had been listening, seeing the man who'd become an ogre in her mind so discomforted. She stooped, rolled snow into a loose snowball, then flung it. The snowball took Kirion square in the face as he began another plea. He spluttered, choking on snow, wiping it in fury from his face and neck. Behind the wall he could hear the howls of laughter. Even his grandmother had a broad grin. Kirion tightened his grip on the reins, swinging his unwilling beast away from the Keep.

It would do no good to remain. Mentally he notched up another score against Aisling. He spent the days riding back to Iren Keep in a foul mood. Some of that he worked off on his mount, some on oaths of what he would do if he ever got Aisling into his hands. He returned to study, paying more than his mother could afford for moldering books and documents that might give Kirion the power he craved. He continued to cultivate Shandro. The man was an idiot, but a very well-connected one. He'd make the perfect figurehead duke if Kirion ever unlocked power to raise the fool to that position.

It did occur to him several times that he hadn't seen his younger brother at all of late, not for months, in fact. Kirion ignored that. He'd found what he felt was a promising trail to the knowledge he sought. Whatever Keelan was doing, he'd come to heel as soon as he was called. Kirion persuaded more coin from his mother and vanished into increasingly unsavory places in his search. As he saw it, he was having quite a good—and possibly profitable—time.

12

Keelan's eighteenth name day was a success. Ciara had made one of her hangings for his room. If you looked at it up close it was merely color. But from the doorway across his room it became Keelan, with Aiskeep in the background. Shosho was included in the work, sitting at his feet gazing up. Aisling produced a saddle and bridle. They were plain, but the leather work was of the finest quality. Elanor marched in with several packages, which proved to contain her usual offering of robe and slippers in the Keep colors of gold and mulberry. To these she'd added a saddle blanket of rabbit furs, winter ones dyed the same colors. It looked magnificent.

Hanion appeared with Harran. Their gift was a joint one of a fine bow in a bow case of oiled gut, and a matching quiver of arrows that were examples of the fletcher's art. Keelan found he was standing there, gifts scattered about him, tears in his eyes, and quite unable to speak. These were the people his mother had always condemned as mean, arrogant, and provincial. If Aiskeep was mean, what did that make her? he wondered. He'd never had gifts like these from his mother. If they were arrogant, how was it they'd accepted him?

As for provincial . . . He looked at them. Maybe they were, by her standards. Their clothes were warm and comfortable, not the gaudy fashions of Kars. Their skin was browned by sun, burned by wind, not the pallid shade favored by the fashionable. Their eyes were alive with life and interest in life. He found his face stretching into a slow, wide grin. Provincial? If that was provincial, then he'd take the provinces any day. Aisha could have Kars, she could have dear Kirion, and she could do what she pleased with both. Keelan would stay here, forever, if he was permitted.

It took him several days to come down from the delights of that day. When he did, he shut himself away for the afternoon to think. He feared asking if he could remain permanently. What if they refused? Ciara and Trovagh guessed, both at his desire and his fears. They left him alone. They, too, had thought much about this. Their decision had been made so long as Keelan plucked up enough courage to ask. That would be the final test.

The boy spent the night thinking. He must know. He marched down to the hall the next morning, terrified but resolute. It was silly in a way. His grandparents had shown no signs of wanting him to leave. Why then did he have this need for a formal permission and agreement?

He found Trovagh and Ciara alone. Elanor always broke her fast in her room these days. She was becoming frail and slept late. Aisling had been and gone, encouraged by Ciara to an errand in the upper valley.

Keelan arrived with the air of one who goes to the stake bravely. "Grandmother, Grandfather." He bowed politely. "I would speak with you."

Trovagh nodded, "Sit then and speak."

Neither of them would have betrayed it for anything, but those Keelan faced were deeply amused by the scene. The lad was trying so hard to be formal. Instead, he gave the impression of a badly strung puppet. Keelan talked. He managed to make it brief, just that he'd like to remain here, to make his home at Aiskeep.

Ciara spoke gently. "Have we made you feel you may not?"

"No, Grandmother. But in view of the way Kirion acted, I'd prefer to have everything clear before I send for my belongings. I don't wish you to feel I am taking Aiskeep for granted."

It was a good point, Trovagh considered. The Gods knew that Kirion had done so . . . until a snowball made it clear how wrong he was. The memory almost made him smile, but he must not. The boy would think it was aimed at him. He collected Ciara with a glance and they both stood. Trovagh spoke as Keelan waited.

"It is our decision that you may remain for so long as you wish to live at Aiskeep. It would please us that you learn of the land and the people. We shall make you an allowance for necessities." He broke into a grin as Keelan stared. "What, boy, did you think to be tossed out? Are we both so frightening?"

"N-n-no. But an allowance, and—" He broke off hastily. That bit about learning of the land and people. It was a portion of the formal acceptance of Keep Heir. Not all of it, just a part. Perhaps a hint that if he shaped well, the inheritance might be confirmed. He'd say nothing of that, though. They knew what they'd said. He knew. He'd prove himself before he expected them to say more.

Ciara was talking gently, "Of course you must have an allowance. We can't have you at Aiskeep with holes in your breeches. Don't expect a fortune, Keelan. Aiskeep does well enough, but we aren't Clan Iren."

She named an amount that made the boy stare. "What is it?"

"Do you *mean* that much?"

Trovagh looked interested. "That's each year, Keelan. Not each moon. Doesn't Aisha give you your coin?"

"No, well, not really. If I nag long enough, I may get a little. But she says I don't need it. Iren gives me bed and board, I can use a horse from their stables, drink wine at their table. What do I need money for?"

"Well, you have it now. Come to my study after you've eaten and I'll let you have the first quarter-year. Now eat; here at Aiskeep we don't like to see our family starve."

He drank off his wine and offered an arm to Ciara. Once they were private, Trovagh exploded. "That selfish, mean, cheating . . ."

"Lying, miserable excuse for a mother!" Ciara finished for him. "All this time she's been begging for more and more money from us." Her voice slid into a beggar's whine. "Mother Ciara, I need more coin for clothes for my sons. They grow so quickly. Mother Ciara, I need more money for my sons, they must be able to pay their way in the city. Faugh! And all the time she's given that poor child nothing."

She turned on Trovagh, but he forestalled her. "Yes, I know he could be lying. But I believe him. Haven't you seen the clothes he has, love? And the weapons. His sword looks as if it was forgotten at the back of an armory. His bow was useless. That's why Hanion and Harran chose to give him a new one. I'd say much of the money for Kirion has gone to him. But the allowance for Keelan, Aisha has been using for herself." Trovagh looked at his wife. "Let us talk to Keelan. I suspect the boy has very little to bring back. We'll send Harran with him and a letter. If we work the timing right, Keelan will be out of there before Aisha knows what's happened to her."

It was done. Keelan had a peaceful happy ride over the long days to Kars. There he left Harran while Keelan rode on to Iren Keep. He found his mother as usual, too busy talking to Kirion to listen much to her second son. It was as if they'd barely noticed he'd been gone nearly a year. He bit back a nasty smirk. That would change soon.

Keelan went through his room with care. Really, there was little he wanted. Most of his clothes were fit only to toss to a beggar. He had a few odds and ends.

He gathered those into the saddlebags he'd been given. They didn't even fill one. He shrugged. What did it matter. He was going back to Shosho, to Aiskeep and his family. He left the rest of his threadbare belongings and returned to the stables. They'd ridden into Kars on fine mounts from the Aiskeep Torgian strain. He'd left his mount in the inn stables along with Harran's horse and hired a cheap, clumsy beast to ride the last distance to Iren.

He'd given orders with a new assurance on arrival there. The beast was to be well-cared for and readied for departure again in a couple of hours. Keelan sat on his bed looking down at the lean saddlebags. It wasn't much for eighteen name days. What did he have in Iren Keep anyhow? A brother he disliked, feared, and distrusted. And a mother—Keelan felt sudden tears sting his eyes. A mother who stole from him. Oh, his grandparents had been quick to cover up. But you didn't live in a Keep like Iren most of your life without being able to read faces, hands, and half sentences. He'd seen the fingers tighten, seen the glance at each other. The query: hadn't his mother given him *his* coin? He'd understood in a flare of rage and bitterness.

During all these years, she'd constantly complained that Aiskeep gave her almost nothing. He'd discounted some of that. She had the latest clothes, the trips to Kars. He'd just assumed that Aiskeep made only her an allowance. That anything she gave her sons came from her purse. It had all been a lie. Trovagh had handed Keelan a purse, a mixture of copper, silver, and gold coinage. Then Ciara had called him to speak outside the door a moment.

With Trovagh gone, Keelan had seized the opportunity.

He'd seen the money given him placed down in a big ledger. Now he turned back a page or two. It had been there: steady columns of figures going down the page in three lines. One headed Aisha, another Kirion, the third Keelan. His new allowance was larger, but not by a huge amount. No wonder his mother could afford to dress so finely. He wondered if Kirion knew that the coin he wheedled from Aisha was Kirion's by right. He'd stepped back behind the desk again.

It had taken only seconds, but he knew at last how his mother valued him. It cut the last tie he might have had with Iren, Keep or Clan.

Keelan looked down at the saddlebags. Then he stood with a new resolution. He tossed the bags over one arm, walking to the door to call the nearest servant.

"Come in." He pointed to the scatter of clothing, and other minor gear laying about the room. "See all this, it's yours. Do what you want with it. Sell it, give it away, toss it on the midden. I won't be back." He listened a moment to the stammered thanks. "Never mind. But I'd get it out of here before someone else thinks they've a stronger claim."

Keelan grinned at the scramble that produced. He strolled down the old stone stairs toward the stables. The horse had been cared for, he checked, then tossed the stable boy a coin—to that lad's considerable surprise—then mounted and rode quietly down the road toward Kars. He'd be there by nightfall.

He slept dreamlessly in the big comfortable bed at the inn. Harran woke him early,

"Ready, lad?"

"Yes." They shared breakfast from the tray the inn sent up, then packed. An hour after dawn, they were on the homeward journey. Keelan found he was singing softly. Home! It was a wonderful word. He remembered the letter his mother would be reading in a few hours. He sang louder. It really *was* a beautiful day!

Aisha read the letter close to sunhigh. As she often did, she'd slept in, then fussed over her meal, her dress, and her plans for the afternoon. Only then was her maid permitted to bring in the letter and sealed purse. She'd assumed it to be the usual allowances, and a note of polite nothings from Elanor. She opened the purse and counted. It was short by a considerable amount. Aisha fumed. Then she opened the letter. With difficulty she perused the lines of neat script. Her reading ability had never been good. It was good enough in this case for her to understand what Ciara wrote—and rather more besides.

Ciara had kept it polite, merely conveying that since Keelan was removing to live at Aiskeep his allowance would be given to him direct. That was all it said. Aisha understood the rest, though. Aiskeep knew that Keelan had been cheated for years. That his mother had given him nothing of what was sent. And moreover, Keelan would know this, too, by now.

She pouted angrily. It was for her to decide how much a son should have. Keelan was still a child. She continued to read and gulped. Ciara had added that in the future the allowances would be sent separately, that Kirion should have his given direct also.

That was serious. If Kirion understood that she'd cheated him for years, he might take revenge. She was just a little afraid of what her son was becoming.

Then it occurred to her. Keelan had appeared briefly the previous day. She'd hadn't seen him since. Ciara's letter said he was living at Aiskeep now? Aisha hurried to investigate. The boy's room was empty of all he'd had. At the stables they told her he'd gone the night before. Further inquiry discovered the inn. Aisha bit a finger. So—Harran had been there. It really did look as if Aiskeep had taken Keelan in, perhaps as heir.

This news would serve very well to divert Kirion. She could mention that the separate—and increased—allowance for him had been at her suggestion. He'd take the coin, but it would also help convince him that Aiskeep was trying to buy him off.

Kirion was away on one of his mysterious errands. She waited until his return, telling him the news of his allowance first. As she'd expected, he was delighted—until she added, quite casually, that Keelan was gone.

"Gone where? You mean he's staying with some friend?"

"Not exactly. The servants say he's cleared all his possessions. In Kars they say he arrived with Harran from Aiskeep. Left with the man the next morning very early." She made her face innocent. "Keelan said something about living at Aiskeep now; you don't think he's entangled with anyone, do you?" She invested the last query with a salaciousness that was startling.

Kirion exploded in fury. "Entangled? I'd wager he's entangled! They'll have decided to make him Keep Heir instead of me." He proceeded to damn every last one of his kin at Aiskeep, with particular virulent attention to his younger brother. "This so-called increase in allowance is to buy me off. We'll see about it. Thank the Gods I have friends."

He flung from Aisha's room in a way that secretly amused her. Kirion would find he had no friends if he started bullying them as he had always bullied Keelan. Perhaps that was why the younger boy had gone?

Kirion stamped his way out to the stables. He had a horse saddled, then rode for the city. He received no satisfaction from his cronies. They could only recite Karsten laws that allowed what his grandparents might have done. Kirion returned in a worse temper than he'd been in when he left. He retired to the tower rooms where he preferred to live. They provided space, privacy, and enough distance from other occupied parts of the Keep to muffle the sounds that sometimes came from Kirion's room late at night. He was making progress in his studies. That at least was satisfactory.

He sat down wearily in a chair. If he could just master the art of influencing people. Not too obviously, but just enough to make them more receptive to what he was asking.

With his anger as a goad he worked for several nights. Then he went back to Kars. He was gone a day and a night before he returned, a sweetly vicious smile playing around his thin lips. Now he could begin his moves. In a year or two at most he should have Shandro on the throne of Kars.

After that he'd plan his campaign against Aiskeep. First he must stir hatred against the Witches once more. In later years it had somewhat died down. It must be kindled to flame again. That would be easy with Shandro; he'd grown up with tales of the mountains' Turning. Half of his clan had died with Pagar. Yes, Kirion would begin with Shandro.

Half done is well begun, Kirion reminded himself six months later. Shandro had been easy to rouse to wrath. All Kirion had done was take every opportunity of mentioning how far down Shandro's clan had fallen.

Of course he'd used the spell whenever he did so. He had that mastered. If only he could have risked the darker, more dangerous one that matched it. That he was not prepared to do. It would be the difference between persuasion and an order obeyed at once. But there were drawbacks. Kirion never underestimated danger to himself. The darker spell could lash back if it failed. It could recoil on the user to his doom. Kirion intended to rule Kars through Shandro, not to lie dead in some ornate tomb.

He used his spell persuading as and when he could. Gradually over the next year Shandro rose in power. His attitude and those of his shadow court hardened against the Estcarp Witches and those of the Old Race who might remain in Karsten. Two years after Keelan had deserted Iren, Shandro became duke of Kars. It was a title of little value as wealth went. The generations of unrest or outright war had impoverished both the city and the provinces about it. All Karsten was poor.

Using his spells Kirion persuaded traders to come more often to Kars. He cajoled better prices for Karsten goods. In Alizon there arose a fad for the felt wall hangings Ciara had made popular many years earlier in the South. A trickle of wealth began to flow into Karsten. It was not a great deal in itself, but it sparked a renewed hope, a rebuilding on the part of those who lived there. In another year the trickle of wealth had deepened and widened. Some of the clans and Keeps were growing rich again. Kirion made sure that the throne took its full share.

At Aiskeep Ciara was torn. She knew from Geavon that Kirion was behind the Kars throne. She heard of the growing hatred against those with the Old Blood. Geavon would have warned her if she had not seen what might come. He was too old to ride any longer, but his mind was as keen as ever, and his fingers as nimble. He wrote more often to Aiskeep to make up for the visits he could no longer manage. His letter this time brought fear.

Trovagh was with Ciara in their own room reading the latest pages. "He says Shandro is considering a new law," she reported.

Trovagh looked up from where he added wood to the fire. "A law on witchcraft?"

"Yes. Not the Horning again, but the result is likely to be the same. They offer half the goods of any found to be of the Old Race and practicing witchcraft, to those who denounce them."

Trovagh was startled. "But that's wicked. They'll have half of the land denouncing the other. A good number of people have that blood. Any can add an accusation of spell-casting. How will they judge?"

Ciara's voice was dry. "Probably by how much those denounced can contribute to the duke's coffers. I smell Kirion's hand in all this. He knows who and what I am."

Trovagh grinned suddenly, "I don't think he'll even look at Aiskeep, dear heart. He's your grandson. If he allows you to be denounced, he names himself. From what Geavon writes Kars is rapidly becoming hysterical on the subject. I wonder just how safe even Kirion may be."

Kirion, too, was wondering of recent weeks. It seemed that one could start a fire that was far harder to put out again. He sat glumly in his room at the palace worrying. It had seemed such a good idea when he began it. Now it looked possible even he could come under suspicion. He hadn't bargained for that. He'd better work out a way to decrease the hysteria. He worked hard most of that winter. He succeeded eventually in convincing Shandro that the idea was not to wipe out all those with any ability.

No, far better to get them under the duke's hand. Use them to aid Kars. It took time but at last he was able to persuade the duke into revoking the law. Kirion took over the lists as yet unused. There were sure to be a scattering of those who were genuinely of the Old Race. He scanned the lines of names. He'd find those, then wring from them any indication of their abilities. Their families would stand hostage.

Here and there he did find a man or woman of the Old Blood. None of the pure line but occasionally one of part-blood who had chosen to remain.

It did Kirion little good. The less of the blood, the less chance that they'd be of use. Most of those he found practiced healcraft in some way. That was not what he wanted. Where they had money he saw to it they vanished. His pockets were filling, as was Kars's treasury. But it gained Kirion no power. He knew an old poisoner in the lower city who could do more than any of these pathetic remnants of the Old Race. He decided to move more openly against Aiskeep in ways they would find it harder to counter. He chose a man of Shandro's clan to make the offer. A very carefully chosen man.

The messengers arrived the day after Aisling's sixteenth name day. Trovagh watched as Ciara read the beautifully penned letter. Her eyes blazed in disgust as she turned to him.

"Ruart! I'd rather give her to a pig. You'll tell him no, of course?" Trovagh hesitated and his wife stared at him.

"Tro? You aren't going to agree, you can't!"

"Don't be a fool. No, I wouldn't dream of agreeing, but look at the consequences. We can't say the girl is too young. She's sixteen. Kirion knows that even if Ruart doesn't. So what *do* we say. A flat refusal is likely to bring half of Ruart's clan about our ears at the insult."

"Say she's sick, loose of morals, mad, or promised elsewhere. Anything, Tro. But she doesn't go to that man. He's the one Geavon told us about two years ago when all that witchcraft fuss was stirring in Kars. I will *not* have Aisling wed a man of that sort even if the girl would agree. And as yet she's shown no sign of looking at any man with much interest."

"I agree, but we must move carefully," Trovagh said quietly. "One thing, too. It's to my mind that we should bring Keelan into this discussion. We made him Keep Heir over a year gone. Aisling is his sister, and he has a right to know what is asked and by whom."

"This offer was probably instigated by his brother anyway. Yes, Tro. Call him."

Keelan came, read the letter in silence, then stared at the fire. It was a fair offer if you disregarded the character of he who made it. Aisling was offered honorable marriage into a powerful clan. They'd accept her with only a small dowry, and they offered several sweeteners for the contract. And if she gave Ruart a son, she was then free to depart should she choose to do so. With her would go a large sum of money as largesse for the clan heir. That last was supposed to help convince Keelan.

Persuade your sister, pressure her if need be. And we'll make you rich in a couple of years. It was well worded, of course. It could equally read that they'd let Aisling free if she wished once she'd given the clan an heir. The coin was to support the heir's mother in her old home once she returned there. That was what Ruart would claim was intended if he was challenged.

Ruart. A crony of Kirion's but almost ten years older, he must be around thirty-five by now. Keelan had seen more of the man than he'd wished in Iren Keep. Not a nice type.

Then, too, there was that business Geavon had mentioned. Keelan remembered thinking at the time that no matter how it had been covered over, he'd wager it had been true. But if they simply refused the offer for Aisling a storm would be raised. Ruart would demand a good reason. What could they say—we'd rather cut Aisling's throat than throw her into your bed?

He grinned; he could imagine what Aisling would say if she saw Ruart, too. His head jerked up.

"I have an idea. I don't think it will put him off forever, but it can buy us time. Grandmother, would you be fit to ride to Kars?" His face became solemn. "After all, Aisling has been reared here in the provinces. She should know her prospective betrothed before any contracts are signed." His voice became meaningful. "Perhaps he should meet her as well."

The two faces opposite him crinkled into identical grins. "You mean Ruart may not like a wild, uncouth girl from the far South?" Trovagh asked.

"Either that or we can hold him off with tales of improving her. More—um—Kars city polish?" Keelan assured him grinning.

Ciara smiled at them both. "It may work, but we'd have to tread a fine line between disgusting him, and angering him to where he'll take her from spite to teach her once she's in his hands." She flattened her palm against the stone wall behind her. "If all else fails, we can stand siege. Aiskeep has outlasted many of those across the centuries."

"We stay with old Geavon, I presume?" Trovagh queried thoughtfully.

"We do; write him now, love. Get the message off as fast as you can. As for Ruart, we can delay a few days before his messengers will grow too impatient. We have to play for time. Every move must be drawn out as far as possible. With luck, Ruart will become bored and drop the idea. We may find a way to refuse without war. Just let us buy time."

They did so. It was high summer before they arrived in Gerith Keep to an enthusiastic welcome from Geavon. Once the first excitement was done he looked at Aisling. Hmm. Her looks certainly wouldn't put Ruart off the wedding. Aisling was slender, as lithe and supple as Ciara had been at that age. Like Ciara, the girl had eyes of a warm hazel. Her hair was a curtain of brown. An odd shade. There was fire under the darker hue. Her face was rounder than that of Ciara, but she had her grandmother's long, swinging stride. The walk of a girl who was fit and healthy.

Keelan hadn't enjoyed the journey. He was too worried about Shosho. She'd vanished just before they left. Old Hanion had promised to look for her, and care for her once she was found, but Keelan was still worried. She was four and had never bred. What if she had chosen now to do so? She might need him. A cat took only a couple of months to bear her kittens. He'd still be here in Gerith Keep until long after that. Damn Ruart, and damn Kirion, who was undoubtedly behind it all. When would the eager bridegroom appear so they could get on with the farce?

Ruart came a week later. Aisling was as rude as it was possible to be to a guest, and found her manners ignored. Ruart had expected no better. The girl was almost a peasant, after all, and she'd know no better. Her dress, too, was abysmal. That could be altered anytime he cared to buy the clothing. He was at his most pleasant, but Aisling could see the wolf snarl behind the charm. She was afraid of him. The idea of his touching her made her sick with disgust. She told that to Keelan the second time Ruart called.

"I loathe him, Keelan, please think of something."

Ruart visited again and again, each time more insistent on a contract. A betrothal would be so suitable. Kirion stood on the sidelines of all this and smirked. He knew the difficulties his grandparents faced. They'd come around, they couldn't hold off the ardent suitor forever, nor dare they refuse him outright.

He was wrong in that. Trovagh faced Ruart four weeks later, making Aiskeep's position clear. They would not force Aisling to a marriage she rejected.

Ruart snorted. A touch of the whip and the girl would consent. Holding desperately to his temper Trovagh pointed out that a girl killing herself rather than wed Ruart would not add to his reputation.

"There are ways to prevent that, My Lord of Aiskeep. I'd be happy to suggest a few."

"So I hear." Trovagh's tone was chilled over solid ice. "But we do not believe in dragging a girl to her wedding so drugged she cannot speak."

"That is your decision? Nothing will change it?"

"That is the word of Aiskeep. Unless Aisling changes her mind, My Lord Ruart, there will be no wedding between you."

Ruart nodded. Kirion had warned him this was possible. His friend had suggested that there were other ways to reach his desire. He'd use them.

Keelan was now bothered on two fronts. On the one hand, he worried over Shosho. Had she returned, was she all right?

On the other, there was Aisling. Ruart had taken that final rejection too calmly for Keelan's peace of mind.

He went to Geavon in the end. Keelan had slowly developed a hearty respect for that astute old man. Geavon was careful. Nothing too open in his hints, just enough to assure the boy that Kirion wasn't the only clever one about. Keelan left wearing a satisfied look.

That changed abruptly three days later. Keelan had gone in search of his sister. They could ride with Geavon's grandson who planned to circle some of the garths talking over the coming harvest. With him went several men at arms. Aisling would enjoy the ride and in safety. He was well aware that of late she had been fretting at her confinement within the Keep. And it would take Keelan's mind off Shosho.

To Keelan's surprise, his sister was nowhere to be found. He hunted, growing more agitated until at last he went to Geavon. There, too, he found his grandparents as he blurted out the news.

Geavon stared for a second absorbing the information. Then he rang his bell violently, shouting rapid orders at those who came. Questions were asked of all those in the Keep. Some had information, not all of it willingly given. In an hour they knew the truth.

Geavon faced his distant cousin, noting the grim set to Trovagh's mouth. "The girl is gone. A maid and one of the manservants are also gone. I believe them to have been hirelings paid to await their chance. It seems they bought a way in sometime back. Around the time Ruart first offered for the girl." He held a hand up to still the outcry. "I have other ways of finding the truth of this. I am not so sure that it was Ruart's doing. One thing is sure, however. Aisling has been taken."

13

Aisling had gone to her room to change. It had been one of those mornings, and now a maid had spilled a water can all down her skirt. It wasn't the girl's fault, but it just capped a long, boring morning so far as Aisling was concerned. She had the clothing over her head and was squirming out of it when she was seized. She tried to struggle, but muffled in folds of cloth she found it difficult. Then she was struck across her head. Blackness descended shot with red sparks.

The next she knew she was head down still bundled in cloth. It felt like a pony under her. She moved a hand surreptitiously. Yes, that was a pony, with Aisling cross-tied over its broad back. She felt sick, all swimmy. Blurred voices nearby slowly resolved into a conversation she could understand.

". . . easy enough. The old fool of a housekeeper will be in trouble when it comes out." That voice sounded vindictive.

"You're just mad because she made you really work. The coin'll be worth it."

"It'd have to be. If I slaved up them stairs with one can of hot water for them lady-mucks I carried a thousand. All that washing. Rots yer brain."

There was a coarse laugh, "No fear of that fer you. Reckon you'm as smart as a pin. Letting m'lady here walk right into you, then spilling all that water down 'er. Gave us'n a chance to get her aside at last. Damn me, but how that family do stay around one another." The other voice only grunted to that and there was a long silence.

Aisling put what she'd heard together. Someone had paid this pair to abduct her. It had to be Ruart. She shivered. But her family would guess, and they'd not rest until they had her back. She could imagine the hue and cry they'd be raising.

If she could have listened to the talk at Gerith Keep at the same moment she'd have been bewildered. No one was looking for her there. Instead, they were grouped in one room with Geavon, making rather labored small talk. Each was almost frantic but they were waiting. They trusted Geavon, and he trusted those he had in other places. Moving too swiftly could risk everything. So they sat, ate food they did not want, making conversation they hardly heard.

Aisling was feeling sicker by the minute. If she didn't get off this pony soon, she'd be throwing up. She felt the small beast turn, and the sounds of its hooves change. It halted. She was untied and tossed over someone's shoulder. Then she could feel herself carried up a short flight of stairs. Aisling was dumped on a floor. It would be Ruart's home, she thought. There was sheepskin under her hands, a fire somewhere near as she felt the heat.

Above her there was a chink of coin. Then the sound of a cork being pulled. An anticipatory mumble as wine gurgled into glasses. She could hear people drinking noisily. Probably the two who'd stolen her drinking to their success and payment. The next sounds puzzled her. A sort of choking, then a couple of muffled thumps followed by the sounds of coins again.

She was lifted to sit in a chair, the cords unwound. She steeled herself to be unsurprised by whatever she saw. It was Ruart as she'd feared. She nodded politely.

"My lord, an unconventional visit, I'm afraid."

He leered, an aroma of wine preceding him as he leaned close. "But I don't mind that, my sweet. I have a bedroom awaiting you." She saw he was very drunk and despaired. Her head still swam and her stomach rebelled.

"So kind, but I do not plan to use it, my Lord Ruart."

"But I do. Here's a token of it." He drew her to him, kissing her with a wet, eager mouth.

Aisling's stomach finally revolted. She jerked her head to one side and vomited violently. As Ruart released her, she did so again. The sight and smell were too much for Ruart. He joined her and they threw up in miserable unison. From the door an urbane voice addressed the room at large.

"*Not* an edifying sight. But don't worry, I'll take her off your hands, Ruart."

Ruart rose clumsily to his feet. "Changed my mind," he said briefly. "Had a room made up for her. She's staying here with me."

"Why?"

"Because I've changed my mind I told you. She's too good for the games you play, Kirion. I'm not wasting a girl like this on a lot of chanting and spell-casting. You can have her afterward."

Aisling had glanced about the room in intervals between her misery. Two bodies lay twisted to one side, wineglasses beside them on the floor. The two who'd stolen her, she presumed, paid off in a more permanent way than they'd expected.

It was Kirion in the doorway. His face bland but the beginnings of dangerous anger in his eyes. Ruart should be careful.

He might think himself safe in his own home, but not for long if he crossed Kirion.

She heard Ruart raise his voice. He'd moved over by the door to join her brother.

"*No*. That's my word on it. You can have her once I'm tired of the girl. D'you think I paid out for weeks just to watch you draw circles on a pavement? I want her first."

Aisling understood enough of that to turn her cold. Kirion was dabbling in real sorcery. It wasn't anything she'd disbelieve of him, but it made her feel like a mouse between two cats. Of course he wanted her untouched.

She felt sick again. She darted a glance about the room. No way out save past the two still arguing. She was badly cramped from the ropes and long journey. Her stomach rebelled whenever she moved, but she must try to find something to help her escape.

She was unable to reach out to the table near her without being noticed. But she knew from experience that people often dropped things down the backs of this new kind of seat. The wife to Geavon's grandson had a set of them. Astia had asked Aisling only a few days ago to help search down the upholstered back for a lost needle. She'd found it by running the point painfully into a finger. And before that they'd also discovered two walnuts and a gaming counter.

Her fingers twisted downward, being careful not to let them see her moving. Her hand scrabbled slowly along the edges of the upholstery. Ah, no, it was only a coin. Still it might be of use in some way, she thought. She moved her hand up to drop it into her boot top. Another coin and then a third.

Then her questing fingers touched something else. It was long, perhaps the length of her hand. Narrow, thin, pliable. At first she could not guess what it might be, then she managed a look down from the corner of her eye.

She knew now. Yes, that really might be of use. She might be able to sharpen it on stone if she was ever left alone. Doubled for strength it would be perhaps three or four inches in length. But hadn't Keelan once said you could stab to the heart in less?

You could do other things with something like that, too. Hanion had taught her years ago as a kind of amusement one very cold winter when she was bored. The argument was growing more angry. She caught enough of it as it also grew louder to guess what might be the outcome.

Kirion was furious. What? Were his plans to be thwarted by the tool of his, this womanizing idiot? He was unpleasantly surprised to find they were.

Ruart was equally furious. His demands for anything he wanted hadn't been refused since he'd risen to rule in his Keep. Now, and in his own home, mind you, this unpleasant little panderer was trying to keep the lord of his Keep from his desires.

He was angered enough to press the demand. He was afraid of Kirion—well, not actually afraid, he told himself, just wary. The man did have some kind of power. But nothing could happen to Ruart here. He had only to call and fifty servants would appear. He could have them do whatever he wished with Kirion then. He could even have him tossed into the special cell below. That thought sparked another.

His voice became quieter. "Listen, Kirion, are we to fall out over a female?" Soft talk never hurt, Ruart thought. "I can toss her in the cell downstairs. You know the one," he said, leering. "No escape there. Then we can talk this over in comfort. I'll throw dice against you for her if you like."

Kirion paused in midshout to consider. It was true his sister wouldn't be escaping from *that* cell.

"Very well. We could gamble for her, as you say, my dear Ruart." My dear Fathead, his mind added. Something in your wine and you can sleep away a day and night. I'll be long gone with her. You'll get over it the next time you need me to persuade someone around to your way of thinking. Aloud, he added,

"I'll come down with you. Two will manage her more easily in case she tries to escape." Or in case you try anything, either, he added silently.

Aisling was dragged down stairs, stairs, and yet more stairs. She allowed herself to go almost limp, letting her feet stumble convincingly. The men were half carrying her and panting at the exertion. But with her head bent she was able to scan the levels she passed.

Like some old Keeps, half of this one was underground. Three floors, she estimated. The lowest would be where siege supplies were stored. The wine racks would be here, and any dungeons. Here, too, would be at least one secret escape route.

She had time for a quick look through a window slit as they dragged her from the original room. It was early afternoon. She calculated swiftly. She'd been taken soon after her morning meal, which she'd had quite early. She didn't think she'd been unconscious long on the pony. Nor had Ruart and Kirion been fighting over her for much time—although it had seemed hours.

So Ruart's Keep couldn't be more than three or four hours' walk away from where she'd been taken. She knew the direction, too; on one of his visits, Ruart had gone on about his Keep. How convenient the location, just to the northeast of Kars. Gerith Keep was also northeast of Kars. If she managed to escape, she'd know which way to go.

Her family wouldn't have been twiddling their collective thumbs in that time, either. They probably had someone keeping an eye on the Keep outside right now. If she could get away, she was sure there'd be help waiting.

Ruart shook her hard. "Take a look at this, Lady." He pointed. "See, we drop this bar across the whole door when we leave." He hauled her onward, halting again, "See this? A good strong lock." He grinned in an extremely unpleasant way. "I lock all the doors down here or the servants get into the wine—and maybe other things I don't want broached." He leered suggestively.

Aisling felt sick again. Kirion snorted.

"When you've finished showing off, Ruart, let's get on with it."

His target grunted, pushing Aisling ahead of him through an open door. "You'll be safe here. Just wait until I come for you. Don't go running away now." He bellowed with laughter as he slammed the door. A key turned with a loud clunk. Aisling flung herself at the door to listen. She heard a second lock clank and then in the distance a dull thud as the bar went into place. Her eyes flicked about her prison. A heap of moldy straw, a bucket, and an empty tin jug and plate. Nothing she could use.

But in her clothing she had something that might aid her. Aisling still felt sick, and to that was added growing hunger and a tormenting thirst.

She dug hastily into her boot to produce the item she'd found. At some stage a woman had been in the room upstairs. She'd been reboning a bodice in the fashionable way. One of the pliable strips of metal 'boning' had been dropped onto the chair, to make its way down the back out of sight. Probably the owner had never missed it.

Aisling bent it into a right angle toward one end. Then, very slowly, very carefully, she began to pick the lock. The lock was old, hence it was clumsy with large, easily felt wards and only two of them. It had been kept well oiled as well. It had been a long time since Hanion had taught her this as a game. But in a short time she had the lock open.

She glanced back at her cell. Play for time, Ciara always said. If you aren't sure what to do, play for time.

Aisling went back. She humped up the straw into a curl, then covered it with the outer skirt. She stared down. What else? She wrenched at one sleeve until the stitching tore at the shoulder. Then she stuffed the sleeve with more straw. She laid that over a small ball of straw. From the door it looked like Aisling asleep, an arm thrown over her head in despair. It would suffice if no one looked long or too closely. She found her head was whirling. She must have something to drink. Hadn't Ruart boasted he kept his wine down here?

The locks on the other doors nearby were also of the older, more simple type. She shut the door of her cell, locked it with her pick, then started on another door. Behind that was the wine. She chose a bottle of a lighter wine and drank carefully. Being drunk certainly wouldn't help, she mused. She tucked two of the bottles in a corner and tried a third door. Thank Cup and Flame for that. The siege supplies, some of them anyway. She took a round of bread and a small cheese. Both went to join the bottles in a corner in the main part of the outer room. Then she locked both doors again.

She sat quietly for almost half an hour. With bread and cheese inside her, a quarter bottle of the wine on top wouldn't make her drunk. Somewhere there'd be water, probably the next level up. Now if she could just get that door open, too—

The lock on this was newer. More wards. More time. By the time it opened, she was sweat-soaked and shaking, knowing that any minute a triumphant gambler could reappear to collect his prize.

Still no one. She dodged through the door and turned to work on the lock again with growing hope. If only one man came to get her, she might be able to shut him in. She'd seen Ruart leave the key in each lock as they took her down. She could wait until whoever it was entered the cell. Then he'd be too far down for any to hear his yells for release.

She opened doors hurriedly. Water. It was in large barrels and stale, no doubt, but with a little wine it would do. She opened a barrel to check. Yes. Her hands were shaking. Keep them steady, she told herself. Within seconds she had poured out most of the remaining wine, filled the bottles with water, and recorked.

She had enough to drink for as long as it might be before they came for her now. The bread and cheese had put new energy into her, too. She studied the situation. She'd come back up two of the three levels. The problem would be this last level. That was the one with the door barred instead of locked. She wiggled her metal strip through the gap, lifting upward. The metal bent. It was strong enough for its original purpose, strong enough to turn a single ward at a time. But raising a heavy bar was beyond it.

Aisling said several words she'd once heard Grandfather Tro say. All of a sudden she found she was kicking frantically at the door. She must get out of here, she must! Fear that she would be heard stopped her attack on the wood. She slumped to the floor beside the planking. Where were all the heroes when you needed one? Did she have to do it *all* herself?

It seemed she did. She ate a little more of the bread and cheese as she thought.

It was clear why Ruart wanted her. She'd wondered about Kirion, but something he'd said had given her a hint. Some half-caught comment about her being of the Old Race.

Aisling knew the story. Centuries ago only the Old Race had lived in Karsten. Then incomers had arrived. People from elsewhere who joined them to live in the mostly empty lands. The two races had lived in peace a long time. Then in the time when Grandmother was a little girl the current duke had gone crazy. He'd called the three-times Horning on all of the Old Race. That was a form of outlawing. After that anything could happen to them and it was lawful. It had been a bad time.

Many had died, and most of the others had left Karsten to live over the border mountains in Estcarp where it was said all women were Witches. It was also said that one day there'd be a blood debt called in. That was why most of Karsten was still against the Old Blood. They were afraid.

And guilty, her grandmother had always added. Too many families had got a start up on the backs of those they'd murdered, with the goods and stock they'd stolen from them.

Ciara was half of the Old Race. Aisling had always known vaguely that she must be partly of the blood, too. Lately it had been difficult. It was as if something inside her stretched, awoke, and demanded from her things she didn't know how to give. Grandmother had taught her to use some of the power. Aisling could drop into the mists when she wished. Once she'd been allowed to help heal an injured horse. Grandmother said horses didn't talk at least, or fear you afterward. It had felt good to do that. To use what she was.

Kirion wanted to use her, too. She remembered his grasp on her the time she'd beaten him in a race. She'd used her power then. Called fire from the mist to his hand so he'd let her go.

The two events came together with a mental crash. She could help a healing, and call a kind of fire. Was there any way she could use her powers to get her out of here?

The simplest and most obvious use was to open the door. She'd seen the bar as they dragged her by.

She stood against the door, palms flat to the wood. The bar had been held on two brackets, one on either side of the door. There were two more on this side and a bar leaning against the wall. That would be to bar the door against invaders if you escaped down here. Good. She could use that to give her a position. She lifted the bar into place. Now, if she was right, the other bar would be here. Dropped into a bracket just—her finger touched lightly—there!

She drank a little more of the watered wine. Then she stood, hands touching the door just where the bar should be in the bracket. She imagined it, and made a picture of it in her head. She gathered herself, then allowed the silver mist to rise in her mind. Now! She strained; the bar had to rise up, then fall so she could be free. That desire grew. The bar had to let her go. Up. *Up. Up!*

She could not have said later how long that struggle went on. It seemed forever, timeless. But at last there was a feeling as if the bar yielded to her demand. In her mind it rose, just far enough to clear the metal that held it. She thrust outward using the dregs of her strength. Beyond the door there was a dull thump as the bar fell. Aisling fell, too. She slid down the wooden planking until she rested sitting against the door. It swung partway open before the movement halted. She could see out. She sagged back.

So that had been what Grandmother meant when she warned using power demanded a price. Aisling managed a tired grin. It would be ironic if she was now too exhausted to leave. She reached for the wine bottle, draining it. She still had a bottle left.

It would be wise to look for a place to hide. Still sitting, she studied the area outside the door. There was a short stairway leading down to here, a good-size landing in front of this door. A pity she didn't have sufficient strength to bar the door from the inside again. That would baffle everyone. No use in wishing, though.

Aisling forced herself to her feet, then dropped the outer bar back into its brackets. After that she collected her bottle and food into a fold of her petticoat. She must look quite mad, she thought. In her petticoats, with a sleeve torn from her bodice, probably reeking to the skies, and straw sticking out of odd bits of her clothing.

She looked down at her boots. They'd make a noise on the stairs. Better get them off, she told herself. She could carry her food and wine inside them. Removing them reminded her of the coins she'd found. She tipped them into her hand and blinked. Two gold and a silver. *Very* nice.

But she hadn't time to think of that. With her footwear tucked under one arm, Aisling scooted silently up the stairs. No one appeared to announce her escape. She stared out of the window slit as she passed by. It was almost dusk. If she could get out of here into the countryside there was a chance she could elude any possible pursuers.

She checked a couple of the rooms at this level. There were ample places to hide from anyone just walking about. She prowled cautiously to where she thought the front entrance had been. Two servants were there energetically polishing. From the look of it, they'd be there some time. She picked a place to watch them, then tried to relax.

Somewhere upstairs Ruart and Kirion must still be gambling. If the servants finished before the gamblers did, Aisling might be able to slide out of the door to freedom. She crouched waiting, wondering what was happening at Gerith Keep. Old Geavon would have been furious when he found out. He'd take it as a personal insult. He'd never liked Ruart, with this business he'd be almost ready to call feud.

Aisling hoped she'd be able to tell Geavon it had been mostly Kirion from what she knew. It would be satisfying to know she'd brought trouble to her older brother. At least as much trouble as he'd brought to her if luck continued to hold.

It was holding better than she knew. Upstairs both men no longer gambled. Instead, they lay sprawled on the floor, faces each wearing an identical look of frustrated fury. Between them a small table had been upended, dice and glasses spilling onto the sheepskins. The fire was almost burned out. Ruart had given instructions that no servant was to interrupt him as they gambled. None would dare go against that order. Kirion had agreed. It suited him to be private. He hid a sly smirk. Ruart was being far more helpful than he realized.

Unseen by his comrade Kirion had slid open a tiny compartment on his wrist ornament. It opened with a twist of his thumbnail to allow a pinch of grayish powder to drift down. He turned, proffering a glass as he drank from his own.

The powder would take a short time to work. Ruart would only think the wine unusually effective at first. By the time he knew otherwise, he'd be helpless. Not that Kirion intended him any harm; he'd just collect Aisling and head back to Iren Keep.

In the solitude of his tower he could wring her power from her. Use it to buy more of his own. He'd found a way to do that without risking anything himself. Aisling would lose a lot, including her life and soul—if there really was such a thing.

He grinned as he rolled the dice again, accepting more wine from Ruart. Was the man beginning to look dizzy? He thought so.

Ruart had eyed Kirion thoughtfully. That powder he'd dropped in his third cup of wine would take a while to work. It cost, too. The old woman by the Kars gate charged high.

He hid a leer. But you got what you paid for. The stuff would work quite swiftly. Another minute or two and the girl would be his. By the time Kirion revived it would be too late.

This wine was strong. He drank off the remainder of his glass, finding himself staggering as he walked to open another bottle.

It shouldn't be that strong, though. He'd ordered the lighter wine. Better not to be too drunk, he thought. He focused on the bottle. Strange, it *was* the lighter wine he was drinking—why then did he feel so dizzy, so weak?

He understood just as his knees gave way. His face creased into helpless rage as blackness enveloped him.

Kirion watched Ruart slump to the floor. He rose to stand over him watching the glaring eyes slide closed. That was that. Now he'd just have one last glass like a lord should. No need to hurry now. He had all the time in the world; it would be tomorrow evening before Ruart awoke. By then Kirion would be back in his tower, his sorceries completed.

He drank his wine. Strange, that may have been one too many. He felt dizzy, weak at the knees. He leaned on the table as it gave way, dropping glasses, dice, and Kirion to the floor beside it. Kirion's face wrenched into a snarl of frustrated fury. Damn false comrades. The bloody man had *drugged* him! His mind slipped into night still yelling its surprised indignation.

Aisling crouched by her door. Through the door curtain she could see the servants had almost finished their polishing. She'd spent part of her time checking for anything that might help her here. She'd found an old cloak dropped in a corner. That would help to hide her unconventional attire. The cloak was dusty and mouse-smelling, but anything was better than trying to march through the door in her petticoat. That betrayed too much to anyone who saw her. The cloak betrayed less—unless they got close enough to smell it.

Kirion and Ruart must be gambling-mad up there, she mused. It had taken her hours to get this far and still no sign of either.

She had finished her drink. If she didn't get out of here shortly, she was going to be in the very unladylike position of having to use a corner. It would be just her luck to have someone walk in at that moment.

The servants were actually leaving. Aisling gathered herself by the door curtain. One was gone, then the other. She dived for the door just as the first returned.

It was a woman. Not young, not old, but her face was lined, bitter and weary. Aisling held a finger to her lips imploringly.

The woman's eyes summed the girl up. Another of his lordship's playthings. Not a willing one, either. Somehow she'd escaped. The servant nodded to herself. She'd call for help to stop the girl; his lordship had given one of the men a whole silver piece for that last time. She opened her mouth to yell, then paused as the girl moved.

Aisling dug frantically into her boot. Where had she put the coins she'd found? They slid into her hand and she held out the two gold ones. Gold! The servant gaped. That was more than Ruart would give her. Aisling smiled and held out her hand offering both gold pieces. The servant edged close enough to snatch them from her.

She could still call for help but she had grudges of her own against Ruart. More silver was a temptation, though. Aisling guessed her thought. There was one coin remaining; she tossed it to the cupped hands.

"Call, and share them, or have to give most of it back to Ruart. Keep silent, keep it all."

Before the servant could make up her mind the girl was gone. Oh, well. Gold was gold. One piece was a year's wages. Two would buy her a different life. Even the silver was a month of hard labor.

Ruart would never know she'd seen anything. She would leave at the end of the year when she was paid her wages. With those and what the lass had given her, she had a way of making something better of herself. Good luck to the girl, whoever she was. She tucked the gold into her bodice carefully, returning to her work.

Outside it was dark. Aisling looked up at the stars, southwest would be Geavon's Keep. She found a bush and used it urgently. Then she began to walk in her chosen direction. She could be home before dawn if all went well.

14

Behind Aisling a spy padded silently along. He had no idea how the girl had freed herself. It had taken him hours to gain access to the keys, and now he, too, had to be gone quickly. Just as Lord Geavon had sniffed out spies in Gerith Keep, so, too, would Lord Ruart once he woke.

The spy grinned to himself. That had been a great sight. Both of them fast asleep and the girl gone. He wondered where she'd got the money for that last part of her escape. But wherever it had come from she'd handled it just right.

He'd follow her. It was a pity she hadn't got free earlier, before he'd gained the keys. Then he could have stayed in Ruart's Keep, watching for the old lord. Geavon was a good master. A fair man, and he paid promptly—in coin. Not the way Ruart had paid off his own pair of spies.

He slid through the darkness listening to Aisling as she stumbled through the brush. At least she had some idea of direction. Another half hour and she'd arrive at the road.

The thought occurred to him then that the road might be dangerous. Not from Kirion and Ruart, but there were others as bad out in the dark of night. He stepped up his pace. With luck he'd find someone before she arrived on the road. His pockets had coin enough to buy a mount if he must.

He was fortunate. A drunken garthsman heading home gleefully sold the spy the farm pony. It was fat, shaggy, and lazy; he'd paid half as much again as it was worth, but it would do. He left the farmer to walk while the spy swung into the old saddle.

He walked the beast a short distance, then halted it to strain his ears. There! The sound of someone pushing through the head-high brush near the road. He called out, keeping his voice low and gentle,

"Is someone there, do you need help?"

Aisling hesitated. It wasn't anyone she knew, but at least it wasn't Kirion or Ruart, either. If she crouched it would be hard for them to place where the voice came from. She called back softly.

"Who are you?"

Good girl, the spy thought. He answered softly, "One who's been sent to look for you, I think, Lady. Make no attempt to see my face, it could be dangerous for me. I have a pony that will carry two." He waited. There was no sound. She was still waiting for more. He nodded. Geavon's kinblood, all right. He lifted his tones to an approximation of the old lord's voice.

"I say I don't trust him. Boy's a rogue however you look at it." He heard the light patter of footsteps in his direction.

Aisling arrived panting. It was almost an hour since she'd escaped, and she was tiring again. Even the delights of freedom were not able to keep her going much longer. She could see nothing of the man in the dark, but it didn't matter. That mimicking of Geavon was only likely to be done by one of his men.

She held up her hands, sagging exhausted by the pony. The spy aided her up behind him. In a mile she was asleep. He kept the pony to a steady walk drawing Aisling's arms about him to keep her in place. It felt good to know she was safe.

He'd watched Ruart for years now. One of those who'd vanished in the witch-hunts then had been his betrothed. Later he'd heard a rumor. He'd known it for truth in the end, after that he'd followed a trail. It had never mattered to him what blood she bore. He'd loved her.

Things like that spread. There were those who died, those who'd spurred on the killing, those who used it for their own ends—and those who mourned their dead and swore revenge. He'd heard Geavon was keeping an eye on Lord Ruart. The spy had gone offering all he knew. He'd been taken in, treated honestly. He'd talk to the old lord once he'd got the girl back. It would be a pity to lose his chance at Ruart and his companion now.

He walked the pony in through the small postern gate. He had the right words for it to be opened to him. He had others once he was inside. Geavon arrived to look at the still sleeping Aisling.

"I owe you blood debt for this."

"Nay, Lord. It's Ruart who owes the blood. This is just some of the payment."

Geavon whistled to one of his men softly. "Call Lord Trovagh and his lady. Tell them the news is good." He handed over Aisling to Trovagh when they appeared. She murmured sleepily but did not wake.

"Take her to bed, Tro. Stay with her. I have things to do here as yet. I'll join you once I'm done." He turned to his spy once they were gone with Aisling. "Tell me, what occurred? Was Kirion there?"

The tall, scarred man he questioned nodded. "He was there, Lord. But it was to Ruart's Keep they took her." He told the tale as he knew it from the beginning. "Likely I can't go back. I've racked my brains and can think of no tale they'd swallow. A pity."

"A pity as you say. But with what you've discovered over the time I can get another into Ruart's confidence. I'd rather have her back safe than bring down that pair if I must choose. As for you, a gift from her kin." He thrust a fat purse into the man's hand. "I still have work for you though. Just of a different kind." The spy found he was holding a roll of parchment.

"What's this, Lord?"

"Your own land, the purse will stock it." He smothered protest. "No! It's a wage. You'll understand when you see where the holding lies. I'll risk you no further with Ruart, but there'll be others you can shelter. Go now and my thanks go with you. Send word once your garth is established."

He heard the hooves plod away and sighed. A very good man. He could still use him as he'd said. He looked up at the stars. Thank the Gods for good men when so many bad ones were nearby.

He walked slowly back inside. It was late and he was an old man. Too old for many more nights like this. He halted at the room where Aisling lay. She still slept. Ah, well. The tale would be the same in the morning. He retired to sleep himself after leaving orders with those he trusted. It was always better to be careful than regretful.

Aisling woke in her own bed early. She looked around as events rushed back into her mind. Her grandmother slept on a bed beside her. Ciara's face was tired, she looked older than Aisling had ever seen her appear before.

On the table between them rested a jug of fruit juice, a platter of bread and cheese. Aisling ate, drank, and lay back once more. She fell asleep almost before she had pulled the covers up.

This time she woke soon after sunhigh. Beside her Ciara stirred, turning to smile at her granddaughter.

"Bright sun to you, dearling. Are you hungry again?"

Aisling was suddenly aware that she was starving. "Yes. Where's Grandfather Tro?"

"Sleeping. He'll come now that you're awake. Just let me call for something to eat for us all."

She did so. Trovagh and Geavon arrived with the meal, Keelan strode in a few minutes later to hug his sister savagely.

"Praise Cup and Flame you are unhurt. Something that will not be said for very long about that pair who took you."

Aisling eyed him over a succulent honey-coated bun. "If you're thinking of the two servants, you can forget them. Ruart poisoned them. I'm not sure why. It might have been so he didn't have to pay. I know he took the money back when they were dead."

Geavon grunted. "More likely to make sure they couldn't give evidence against him. Shandro is duke. Kirion may have a lot of influence there, but the duke would have to listen if we made a formal complaint through the shrine at Kars." His mouth stretched into an unpleasant smile. "His own clan don't much like Ruart. If we took a complaint to Kars courts about this, the clan wouldn't support him."

Ciara shook her head. "We can't afford to risk that and well you know it. Opening a bag usually lets all the cats out that are inside, not just the one. Shandro fears the Old Race about as much as he likes Ruart. Tro and I have talked this over. We shall leave for Aiskeep tomorrow. As soon as we found Aisling gone, I sent a swift rider relay to the Keep. Half our men ride hither, Harran leading them." She touched Geavon's arm gently. "No reflection on you, kinsman. If you can provide a few of your men to escort us until we meet those who ride to our aid, I would be grateful."

Geavon agreed without protest. "But leave it to me to deal with Ruart should he return to speak of a betrothal again."

Trovagh smiled wryly. "I do not think he will be so bold. But yes, to you the handling of him if he dares."

The following day they rode out without fuss at first light.

Geavon's men, headed by his grandson, escorted them, acting as if they expected bandit hordes to descend ravening at any moment. Harran met them halfway to Aiskeep. Aisling was delighted to see him. She listened to all the small news of home before Keelan interrupted urgently.

"Did Shosho return, Harran?"

The Armsmaster grinned. "She did indeed, Lord Keelan. Where she had been I know not. What she had done there I *can* tell you. She's heavy in kitten. She seems well enough but she is missing you, I believe."

Keelan gulped, looking hopefully across at his grandmother. It would be Shosho's first litter, and his cat was already four. He knew it could be dangerous for a cat to bear kittens for the first time when she was older. Ciara nodded to him.

"I'll look her over at once when we're back at Aiskeep. Don't worry. Most cats kitten easily. They know what to do, they've been doing it without humans for a very long time."

Privately she wondered. No use telling the boy all that could go wrong, though. They'd be home soon enough. She stretched, she was so tired. Her own bed at Aiskeep with Tro beside her would look wonderful. For now they'd have to make do with the tent.

Being home was one of the best things in the world, Ciara thought a week later. Of course there were problems. Shosho would kitten any day now and Ciara didn't like the look of things there. Then there was Aisling. Using her gift so frantically to open that door seemed to have started something.

Twice Aisling had given someone a shock. Keelan had been the first, the day after they got back. The girl had been tearing from place to place and finally Keelan had seized her hands and whirled her around.

"Slow down, you're making me giddy." Then he'd released her with a surprised yelp. "Ouch! What was that for?"

Ciara had been close enough to see silver fire glimmer briefly about their clasped hands. Aisling had been upset and apologetic. It had just happened, she insisted. She hadn't willed it, hadn't even been thinking of it. Two days later it had happened again when Trovagh hugged her good night.

Ciara had wondered if it was some kind of overflow effect. Use it or it uses itself. She had taken her granddaughter out quietly the next morning at dawn. There she'd thrown most of the work of healing a sick lamb onto Aisling. It appeared to have worked.

For a few days. But today Ciara had hugged her good morning and felt the sudden flare. There seemed to be a circle. Use the power to damp it down. But the more it's used the faster it builds. The more you damp it down with use, the faster it returns and at higher levels.

Ciara had an unpleasant feeling that it could end in Aisling burning up. There must be controls, but she'd never learned them. Those in Karsten who might have known and been able to teach were gone, either by death or departure.

Ciara sighed. Life! Just whenever you thought things were going better, something came along to prove you wrong. From the sound of pounding footsteps racing down the passage toward her room, that was about to be verified. Keelan arrived through the door opening already yelling.

"Come quick, come quick, Shosho's started."

The small cat had. What was worse, Ciara thought an hour later, they did have a real problem. From careful investigation she could find only one kitten present. It was huge. Keelan was getting under her feet, Aisling had vanished. And right now Ciara wanted one and not the other.

"Keelan, listen to me. I need Aisling. Go and find her as fast as you can."

That got him out of the way. Ciara soothed Shosho. "Steady, my sweet. I don't know what you found out in the hills but you should have thought twice. I know what needs to be done, but I need Aisling's power to do it. Pray Cup and Flame she hasn't used up her gift on something already."

Keelan arrived back with Aisling in tow. "I found her. What now?"

Ciara had had enough. "Now, my lad, you go out to the stables. I want a comfortable nesting box for Shosho and her baby when it arrives. Make a step half height at the door. That way she can go out but the kitten will stay in for a few weeks. Pad it inside with carded wool. Eshwin's garth may spare you some. When you get that done I want a fire in the smaller hall and water heated there. Now get on with it."

"Yes, yes. I'll get it done at once." He was bustling out of the door leaving Ciara and Aisling in peace.

Aisling grinned. "How much of that is necessary?"

"Well, the nesting box will be useful. But Elanor probably has carded wool. He doesn't have to go half an hour's ride to find that."

"What about hot water, we don't need that, do we?"

Ciara snorted inelegantly. "Oh, yes we do. Once we're finished here we'll all enjoy a rest and a hot drink." Aisling giggled. "Now, I want you to relax, slide into the mists, and let me use your power. You can watch what I do. But try not to tighten up or stop the outflow. I know what needs doing, but I just don't have enough of my own gift. If Shosho dies, Keelan will be devastated. Are you willing to do this?"

"Of course."

"Then begin." She watched Aisling's breathing slow. She reached out to take the young hand, placing it on her shoulder, positioning the girl just behind her. "Keep your hand there until I say you can remove it."

She called her own mists, dropping into them with the ease of long familiarity. She turned her concentration to the cat. The kitten lay in the right position, it was just too large to be birthed normally.

What she was about to do was unorthodox. But it was all

she could think of. She drew on Aisling's power, mind sinking deeper into the small cat's tissues. She gathered the process up, she must do this and this. Then she drew hard on her granddaughter's gift.

The silver mist came to her calling, and poured into the cat. Under that demand, that impact of power, tissues became elastic, almost fluid. They stretched far beyond normal. She held them, then nudged the contractions.

Shosho strained. Slowly her kitten appeared; it gasped, squirmed, and came free. Ciara reached again, drawing more power. They might pay for this once she was done, but for now she would use what they had. She poured more power into the stretched tissues as they returned to normal slowly, then she added strength to the exhausted cat. She monitored her granddaughter. The girl was power-drained but not exhausted. Ciara was the same.

It was well. Finally she withdrew, touching Aisling's hand. "You can let go now."

Aisling did so, folding abruptly to the rug. "Phew. I didn't know power could be combined like that."

Ciara's voice was dry. "Nor did I, but we had to do something. I thought I'd heard my grandmother say once that this was possible. I was very young so I could have misheard." Her voice was suddenly wistful. "We lost so much when Yvian ran mad. My own mother's gift was small and only for healcraft. But she at least was trained. She'd begun to teach me a little, but sometimes it seems that with less than full-blood the gift comes later. I'd barely begun to learn before everything was gone."

And that, she thought silently, may be your trouble. You read as a woman of the Power to me—full power. But it's come late, you're untrained, and I know of no one who may help. But I do also recall Grandmother saying that was dangerous to the one untrained where the power comes suddenly. There's no growing into it.

She thrust away her fears, helping Shosho care for the kitten. As his fur dried Ciara admired him. But looking down at the squeaking kitten she wondered again who Shosho had found as a mate.

The kit was large. Dried now, fur fluffed, he looked even bigger. It was impossible to believe Shosho had carried him. Why he was almost half the size of the small cat. Nor was he the usual color or markings. His fur had dried a sort of brownish-yellow. There was a dark-furred V on his forehead, and another like a necklace upon his breast.

The Aiskeep cats were all of Sulcar breeding, tabbies in differing shades but mainly black or silver. Their heads were broad and their bodies stocky. The kitten's head was more wedge-shaped, his body longer and leaner even so new born. Ciara thought it likely that fully grown he'd be near twice normal size.

Keelan returned then, agog to admire his cat and her achievement. He gaped at the kitten incredulously.

"It's *huge*! Is Shosho all right, will she have enough milk for it? I have the box for them, and the fire's blazing downstairs."

Ciara eased her shoulders, "Good. Put them in the box and leave them. Shosho would like a bit of peace and privacy now. Stay away for a couple of hours. You can come down with us and make us something to drink. I'm not as young as I was for this sort of afternoon."

The kitten thrived. Shosho had milk but the baby turned to meat earlier than usual. He grew fast. In four months, he was as large as any cat at Aiskeep. At the same time he made his choice of human. To Aisling's pleasure it fell on her.

"I don't know what to call him, though." She giggled, "Maybe I should leave it up to him." She nudged the kitten sprawled on her stomach. "What do you want to be called? Half-a-Horse might be appropriate."

The kitten sat up with dignity. Into Aisling's surprised mind came a picture. The kitten whirled in pursuit of a leaf. Spun, leaping high into the air to land with soft paws on the captured prey. Wind ruffled his fur. He leaped at the breeze as it passed, patting out with hopeful paws. Dancing with the stir of air. The girl smiled, touching the soft fur between his ears.

"Wind-Dancer? I'll call you Dancer for short." The kitten purred approval.

Ciara watched. She, too, had seen. That was interesting. She could receive some emotions from animals as could her granddaughter. But that had been more, a strong, clear picture in reply to a question. More and more she wondered who or what Shosho had found as mate.

When Dancer was a year old, Aisling's gift began to wear on her. At the same time Kirion made another attempt to lay hands on his sister. His studies were no longer gray. Now they were black sorcery. He'd discovered ways to power yet he remained cautious. He had also learned too many of the things that might happen to those who were casual.

Ruart, too, had not forgotten Aisling. The girl was seventeen. He'd offered marriage once. Ruart had been ill that winter. For the first time he'd realized that no one lives forever. A man should leave sons behind him. To do that he needed a respectable wife of good family. Aisling would be just right.

To the fury of all at Aiskeep, he renewed his offer. It was rejected firmly. Then two weeks later as Aisling rode alone in the upper valley, two men appeared from the trees. She was seized. In her terror she drew on her gift without restraint. One man died on the spot, the other a day later. But he survived long enough to confirm that Kirion had been his master.

Trovagh called the family together. "I have bad news. Geavon writes that Shandro is favoring Ruart more and more. He has enough influence lately to receive almost anything he asks to have.

"We have just sent word to Ruart that Aisling refuses him. How long before the duke intervenes and insists? Aiskeep can still refuse, *will* still refuse. But what will Shandro do if he is openly flouted?"

Ciara glanced around. "There is also Kirion. As he has shown us, there are ways into Aiskeep other than the main gates. I doubt many men could enter through the hills as that pair did. But what if we were held in siege at the gates, while others attacked in a steady pattern of twos and threes through the hill tracks? We might not be taken by storm through the gates, but we could be worn down over time."

Trovagh nodded. "For that reason I plan to fill the lower storerooms again. Trader Talron arrives in three days. Aiskeep has always held siege supplies, but I will double them."

"We pay with what, my love?" Ciara questioned.

"With horses of the Aiskeep strain. Talron has a Sulcar master who will take them aboard to sell in Es City. If we are besieged, we will be unlikely to sell our beasts, so I am stripping the herd. All trained mounts will go save for one mount for each of us."

Elanor had been carried down to join them. She was in her nineties but while frail of body, her mind was as keen as ever.

"Sell all the Keep's ordinary horses, too, Tro," she said now. "They eat as much as the better beasts. Replace them with the Torgian strain as we train the young ones."

Trovagh agreed. It was something he had not thought about. The Keep had always used ordinary beasts for the work in harness.

His glance touched Aisling. She'd been so quiet lately, ever since she'd killed the men who would have stolen her. He thought the worst of it for the child was that she had not intended to strike. Now she was afraid to touch or allow the touch of those she loved. Ciara said that the girl alternated between refusing to use her overflowing power until her skin shone with it—or using it over and over until she was dangerously exhausted.

Keelan moved to the table to pour wine. He didn't like any

of this. His brother Kirion was a danger to Aisling. Ruart would be more easily handled. Shandro would sit at Aiskeep's gates for months, maybe a year. Once he found what a siege cost, he'd think up some reason to save his reputation and leave, and if he didn't, the merchants would have something to say about it. They wouldn't appreciate being taxed to pay for Ruart's choice of wives.

But Kirion would cling on. There'd be more of his creatures slipping into the upper valley. More people dead. Knowing Kirion, it wouldn't be long before he hit on the idea of hostages. What would that do to Aisling?

If she refused to go to Kirion and people died for that? If she went and Kirion *could* use her power for himself and his sorceries? How long would it be before Aisling came to a conclusion that her own death would solve everything for those she loved?

She'd been hard hit by the death of two men—men who, Keelan thought, were probably better dead for the sake of others anyhow. The one who'd survived most of a day had talked deliriously. His descriptions of what his master had done with those stolen had almost made Keelan sick. The brute had been Kirion's supplier and had a lot to tell.

Talron came and went. The lower storerooms bulged with what he left. Dancer had a wonderful time assisting, being shut into every room in turn and bawling to be released, only to be shut in the next and the next. He kept Aisling distracted for several days.

But once the supplies were in, the horses handed over, Talron and his men left. Now she had time to brood again. Dancer did his best, but Aisling was too unhappy to be distracted.

The truth was that she feared her gift now. She had killed with it. She'd been terrified when she was seized, but she might still have kept the fire under control. Then one of the men had twisted her arm, the pain had sickened her. With the pain she lost control. Her skin had flared with silver light, both men had fallen screaming, one was dead in seconds. The one who had hurt her. The other died before the morning. She intended none of it.

If it came without her willing it there, what of her grandparents? What of Keelan, old Hanion—any of them might touch her. Hanion always liked to throw her up onto her mount if he was by. It was his privilege. He was almost too old to lift her now, but he'd taught her to ride. How could she tell him to stand away from her? Keelan, Grandmother Ciara, Grandfather Tro, Great-Aunt Elanor, they all hugged her often. Was she to thrust them back? Demand they never come too close to her?

Worse yet, she'd begun to dream. She guessed where the place was the third time. Mountains like that weren't natural. They had to be the border where the witches had turned all the land between Karsten and Estcarp. What were the dreams saying? That she should go to Estcarp? She probably had far kin there, distant cousins or something. Ciara's grandmother had been of pure blood. There were sure to be kin of some degree there. Was she to go to them? But she didn't want to leave Aiskeep.

It was midsummer when the duke arrived. He sent polite messages. He would be pleased to meet with Trovagh and his lady when it was convenient. There was a hint of steel in that: it had better be convenient quite soon. They went the following morning.

Shandro was still polite but firm. There was no good reason why their granddaughter should not wed the duke's most loyal and trusted Ruart.

They mentioned the scandal of the witch-hunts some years ago. Shandro scowled. Ruart had been much younger. Rumor had greatly exaggerated events.

Ciara leaned forward. "We do not believe it did. Aisling is unwilling to wed Ruart. To be blunt, my Lord Duke, she says she would prefer death as a bridegroom. We do believe *that*. We are prepared neither to drag a drugged girl before the priestess, nor to attend her funeral. Apart from which," she added tartly, "you are talking of a large and respectable wedding. Not some affair in the dead of night with a priestess and the couple alone. What priestess would consent to officiate in such pomp where a bride is clearly drugged until she cannot stand?"

Shandro shrugged. "You will persuade the girl it is in her best interests to wed. In the best interests of all of you. I will hear her reply in two days. If it is a refusal still, then all Aiskeep shall regret it."

They left wordlessly. Once they were back in their rooms Trovagh stared down at the wineglass he turned in his fingers.

"A winter siege and Shandro will change his mind. Geavon's last letter dealt with this. Once full winter closes in, the duke and his lords will be back in Kars in the warm. Geavon has a girl in mind then. He'll aim her at Ruart. If all goes well by spring, it will be her Ruart wishes to wed.

"That'll call off Shandro. But not Kirion. Geavon's sure this latest business had Kirion behind it."

Ciara snorted, "Almost certainly."

"So what do we do?"

"What Aiskeep has always done. Play for time. If we can get Ruart and the duke off our backs, then we can turn all our resources to Kirion."

Trovagh sighed. "Meanwhile we're under siege—again. I must find something important for Keelan to do. He's fuming so much I fear he may start taking risks."

The siege began two days later when a message was sent to the duke. It was a polite but very final refusal of Ruart's offer.

Over the next few months, summer faded into fall, and fall toward winter. With them Elanor also faded. Aisling said nothing, but privately she feared it was the worry of being under siege. If so, then it was all her fault. Elanor died as the first snow of the winter fell. They buried her in the Aiskeep graveyard. All of them wept. None had ever known an Aiskeep without her; she would be greatly missed.

But it made up Aisling's mind finally. If she stayed here, she would only bring more trouble or death to her family. It would be best if she went away. Not to Ruart, she couldn't. Nor to Geavon and risk yet another Keep.

Her gift ached at her. It made the decision easier. She'd go over the mountains to where she could learn to use it properly. To where they could train her to control it.

Her decision firmed. She'd go in secret, leave a note for her family. She'd go alone from the upper valley through the hills; on foot with a pack no one would know her.

She'd have to leave Dancer behind. That would hurt. In the year and a half since his birth, she'd grown to love him as much as Keelan loved Shosho. To leave Dancer behind, to turn her back on Aiskeep would tear her heart. She would never forget them, never be as happy anywhere else. But she must go.

She began to gather the things she would need. A pack she could carry, a spark striker to light fires, cooking gear, bedding, heavy clothing, and her weapons. She would need a sword, bow, and dagger. It was a long journey, and she would have to hunt some of her food as she went. Aisling hoped she would be able to carry everything she'd need. Winter was closing in. She must act soon or it would be too late. No one must know what she planned until she had gone. She reckoned without Ciara.

15

Aisling had her pack prepared. She could lift it—just. That was no good. The pack was emptied and Aisling stared in despair at the contents. Dancer sat on the bed glaring at her. Now and again he gave a small growl. There was a light tap at the door, Aisling turned to toss a blanket over the pack but it was too late. Ciara was already looking at both pack and her granddaughter, knowledge and gentle amusement in her face.

She walked to the bed, pushed Dancer up gently, then sat. "I guessed you had this in mind. Where do you plan to go?"

"To Estcarp. I keep dreaming of the mountains where they turned." She looked at Ciara. "Are you going to stop me?"

Her grandmother shook her head slowly. "No, dearling. But I have a tale to tell you. You know how I came to live at Aiskeep?"

Aisling nodded. She'd grown up knowing the story of that time when all was death and destruction for the Old Race in Karsten.

"I saw my mother Lanlia die. At the time, I saw only that she fell in silence from our watchtower, no cry of fear or horror. Some years later, I dreamed of it. A true dreaming. My father's mother lived with us until she died two years before our blood was named outlaw. She loved us all deeply. She was of the old pure blood and held Power in her time. I dreamed that my mother stood waiting at the tower's edge. Then Grandmother spoke to her."

Aisling was engrossed. "What did she say?"

"She said 'The blood shall come full circle. It shall rise to flower again.' Then she called. I was in my mother's mind as she fell. Her spirit was taken before she reached the ground."

"What does that mean, about the blood coming full circle?"

"Wait. I dreamed again, many years after that. I saw the mountains turn. I heard the same voice repeating those words. But when I assumed it meant the blood should go over mountains to Estcarp, it said no. It added then 'Not to Estcarp but to the East shall the blood seek. There it shall flower in freedom. When the time comes, give what you treasure that one you love may fly free.'"

"East—but there's nothing east, is there?"

"There is far more to the East than any once believed. You were too busy at Gerith Keep. But Geavon has long ears. So, too, does Trader Talron. Between the tales both have heard, I can say that eastward there is another land. Old, not new. It was from there that those in Estcarp once came. And since we, too, are of their blood the land may yet welcome you. I have dreamed of mountains even as you. And more."

Ciara held up a hand. "Last night I dreamed a third time. I saw you ride out with Keelan and Dancer." At her side the cat gave a short chirp of approval. "I looked close, my child, I saw, too, the treasures you shall bear."

Aisling bowed her head a moment, then she looked up. "I can't take Dancer. It's winter and getting colder every day. How is he to keep up with horses if we ride?"

The cat rose on his hind legs patting at her braids. Ciara smiled. "I think you may not find it so easy to leave him behind. As for his being able to keep up, once you reach the mountains it may be best to go afoot. Until then, he can ride with you in a carrysack the way babies do. Let us look over your pack."

Aisling opened her mouth and shut it again. No one ever bested her grandmother once Ciara was determined on something.

In the end it was several more days before Aisling departed. When she did, they left by the upper valley, both she and Keelan astride horses of the Aiskeep strain. Dancer rode her shoulders in a padded baby sack. But before they were gone, Ciara took Aisling aside.

"Give me your dagger." She accepted it, producing a second knife, which she offered. "This belonged to my own line. Legends say it was made by an adept so long ago the years themselves are dust. Whatever the truth of that, it will never require to be sharpened. Where you go, that is of more use than legends. There is also this. It was my mother's. Elanor laid it away in a chest. I found it after her death."

Aisling gasped at the cloak. It was of riding length. Astride it would hang almost to her stirrups, knee-length when she walked on foot. It was woven of a fine gray wool, lined with white fur, and made skillfully so it could be worn either side out.

Ciara stroked it as she held it out. "I remember my mother making that, spinning and weaving the length of wool half of the previous winter. I wore it when I left Elmsgarth with Tarnoor and Trovagh—afterward." Aisling did not ask after what. She knew it had been after the deaths of all her grandmother's family.

She saw that Ciara still held something. It was within a small bag of embroidered silk. A finely wrought tempered-steel chain hung from the bag's opening at the top.

"Is that for me, too?"

"Yes." She lifted it toward Aisling as she lowered her head. As it settled on her breast the girl felt a surge of warmth.

"Oh, what is it?" Her fingers widened the opening as she peered down. "Grandmother, I can't take this. It's your pendant. The one your brother gave you."

"And now I pass it on. In my dream I saw you ride, child. My mother's cloak about you, Dancer at your shoulder. Fire shone at hip and breast where dagger and pendant hung. I do as I was bidden once. I give what I treasured, that one I love may fly free."

Aisling bent to hug Ciara hungrily. This would be the last time she'd see Aiskeep, the last time she saw the love in her grandparents' eyes, felt their arms about her. Trovagh saw his wife was done and joined them, hugging Aisling lovingly.

"Take care, my dear. May you find your dream."

Aisling nodded, her throat aching too much for her to speak. She turned her horse toward where Keelan waited. Behind her Ciara whispered.

"Fly free. Find your dream and be happy."

She linked her arm with that of her husband. They stood watching until there was nothing more to see. Then they sought the shrine to pray.

The air was cold but not the icy chill that would grip later in winter. At first Aisling was somber but then her mood lightened. It was an adventure. Besides, she had to go. She couldn't be miserable all the way to the border and make poor Keelan unhappy, too. She began to sing, then choked off the sound hurriedly.

Keelan laughed. "Yes, sing, little sister. There are no enemies about to hear you."

"How do you know?" Despite her resolutions her tone was sharp.

"Grandmother leaves no more to chance than she must. Six of the guards rode out yesterday. They travel in a screen ahead for the next few days. Once they turn back, we'll disguise you and the horses. It's mostly their color people remember. With you, they remember you're a girl." Aisling looked at him in surprise.

"I'm going to be a boy?"

"Yes. I'll be a blank shield, you'll be my younger brother learning the trade." His voice dropped in regret. "We'll have to cut your hair and both of us will be bleached blond."

"Why didn't we do this before we left Aiskeep? It would have been easier."

Keelan nodded. "And people would know. Kirion's still about. He's very good at persuading people to talk one way or another. You'll notice Ciara didn't give you the cloak until we were past all the garths."

He glanced up at the sky. "It's going to snow again. We'll keep moving until we get to shelter. I've kindling in my pack."

They rode in silence then, Aisling thinking as she moved automatically to the swing of her mount's steps. In a way she supposed she'd been naive. She'd somehow imagined that she would just walk out of the valley alone. Walk all down the line of hills to Geavon's Keep, then up along the border to some place she could cross into Estcarp. Just as if she was out for a ladylike stroll in her own Keep.

She gave a slightly bitter smile. And she had probably expected a complete Keep of relatives to be waiting at the pass to greet her. She took a deep breath of the cold air. Thanks be to Cup and Flame for her grandmother. Without her, Aisling would still have been walking to the border a year hence.

They camped in a shallow cave that night. It was quite comfortable, Aisling thought, if you didn't mind sleeping on rock in a draft. It reminded her all over again that even so, this would be easier than the trip *she'd* planned. Keelan was quietly confident.

"If there was any trouble ahead, one of the men would have

come back to warn us. Sleep all night. Later on we'll have to take it in turns to stand watch."

Five days passed in peace as the horses plodded through the light snow. On the fifth night one of the guards from Aiskeep appeared. Keelan looked up in query.

"No sign of anyone, my lord. A couple of the others have gone another day ahead just in case. They'll watch the road you'll be joining then. They can tell you who's ahead of you. I've sent others back to see who comes up the road behind you."

"Good. Share the fire, tell Keep's lord and lady we were well when you saw us last." The man nodded agreement. When Aisling woke, he was already gone.

They found the other guards at the road. Harran greeted them, quietly waving them to camp in the lee of a large lawleaf thicket.

"Very little traffic on the road," he told them over stew. "Ahead, there's a small group of merchants hurrying to winter over in Kars. Coming up behind you there's several single travelers. None look to be a danger." He looked at Dancer. "Just don't let any of them see that cat. It isn't exactly the sort of companion mercenaries ride with. Move along briskly, though, and likely they'll never catch you up."

Keelan and Aisling did so. The roads were wearying since they kept more to the lesser trails and stayed from the main road direct to Kars city. They arrived at Geavon's home to good news once the old man had them alone.

"Ruart has taken the bait I have dangled before him. He will wed the girl and Shandro will call home his soldiers before the winter is done. But be wary. I have heard nothing of Kirion of late; that I dislike."

Keelan looked thoughtful. "Did you not have a spy in Iren Keep?"

"I did. He vanished," Geavon said briefly.

Keelan whistled. "I dislike that myself. How much could he have said if forced to speak?"

"Too much. Yet he disappeared on the way here. It may have been bandits. His horse was a good beast."

"And if it was not?" Keelan queried, leaning over to stroke Dancer.

"Then he could have said you were on the way here. That you were expected before the worst part of the winter. I made inquiry when I discovered he was nowhere to be found. He should not have known these things, but someone spoke too carelessly." Geavon gathered himself to stand slowly. "I think it best that you, Keelan, remain here. If there are watchers, let you appear careless just once. They will believe Aisling remains here with you."

"But she does not?"

"No, there is a garth along the river. It is well on the way to the mountains and east. She may spend the remainder of the winter there in safety. In spring, she can travel on as she wishes." He bowed toward Aisling. "That is, if this accords with your desire, my dear."

She had been listening carefully. Now she bowed in return speaking formally, "It accords with my wish in all ways save that I may have brought trouble to Gerith Keep and its lord."

Geavon chuckled harshly. "The trouble is an old debt, child, and none of your making. Tarnoor whom you never knew was like a brother to me and distant kin also. I may not live to see the end of this, but when our spirits meet I would not have him feel I had done less than he would have done for one of *my* children in need. Go now and rest. I will see that messages are sent."

He smiled as they trotted obediently away. They were good children, healthy twigs from a rotten branch. He'd always known the father would bring death or disaster, but these two were sound stock.

Messengers left before dark and a watcher saw. He went to

report, not to Kirion but to Ruart, who found it interesting. He listened and smiled slowly.

One messenger to the south road. That would be to let Aiskeep know their lambs had arrived safely. The other messenger to the hills, luckily there had been two watchers. The leader was intelligent, and he'd sent his companion to follow the hill rider. Ruart had long suspected that Geavon had some holding there. The old man had been clever, but not quite as clever as he thought.

Ruart had guessed that Aiskeep might find a way to get Aisling out of their hold. The watcher had recognized Keelan. From the description, the other with Keelan could well be the sister in disguise. Ruart grunted to himself. The border was wide and lawless. Who would know what had happened there to a girl who vanished in the hills? Certainly none had known what happened to a spy riding back to his lord. And that had been in more populated lands.

Ruart's smirk widened. He'd been visiting Kirion at Iren Keep when he'd seen the man where he should not have been. He'd said nothing to Kirion, but had the man watched. When the time was right he'd had him taken.

The spy had talked. From that Ruart knew more than Kirion for once. Let his friend find his own trails to hunt. Ruart would follow this one.

Besides that, Ruart had a grudge. He'd gone to his clan head to ask for aid in forcing Aiskeep to give up Aisling. He'd been told briefly that the clan did not care to become involved. Ruart was making himself a laughingstock, now he was making his clan a laughingstock as well. Nor did they like other comments that were said of him. Flung mud stuck—to his clan as well as Ruart. Let him choose another wife and be less obvious in his dealings.

For most of his life Ruart had had his own way. To be scolded like a naughty child drove him to utter fury.

He left, determined to have all he wanted. The girl Geavon

dangled before him—and Aisling. He spent coin to hire men who would watch. They had done so to some purpose.

Aisling rode out quietly a day later just as the sky brightened. There were none to see her go. Ruart had spread his watchers along the hill trail the messenger had taken. They told him swiftly enough when she passed, though they did not see the cat, deep in his baby sack.

Ruart would have followed at once but for Shandro who insisted his favorite remain at court another few days. By then the girl would have reached her shelter. Well enough. Ruart would wait a while. There was usually a lull in the weather around midwinter. When that came, he would ride swiftly.

Meanwhile, Aisling had ridden three days along the river before turning up along the left fork that led to the higher hills. During her halts to camp, Dancer was free, returning often with some prey to eat alongside Aisling as she cooked for herself.

Geavon had drilled her in the landmarks and in what words to use when she came to the garth at last. She rode in with failing light, sitting her mount in the yard as she watched a bobbing lantern approach.

"I come from an uncle," she said softly to that haze of light. "An uncle who dislikes a rogue."

The light jerked sharply as the spy recognized the girl he had aided to Gerith Keep. He collected himself to reply. "All who dislike rogues are safe here," he said clearly.

Aisling peered at the figure behind the lantern. The voice was somehow familiar. She dropped from her weary horse to walk it toward the stables. The spy spoke again and the scent of the horse, the dark, and his tones came together.

"I know you," she said slowly. "You're the man who helped me the night I got away from Ruart."

In the edge of lantern light she saw him nod. "That I was, my lady. Pleased to do it, too. I have an old score against the man. I'd have aided you for that alone even had I not been

Geavon's man. Let us get the beast inside, and a meal on the table. Time for talking then and longer than we may want."

"Why?"

"Storm's coming. Up here they can last for days, even weeks."

It lasted only days. By then Aisling had his story from him. A decent man, she believed. One who'd been cruelly wronged by Ruart, too. They had that in common. She liked him, trusted him even here alone on the garth with no other.

It pleased her that he liked Dancer. The cat had refused to be left again, despite all Aisling could do to persuade him. He'd arrived in his baby sack, much to the spy's amusement once they reached the house and the cat had emerged.

That Dancer made it plain he liked this human was good enough for Aisling. The cat had proved to be a good judge of character in the past. After a short time, she liked the man for himself. But this past week Dancer had been fussing. He would run to the door wailing urgently. Aisling would allow him out, only to be howled at in exasperation. It was not that which he wanted of her.

Temon watched the cat thoughtfully. "I think, my lady, he wishes to warn you in some way." He left her with the cat, vanishing into his storeroom to collect supplies. These he sorted slowly into a shoulder pack. Into that went all the small odds and ends that can make a camp comfortable. He added bedding, lightweight but very warm and proof against any but the longest, most driving rain. He hefted the pack then, scarred face expressionless.

He reached down journey-cakes, each wrapped twice over and sealed. Two water bottles were stowed, each into a different pocket on the outside of the pack. One was empty, but a fiery cordial went into the other. Taken in sips, it was a restorative. Poured over a wound, it would cleanse. She'd come with a short bow and arrows, that would do well.

Should he add a sword? he wondered. But to carry one she could not use would be of no help, only useless extra weight.

He tipped the pack empty, checking all it had contained once more. Then he stowed the items one by one. He'd done the best he could do for her. The cat was a canny beast. If it saw danger coming, it was likely right.

He sighed quietly. She reminded him of the girl he'd loved so many years gone. This one, too, had power, fleeing Ruart. But he would see that this time Ruart did not catch her. That he swore by the Lady of the Hills. He'd hunted deep into them. He could put her on the path as far as the ancient ruined Keep far into the mountains. After that, she must make her own trails.

He walked back to give her the landmarks. He made her repeat them again and again. Then he showed her the pack made ready. Aisling added her bow and quiver to it. Dancer still fussed; indeed, as midwinter approached he became still more insistent.

Temon made up his mind. "I think the beast senses danger. In midwinter, there is often a time when the weather clears here in the mountains. The wind blows from the North then so this side of the hills is sheltered. Be ready. You know the way as best I can tell you. Your pack stands waiting. If danger comes, get you gone. I'll do my best to delay it."

It was well planned, but Ruart was already riding. Nearer Kars the weather had cleared earlier. He had ridden out at once.

He had no way of knowing that his spies were not the only men to sell their service in odd places. One of them had sold word to Kirion. Ruart rode hard upriver heading for the garth deep into the hills. Kirion was two days' ride behind but in more haste on a better horse.

Ruart came in sight of the garth in late morning. The snow had only cleared this high up that day. He knew his prey would still be here, he was sure of it. He watched as Temon walked across to the stables. Ruart's breath hissed from him. That was the man who'd freed the girl before. By Alizon's hounds, he had both of them now!

He moved to his horse, mounting quickly to set the horse down the slope. Below Aisling had just walked out into the yard. He made for her. Temon was a garthsman, not a fighter. A sneaking tricky spy. If he tried to interfere, Ruart would know how to deal with him.

Temon was in the barn when he heard Aisling scream. Over Ruart's shoulder she saw him running toward them, a terrible look on his face.

Her powers were almost to nothing. She made a habit of using them as much as was possible when she was near people. It ensured, or so she hoped, that she would not accidentally harm a friend. That morning while Temon was cutting wood she'd used her gift in various small ways, just enough to empty most of it without tiring Aisling too badly. Now she called the silver fire desperately, just as Ruart struck her across the side of the head.

The garthsman arrived as Ruart screeched and dropped Aisling. Temon raised the hammer he still held, then halted, collapsing slowly to the ground. Ruart stared in satisfaction. The fool had underestimated a man who'd fought a score of duels. A dagger in the sleeve had been useful in the past and Ruart always had one ready.

Ruart smiled, a slow, anticipatory smile. From behind him came a low, vicious snarl. Dancer had arrived.

The cat attacked in a flurry of feints and evasions. Ruart wove steel before him, but this was no short duel. The brute seemed tireless. Behind him Aisling staggered to her feet. She felt dizzy, but she would not let Dancer fight alone. She scrabbled in the snow finding stones beneath the whiteness. Then she began to fling them. One at a time, each carefully aimed. The second crashed into Ruart's leg, he yelped, stepping further back from her. Before he recovered, Dancer scored home on flesh beneath the clothing.

Ruart slid back again. Behind him a terrible figure arose. Blood poured from Temon's chest to redden his clothing. His eyes glared with the effort as he dragged himself to his feet. The hammer lifted—and swung down. Ruart went soundlessly to the ground, his head broken open in that single, awful blow.

Temon slid quietly down to lie beside his victim. A long hatred was assuaged at last.

Aisling stumbled toward Temon, Dancer at her side. She would have fumbled his clothing open but he shook his head.

"No use, girl. I know where the blade went. You'd exhaust yourself for nothing. Listen to me. You wouldn't take Geavon's horse on because you could not bring it back. Take Ruart's." Temon's face twisted into a wry smile. "He won't be needing it. When you're as far as you can go afoot, strip the beast and let him go."

Aisling was crying now. "And don't cry for me. I only stayed alive for this. Leave the barn door open, the cow will have enough hay to last until spring."

He paused to gasp for breath. "Let Lord Geavon's horse go. The beast will go home as soon as you do. Geavon will send someone to sort things out. You can leave a message for him in the secret place. Whoever comes will know where to look."

His voice was weakening. Perhaps the lass could have saved him if he'd let her, but he hadn't wanted her to try. He'd known what happened to his betrothed, his beautiful Ismene. At first he'd only known that she was dead, and that she'd been in Ruart's hands. Later, after he'd joined that household, he'd heard it all. A comment, a few sentences at a time. He'd planned to kill the man one day but by the time he knew it all Aisling had escaped and Temon could not return to Ruart's Keep.

He smiled up at her. It hadn't mattered. After all, she'd

brought his enemy to him in the end. He lifted a hand to wipe her tears. It was so heavy, so hard to raise. He felt oddly light though, as if he was floating above the snow. Beside him a figure slowly came into focus. He looked up, his voice a glad cry,

"Ismene!"

Yes, beloved, come with me, now we are together again.

He rose to follow, the heavy weakness gone. Behind him Aisling closed the open eyes with gentle fingers.

Moving slowly throughout the remainder of the morning, she did as Temon had requested. But first she dealt with his body. It was difficult, but she managed to bring it into the storeroom against the side of the house. There she laid him out on a table on the coverlet that was all he had of his betrothed. Aisling placed ice-flowers in his hands, the hammer she laid at his feet. Let the Gods know he had died as a warrior fighting to protect the innocent.

She mourned for Temon as she stood there. He hadn't deserved to die that way, but then she remembered his words. He hadn't needed to live on. Hadn't even wanted to once he'd paid the debt. And he was with his Ismene now, that she never doubted.

The cow was given access to hay. The Gerith Keep horse was freed. It wandered off to the West at once, stopping to graze now and again but always heading back. She wrote a hasty letter, placing it carefully within the secret cavity in the wall.

Dancer was fussing again. Aisling glanced over to where Ruart still lay tumbled in the snow. She could do nothing for him. Let him lie. If Geavon's man arrived before thaw he could do whatever appeared seemly for Ruart. If thaw came first, let the foxes have the body. She didn't care.

She dug out Dancer's baby sack. According to the landmarks and places to shelter Temon had drilled into her, there was a good place she could reach on horseback before nightfall. Last time Dancer had fussed, Ruart had been on the way. Who was coming now she had no idea, but she'd trust Dancer.

She emptied the pack into two saddlebags, added the empty pack, then swung into the saddle. From the baby sack on her shoulders Dancer gave an approving chirp.

Aisling halted the horse at the top of the small hill. From there she could look back over the deserted garth. It looked no different.

She lifted her hand in a blessing, the last part of the sign leaving a faint glint of silver in the air. But Aisling noticed nothing; she had already turned the horse away to plunge down the slope. She prayed for Temon again as she rode.

The shelter was rough but it did well. Aisling found the crude windbreak at the back of the shelter. She stood it up carefully again by the entrance against the prevailing wind. Snow packed against it swiftly. Behind that Aisling lit her fire, keeping the circle of coals small. Dancer moved to sit by the flames at once, his purr amusing Aisling.

"You might well purr. You insisted on coming along. There may not be a fire every night, you know." She laughed as he thumped her with his head. "All right, all right. Food next."

The weather continued fine and she made distance at her mount's steady walk. She had taken all the oats Temon had. It meant she could ride the whole day and let the animal feed well at night without the need to stop and graze. She was pleased she'd thought of it. In a couple more days, she'd have reached as far as it would have taken in weeks on foot.

After that she would have to leave the horse. A pity, but Temon had said there was a place there where he'd manage. Come spring he'd probably start back, too. She fell asleep that second night listening to Dancer's purr and the sound of crunching teeth as her mount relished the hard feed.

Kirion had drawn up at the garth the previous morning. He'd looked down at Ruart's sprawled body and snorted. The man had been a fool but useful. Still, there were other useful fools to be found.

He stamped inside the house, checking each room. There was only the body of the garthsman. From the look of it, he and Ruart had killed each other. But the girl had been here all right. Ruart hadn't moved after the blow that had killed him. Someone had laid the garthsman out. Someone who'd cared.

He'd seen the Gerith Keep horse, too, as it headed west. He'd tried to catch it, but the animal was too wary.

Kirion considered. Ruart's beast was missing; she must have gone ahead on that. He could follow. If he pushed, he could probably catch up in a day or so. He checked the barn, he was out of grain. He found none and grunted irritably. His mount would just have to manage.

He pushed his horse all that day but he had to pause in time for the hungry animal to graze. Nor did he know the landmarks Aisling had been taught. He wasted time in dead ends, in following trails that led nowhere.

All the time a light snow fell. Not enough to slow a rider greatly, but it erased hoofprints in hours. He found her second shelter, but by then he was a day further behind and he knew it. Kirion spent the night there, but in the morning he turned back.

He'd lost his chance at gaining stolen power from his sister. But there'd always be others. He was learning all the time. It was sorcery, but what matter. It was also power.

Aisling followed the river. Even here it was a rush and tumble of powerful current coming down from the mountains from the East. She wondered if it could speak what tales it would tell of that mystical land she sought.

Geavon had learned patches and tatters of news from traders and merchants who gossiped more than women ever did. The land was called Escore, ancient, holding powers unknown in Karsten. They said that there those rode to war, some not even of humankind.

Her hand stole up to clasp the pendant. Her fingers dropped to touch the dagger hilt. They said that those of the Old Blood had come from that place. Could these have come with them?

Did she but return them to an ancient home? The trip thus far had been tiring, but apart from Ruart, not so impossible. Would that change when she went afoot? She scanned the landscape.

Light snow continued to fall. Ahead lay a wood and into it led the old trail. Aisling shivered. There was a menace in the lowering trees, as if something within watched and waited. There was the feeling of eyes, unfriendly ones. The idea of entering the wood, moving beneath those dark trees, was unpleasant.

Dancer, too, seemed uneasy. The cat had senses one who journeyed would do well to heed.

Aisling considered. It was within an hour or two of dusk. If she must dare the trees, better to have daylight. She knew not how far it might be to ride through such a wood.

She turned her tired horse. Back a mile she had seen a place to shelter: out of sight of the wood and with half a roof yet remaining. Maybe it had been some sort of way station once. Now it was ruins, but it would suffice.

The shelter was large enough for her to bring in her mount under cover. The wood gnawed at her mind. She had liked nothing about it. She must now decide in how much haste she traveled.

Temon had said there were two roads. One was a mere trail that skirted the wood and took an extra day. The other ran through the center of the wood and time would be saved. She might not have much of that to spare. The midwinter lull in storms would soon come to an end. Also she had little grain left: three days, no more. If she wasted a day circling the wood, that was a day she could not ride without time spent letting her mount graze.

In the event it was not she who made the decision. The horse was more nervous the closer they approached the wood with the morning light. Finally he balked. Aisling let Dancer jump from his carrysack. He, too, eyed the wood suspiciously. He approached sniffing dubiously, then led her onto the narrower fainter trail that circled to the left.

The girl sighed. "I understand. You both think there's something in there, too." She shrugged. Animals sensed things people didn't. All knew that. She'd believe they were warning her.

Dancer showed no sign just now of wishing to be riding again. He pranced happily ahead, first chasing a windblown leaf, then pouncing on something small and squeaking. Aisling laughed and Dancer looked up at her. She grinned down, addressing him softly.

"I hope you won't regret coming along, but right now it's very good to have company." He churred in agreement, moving on ahead of the ambling horse.

They skirted the wood over the next two days as Temon had said. The trail swung out around the trees a good distance before it looped back to the older, well-worn trail. Even as she rode on Aisling had the impression that eyes glared after her from its cover, as if she was prey who should not have escaped. She shivered, nudging the horse to a swifter pace.

The road turned around a long, sweeping bend in the river and there before her lay the last landmark Temon had known.

It must have been a great Keep in its time, she thought. It was at least as large as Aiskeep. She wondered who had lived there. She had no need to ask how it had fallen. Here in the North none of the Old Race—Keep, garth, or hovel—had escaped.

Aisling sat on her restless horse, gazing at the building. No breaks showed in its walls, though the major portion of the drawbridge had gone. Near the end of that a small building still stood. Temon had thought it to be a shine of some kind. But whoever or whatever might have once dwelled within, there was only emptiness now.

She slept the night in peace, untroubled by dreams or watching eyes. In the morning she peered up at the sky. Clouds were drifting very slowly into clumps that heaved up into fluffy masses along the mountaintops. It might not snow more heavily today, but snow was surely on the way. Here in the abandoned fields there was ample shelter for her mount. Grass, dry now but still nourishing, remained. She had one more small feed of grain before that was gone. She sat a moment making up her mind.

She would ride, and ride hard for this final day. Then she would let the beast have the last of the grain. She would go on foot after that. The horse would drift back to the empty fields for food and shelter. She called Dancer, tucked him comfortably into his carrysack, and nudged her mount with a firm heel. Where she had level footing, she heeled the horse to a canter. In the course of a day she came high into the foothills, all the time striving to see a way she might take across the mountains looming before her.

Toward the close of light she seemed to see a place where two mountains stood apart. It was possible there was a pass there. She halted, offering the horse the last of the grain. There was a half cave in the hillside that would do. She was too weary to seek a better refuge. Her mount ate eagerly before wandering off to graze on the smaller patches of grass still to be found under the snow. She had stripped him of saddle and bridle. Now she emptied the saddlebags, and sorted the contents into her pack.

She must leave something. The saddlebags were of leather, and heavy. She had no need of them. But Dancer's carrysack was light despite the padding. In the morning she must move upward, seeking the pass she hoped to find. Perhaps she could add the carrysack to her pack for so long as the weight was not too burdensome. It meant that Dancer would sleep warmer if there was no shelter to be found.

She weighed the object in her hand. Let her take it. A thing could always be discarded, but not taken up again if it was left far behind.

The cat sat watching her before claiming his sack to sleep. Aisling placed her pack close at hand, then laid out her bow with an arrow by the string. Wood had been laid in a half circle before her. Temon had told her that she should light a fire. There were strange beasts in the mountains since they had changed. Long ago, too, old Hanion had talked of campaigns when he rode as a lad with Aisling's great-grandfather, Tarnoor. A fire could be a weapon at need.

Tonight she laid out the small core of it, but to either side she added more to make a half circle before her, of the driest wood she could find. She sorted out several very long branches. There was a feel to the night. Hanion had said never to ignore that feeling. It was often all the warning a soldier would have.

Aisling smiled. She wasn't a soldier, but good advice was good advice. She lay down to sleep, her mind turning to her family. Keelan would stay the winter with Geavon. With Ruart vanished, the siege on Aiskeep would be lifted. She prayed silently for those she loved. Let them walk in the light and be well. Then she curled into her blankets. She slept.

She woke several hours before dawn with Dancer patting anxiously at her face. There was a feel to the night. As if it waited.

Moving with silent caution, Aisling sat up reaching for her bow. She'd learned healcraft from Ciara for most of the girl's life, and had listened to tales of herbs that repelled those of the true Dark. Once well onto the trail from Temon's holding she had smeared such herbs over each arrowhead. It might even be that the scent of them would help ward off anything evil. She slid quietly from her bedding, laying her other hand upon the end of one of the long branches left in the fire.

There came a snuffle from the darkness, then her mount cried out in terror. The big horse came blundering toward her, something leaping at its side.

Aisling screamed, a sound half of rage, half of fear. She whipped the branch across the fire, seeing the flames stirred to life. In the firelight she could still not make out what attacked the horse, but the outline of it was there. She shot. Immediately there was an outcry. The thing rolled howling and screeching to free itself from the shaft. Others of its kind set out screams that rent the night.

The terrified horse seemed to understand that here was help. It leaped past the fire to stand partly sheltered. Aisling waited. Out in the darkness whatever she had hit was still wailing.

It may have been that which incited the second attack. They came toward the fire, circling from either side. Dancer rose to send a long, challenging shriek raw with fury into the night. The creatures paused. Then Aisling caught up her branch. She ran the flaming end along the dry wood laid ready. In seconds it flared into a half circle about their refuge. She had rubbed herbs along a branch at each end of that and added a bunch of angelica. There had once been a herb garden by the drawbridge shrine where herbs still grew.

The fire and smoke from the herb maddened the attackers. They raced howling back and forth in the darkness, but it seemed none dared face her defenses. The girl found she was shivering. The sound of their cries was terrifying. Perhaps that was their intent? She waited, an arrow half strung. From the dark came an outcry that made Aisling jump before she understood. Balked of their chosen prey, the attackers had turned on the one she had injured. Its wailing ceased abruptly to be replaced by the sounds of feasting.

She was sickened, but it was better they killed their own

than Aisling or one of her companions. The horse crowded against her. She patted it comfortingly before adding wood to the fire. She might as well use it all. She could hardly drag it with her. The flames brought another irritable chorus of shrieks, which she ignored. She leaned against her pack, half drowsing. The beasts would warn her at need.

Morning came reluctantly in clouded skies. She eyed that with foreboding. Tomorrow it would snow for certain. Best be on her way. She patted the horse, then chased him back down the trail. He got the idea after a few yells, and trotted off, heading steadily to the West. She hoped he had a peaceful winter back in the fields of the deserted Keep.

She ate swiftly, tied the gear she was leaving up into a tree nearby. Someone might find it useful. Then she shouldered her pack. Ahead of her lay the two mountains. She could only pray that a pass lay between them.

Dancer galloped ahead leading the way. He appeared to have no doubts. She admired his lithe form as he bounded upward. He'd grown to look quite different from the ordinary Aiskeep cats. They were round and comfortable. He was leaner, more rangy. His eyes were not the amber of the Aiskeep cats, but a clear chartreuse green. Even more than other cats, Dancer gave the impression of knowing secrets he wasn't telling. Aisling loved him as she knew he loved her. But there were times when she wondered just who or what Shosho *had* found as a mate in the Karsten hills.

She halted to stare up at her path. Her feet seemed to be finding some kind of a trail under the snow. Probably a deer trail. She would keep to that so long as it lasted and give thanks. She plodded on, the pack heavy as she toiled upward. At her breast the pendant gave a sudden throb of heat.

Aisling halted at once. Her hand went up to close about the silken bag. Gently she freed the pendant holding it out in front of her. It flared into light, the tiny blue gems seeming to catch fire. It flamed higher. Now a noxious scent met Aisling's nostrils. She gave back hastily as Dancer leaped to her side.

Ahead of them a jumble of snow-covered boulders loomed. She could circle those. She moved to do so. From the boulders something that looked like one of them moved downward. It leaped at her, teeth in a suddenly open mouth clashing and reaching. Aisling screamed, dodging as it swung toward her. It swept back, halted and returned. The pendant was hot against her skin. Dancer was howling his battle cry; Aisling felt besieged.

Dancer's carrysack was coming loose. She remembered that it was padded. It would help to ward off that thing's teeth. She snatched the sack from the pack strap, wrapping it around her arm. It would act as a shield at need.

The boulder leaped for her. Aisling swung her arm hard, thrusting it away, feeling the creature's teeth clamp home in the padding. It spat that out, springing in again at her. She dodged, but felt teeth score her ankle. Dancer lost fur but no skin as the false boulder snapped at him in passing.

The girl stumbled, her leg felt numb, her feet kicking at dangerously rough ground. She glanced down. The thing was driving them to the boulders. Why? Judging by the pendant it could be for no good reason. Maybe the boulders were all of its kind, a nest. She preferred to die in some way other than being devoured alive by boulder creatures. In bed at a hundred and fifty surrounded by adoring family would be nice. Dancer was moving to the right away from the rocks. With grim determination, she fought her way across the slope following his path.

The boulder leaped, slashing more savagely, but somehow she held it back. It bounced high, teeth obtaining a sudden grip on one sleeve. As she jerked away her hand fell to her dagger. It burned even as the pendant. Without thinking, Aisling drew the blade, swinging it around at the boulder thing.

To her amazement, it bit in. The boulder uttered its first

sound, a cry that she felt in the pit of her stomach, more a vibration than a sound. Then it retreated hastily. It merged into the jumble of rocks to become just one more.

The girl stood panting. From the dagger a gray stinking ichor dripped slowly. Dancer's carrysack was ripped almost to shreds. It would be of no use now. But she was grateful she'd carried it this far. It had certainly saved her arm.

Aisling moved on hastily. She'd like to be farther away from that thing in case it decided to try for her and Dancer again. Dancer! She halted to be certain he was unharmed. He purred up at her smugly. It would take more than a live, leaping, tooth-gnashing boulder to faze *him*.

The delayed promise of snow was fulfilled the next day. From leaden skies it came, softly at first, then more heavily, turning into a blizzard in which it was impossible to see more than a foot or two before them. Aisling plodded forward, eyelashes frozen with the tears the cold brought forth. Temon had told her to use wood ash and a scarf for the glare. It helped, but the bite the false boulder had given her ached painfully. She'd cleansed it, smeared on salve, but with each step the ache grew.

Around her the snow deepened, heaping up into drifts in the hollows, scouring from the ridges. There was no great amount of wind, but the snow was enough—as was the growing, bone-deep chill. Aisling plunged and plowed her way through the drifts. Dancer was able to run across most of them, although every so often he had to be rescued when he misstepped to one deeper than he'd expected. His expression was comical at such times. But her ankle ached. It had gone from numb to first the ache, then real pain at each step. She was worried about it, but could do nothing. She needed shelter.

Dancer found her a little as afternoon darkened. Two rocks lay in a slight depression and a third had fallen to produce a partial roof. Around and across these earth and snow had gathered to make the half cave windproof so far as it went.

Before the light was gone Aisling heaped and packed snow. It extended the half cave into something that would give her enough warmth and shelter once she had a fire. Nearby was an ancient tree; she dug around the foot of it finding a heap of dry twigs and branches. Some she saved. With the remainder, all she could salvage, she lit a small fire.

Dancer snuggled blinking happily in front of the flames. From her pack Aisling dug a small packet of herbs and dried meat, pounded together. In water it could become a nourishing stew. She was strangely not hungry, but she forced herself to eat. Once the shelter had warmed a little, she gingerly removed her boot to dress the slash across her ankle.

The marks were red, the flesh puffy. She smeared on more salve, donned her boot once more, then fed the fire.

She dozed through the night, dimly conscious that Dancer joined her, his body making a much warmer spot against her stomach. The next day snow fell again. It was hard to find any trail, let alone keep to it, Aisling thought, as she forced her way through yet another drift.

Fear was breaking into her mind more often as she plodded her way upward. If anything happened to her, she would die here without help. If she died here, Dancer would be alone. He'd die, too. Her mind was beginning to blur. It made her more afraid each time she realized she had lost track of her march. The pain in her ankle was worse and she was so tired she could barely force herself onward.

There was no shelter to be found that evening. She heaped snow as Temon had taught her, thanking the Gods for those weeks with him. He had spent much of his time warning her of the mountain's dangers, teaching her how to overcome them. She saved her small bundle of twigs. The bunches of dried moss she had scraped from inside the rock shelter of the night before would burn for only a few minutes. Better to save them until she could find more fuel. Otherwise, she might have that but no tinder with which to catch a spark.

Her ankle hurt now whether she moved or not, so much so that she did no more than doze occasionally through the dark hours. Dancer snuggled close eyeing her with worry. She smelled of pain and illness. Of exhaustion and fear. With morning light she staggered to her feet, moving on grimly. Dancer stayed close to her, lifting his nose to check the breeze. The pain was teeth, slashing anew at every step. She was hot, she was cold, her head hurt, and every step was an effort against the dizziness she now felt all the time. Aisling shivered as she walked.

She found she was repeating words over and over in her mind. They fitted the slow thud of her steps. They were part of a song that Ciara had loved. Her own mother had sung her to sleep with it and in turn Ciara had used it for Aisling.

The song was very old, it had arrived with the incomers to Karsten. There, as they cleared land, built new homes and great Keeps, it had become almost an anthem. It was called "If the Dream Is Worth the Price."

Aisling sang the words in her mind. She, too, had a dream, of freedom in a land where it wasn't death to have the Power. A land where someone would teach her to use the gift that pulsed within her.

Ahead Dancer called. She stumbled toward him alarmed in a few clear moments by her growing weakness. He'd found a cave. It appeared to cut far into the mountain, but she had no time to explore. Her ankle failed under her, throwing her painfully to the rocky floor. Outside of the cave the blizzard was worsening. Aisling sat drawing up her leg to peel away sock and boot. She looked down and stifled a gasp of fear. The ankle was swollen, livid marks showed where the boulder creature had slashed the flesh. The marks were darkening to a green-tinged black. She had never seen anything so horrible.

The pain came in sickening waves. With a frightened determination she dragged herself to her pack. She found the small bundle of dry kindling from the camp at the tree from two nights ago. There was more wood at the side of the cave. It looked like a tangled nest, though nothing would build one so large. She laid scraps of dry moss carefully, snapped sparks from her striker into that. It caught slowly. Forcing herself to keep moving, Aisling produced her water pot, filled it with snow drifted into the cave mouth, then set it to melt the snow.

Her weakness terrified her. She must think out each move, then force herself to it. She steeped herbs in the water once it heated. She drank avidly but put her food aside.

Dancer came to sit by her, his eyes anxious. Aisling leaned back against the rock. She was so tired, so weak. She'd rest, just for a moment. She did not see the cat vanish down the length of the cave. Did not hear his imperative howl. Only when he sank claws into her jacket and began to tug her toward the rear of the dark cavern did she rouse.

"Dancer, what . . . ?"

Urgency. Determination. A demand that his human act.

She felt tears of pain and weakness well into her eyes. "I can't. Maybe when I've rested."

Again the urgency. With it this time came a picture. Sharp, clear, of Aisling dead in the cave, of Dancer crouched dying of cold and starvation beside her. She must move now—to save them both. The girl allowed the slow tears to slide down her cheeks. She couldn't move, it hurt so. But she couldn't let Dancer die. She couldn't let herself slide into death knowing she condemned him also.

Making a great effort, she began to crawl. Dancer followed, teeth firmly gripping the pack. Finally she reached the back of the cave. There she slumped. What was she to do, burrow like a rock-mole? Her mouth curved in an hysterical grin. Rock-moles were a legend, more was the pity. She could use one right now.

Dancer sat up to look at her eye to eye. Then, as her gaze followed him, he rose on long, graceful hind legs to pat at a portion of the wall.

The girl gaped at him. Was it some sort of secret passage? All Keeps had those, but what would one be doing in a cave halfway up a mountainside? Dancer yowled loudly, patting at the rock.

Aisling hitched herself up a little. Her fingers traced the rock where his paws struck. Something was carved there. So mazed was she by the pain from her ankle that it took several tracings before Aisling realized that the figure beneath her hand was familiar.

She blinked. It felt like her pendant, but the shape was carved as a hollow into the rock. Dancer struck at her in exasperation, his claws stinging her from her daze. His head butted at her; she must take her pack, use her pendant. Gather him to her and *now*!

Every move a terrible effort, Aisling lifted her hand. If she forced herself to sit up just a little higher she could lay the pendant in the carved hollow, which fitted it. Dancer hurled himself into the crook of her other arm, bringing a gasp of pain from her.

One of the pack straps was over the arm. Well, what was she to do now? She began to slump again, her hand dragging at the pendant.

Within the rock it turned. There came a slow, soft grating as the rock wall revolved. With its turning it swept girl, cat, and pack within. In the dark something flared to light, a warm silvery glow as the inlaid star on which she now curled came to life.

It was too much for Aisling. She fell into darkness in which someone with a quiet, gentle voice questioned her over and over. She swam in limbo, a place not of her world or any other, where all things were possible.

With the questions done it was as if she was sifted, winnowed for judgment. But when the winnower might have rejected her, Dancer was by her side. His voice was insistent, demanding. Was she the only one to be considered? At last amusement came. Since he wished it greatly it should be so. Both should pass through.

After that the sensations were strange. It was as if she was flung back into the pain-filled, exhausted body, then swept away in a whirl. She could not breathe. Chill air beat at her, a feel of fluttering wings about her cringing body. Then she landed with a groan as she felt the rock beneath her once more. Had passage been denied her, after all? Was she to die in the cave?

Aisling woke finally to the cat as he dragged her once more, muffled growls coming through his clenched teeth. The pain was white fire that consumed her as she managed to crawl a little further. Her pack remained. But she herself must move, one last effort.

She obeyed, tumbling over the edge of a shallow saucer into something soft, which gave way under her. She could go no further. She hoped with the last flicker of consciousness that Dancer would be all right here—wherever "here" was. And wherever it was, at least it was no longer the mountain cave. The questioner had granted her that much. She opened her eyes far enough to see Dancer was safe, then she allowed the dark to rise up and take her.

She roused hungry and thirsty. She would have moved but could not. Fear woke to be dispelled by a soft purr in one ear.

"Dancer?"

The cat purred again, then she felt some vibration as if he tore at her prison. The sounds he made were reassuring; whatever was here Dancer did not fear it. Gradually the stuff encasing her broke away under the impact of eager claws.

Aisling moved to see. Mud. It had been mud that held her.

She scrabbled to sit up, peering down at her ankle. There was no longer pain, the flesh showed white, fully healed scars.

The mud appeared to fall away cleanly, none showed on her clothing; but oh, she felt so grimy. Still unsteady, Aisling staggered to her feet. A small call from the cat led her first to her pack laying within the cave where she had arrived, then to a pool. The water was warm, and silky-feeling. She bathed, luxuriating in being fully clean again after so long. Aisling donned clean clothing, then sat on sun-warmed grass to hug her cat.

"I owe you, Wind-Dancer. I'd have just lain down and died in that cave if it hadn't been for you. Now all I need is someone who can tell me where to go from here. You seem to have found everything else I needed. What about a guide?"

From behind her there came a polite cough. "Will I do, my child?"

Aisling gulped turning quickly to face the speaker. "Who are you?"

He didn't look dangerous. But then neither had her brother Kirion. She eyed the man. He was of medium height, slender, and fine of bone. He was dressed in gray, and his eyes were kind. Dancer was stretching up to the fingers that caressed his ears. The man spoke gently as if understanding her fear and confusion.

"I am often called Neevor. Call me that if you wish."

"Neevor. Where am I, how did I get here, is . . . ?"

He held up a hand laughing quietly. "You are where you sought to be. One who holds a gate chose to open it for you in your need. Your third question was going to be, I believe, is there a place for me? That shall depend on you and on what you are. On what you may choose to be."

Aisling remembered Yvian, Pagar, those who had died in the Horning. This man might distrust her but she would not begin her life here with a lie. Her voice quavered a little as she spoke.

"I'm not wholly of your race. Part of me is from the in-comers in Karsten."

Neevor smiled, and his hand went out to her. "Child, many are accepted here who are not wholly of our kind. The Guardian passed you in." He reached out to touch the pendant. "It has been so long, but the blood answers the call. There are those who will welcome a daughter in power, teach you what you must know. Come."

Aisling caught up her pack, and Dancer fell in beside her as she followed her guide. At the top of the small rise she halted staring down the land before her. The wind lifted small tendrils of her hair.

A new land, a new beginning. Behind her lay everything she had ever known: her home, her family, her friends, even her land. She found she was humming Ciara's song. She'd never been certain, but she'd paid the price. Her dream stretched before her and in that moment she knew. No dream is ever quite ended, there is always another.

She smiled down at Dancer. They would share their dreams.

Below her the land spread out. There would be a new home, new friends, and the learning she craved. She followed Neevor down the slope. She would not forget those behind her, but they had their own dreams, which were different. She must seek her own. With Dancer to help, she would not fail.

She swung down the slope singing softly. Beside her the big cat pranced. He, too, had come full circle. It was good to be home.

Ciara's Song

If the dream is worth the price,
if the singer is worth the song,
let my heart still remember
long after my body is gone.

Let my spirit seek then and find
the place of my dreams apart.
the place I have longed to find
the dearest dream of my heart.

If the price I have paid was enough,
if the song I have sung was so sweet
guide me onto the road
running with eager feet.

For the worker there is an end to work,
to the lover an end to the day.
For the dreamer never an end to the dream
nor an end to the price they'll pay.

For the dream is worth the price,
the singer is worth the song.
I've dreamed and paid, I've worked and I've loved,
Now I *am* the dream and the song!